T0357502

The Last Guy You Kiss

Also by Carla de Guzman

Manila Takes Manhattan

Visit carladeguzman.com or
the Author Profile page at Harlequin.com for more titles.

The
LAST GUY
YOU KISS

CARLA DE GUZMAN

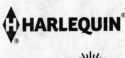

ISBN-13: 978-1-335-57495-4

The Last Guy You Kiss

Harlequin Enterprises ULC
22 Adelaide St. West, 41st Floor
Toronto, Ontario M5H 4E3, Canada
www.Harlequin.com

Printed in U.S.A.

Recycling programs
for this product may
not exist in your area.

To Toni and Lorenz, for always making me believe in 2000s love.
And to the Tea Salon, for encouraging it.

As always, this book has some Filipino words.
A glossary was intentionally not provided.

Content Warning

Mentions of the COVID-19 pandemic. The author chose not to provide a glossary for Filipino terms.

Chester and Laurel Gonzales
and Atty. Martin and Jasmine Barretto

Request the honor of your presence to
celebrate the union of their children
David and Marina Jolene

Madre de Dios Chapel at the Tagaytay Highlands

Reception to follow at Luisa's Restaurant

One

There were many reasons why Mara Jane Barretto loved owning Wildflower, a creative studio and flower shop in the middle of Quezon City. This part of the city was still chill, made up mostly of small businesses set up by upper-middle-class families. It was indie, but unpretentious. Accessible, but still quiet. Mara liked that small things still felt like they could grow on this side of Metro Manila, and she never wanted to leave. Here she could whip up fantasies of spectacular weddings and over-the-top events, and, for the ones willing to pay for it, make them real.

She didn't like that she had to explain to strangers what she did for a living—what is a creative studio? You *style* flowers? What do they need styling for? You used to work in *marketing*? You left *that* for *this*? Are you making money? Ah, you're still single? Oh, single since birth? That explains a lot. Makes sense, makes sense.

Makes sense how, exactly? Mara did not want to know.

Anyway. A list of her favorite things about running Wildflower:

One, Wildflower was on a street lined with little boutique restaurants, other specialty shops like hers. She had a neighborhood café, a neighborhood Japanese restaurant with excellent sashimi, and a bakery that sold the most sinful *pain suisse.* Since she graduated university ten, twelve years ago now, her world shrank quickly from the tall, congested spires of Makati to this quaint little street that she loved being a part of. Every morning, she got up, got dressed and hitched a ride with one of her sisters to the shop on their much, much longer way to work. In a country with an absolutely broken public transport system, this alone was a privilege, and a dream.

Two, Mara *loved* being in charge. She'd been called names for it, of course. Bossy, high standards, mataray. But she liked things to be a particular way, and people who understood that were the ones who stuck around. Her business thrived on being able to understand specific prompts, and one needed a firm hand in order to execute such specific visions. Things like, "I absolutely hate my boss but I have to get his retirement party decorated," and, "Fake flowers for a Dungeons and Dragons session that's also a wedding," or in the case of today's event, "All red, like bleeding love, but with, like, a bit of orange so it's also fall."

But Mara's favorite thing about running Wildflower was when a client looked into her eyes—a little lost, a little helpless in the face of a major decision—and asked her favorite question in the world. One that made her feel competent and trusted, and most of all, needed.

The question being, "What would *you* do?"

It was usually a wedding client, too. *What would you do, if it was your special day?*

Ah, yes. What would Mara do. What *wouldn't* Mara do, really. Some days, she wanted a splashy, classic ceremony at Las Casas Filipinas de Acuzar. The resort had ancestral homes uprooted and shipped from all over the country (wild) and settled into a complex that looked like a world showcase at Epcot. She could picture renting out the place, guests strictly in barongs and Filipiñana. Mara would stay away from any kind of traditional flower and opt instead to deck the warm-toned exteriors in shades of green. She would choose long palm fronds as banderitas across the venue, huge anahaw leaves as a base for the arrangements, ferns to make them fuller. There would still be flowers, of course—maybe a few delicate sampaguita for true Dalagang Filipina elegance. She could picture herself hiring a drum and lyre band for when she and her new husband left the church. For a wedding like that, nothing would be subtle. It would be a boisterous and loud declaration of love, and some days, Mara could see herself with that.

But there were other days she wanted to eschew all that tradition and just go for the big, in-your-face punch of color. Forget the church wedding altogether—they could just get a priest to bless them at the venue, how modern! And because asking anyone to leave Manila was such a hassle (especially during the holidays), she would have to choose a venue that was intimate and elegant at the same time.

There was always the Nielsen Tower in Makati—an old airport since turned into a restaurant, so at least the food was settled. The walls were all white, and it had marble floors and a spiral staircase in the middle of the room. But Mara loved the windows. Big, huge windows with black wrought iron frames, curved around the wings of the building. It was the perfect backdrop to fill with the most colorful flowers in her arsenal.

She could see huge peonies in bright pink. Orchids in magenta, framing the sides of the arrangements. Birds of paradise with their bright pops of orange, yellow green mums and variegated anthuriums. The flowers would breathe life into the venue while matching the wedding party's tropical jewel tones. She could arrange them to descend from the ceiling, adding clouds of baby's breath to make it feel like a floral sky inside an old airport.

Did it matter who the groom was? What he thought about her fanciful notions? For a girl who had never had a boyfriend, that was a minor detail that didn't really matter. That mental role was easily filled by any of her array of Korean crushes via delusion. Currently, for example, it was Jo Yihwan from East Genesis Project. He was appropriately aged, had nice hands, and he could play guitar. What more could a girl possibly want from an imaginary husband-to-be?

"Ate Mara?"

Not that she would know what else one could possibly want. Having only experienced the Eros kind of love from books, movies and music, the idea of romantic love was alien to one who had never experienced it before. It didn't make her less qualified to do weddings of course—did a fantasy writer need to meet a dragon before they presumed volumes of lore about them?

But it did always make her wonder. Would it be nice, to have someone who loved you? Who wanted to gather everyone you loved, everyone important, and tell them that this person was the one for you? That there was no one else, till death do you part.

"Ate? Are you awake?"

It would be nice to have a wedding, to have people around you celebrate the fact that, hey, you found someone you think is wonderful! And your life is going to change, so here we are all, cheering you on!

"Si Ate? She's not asleep."

It could easily devolve into spectacle, sure. A very expensive, high-expectation spectacle that could slip away from you if you weren't careful enough. But Mara had always been a careful person. And she probably wouldn't choose anyone that wasn't worth it.

"How do you know she's not asleep?"

But how would she even know, if she had never dated anyone? Mara was fully convinced of the good parts of a relationship, the kilig, curl-your-toes, happy montage parts. It was the other parts she was unsure of.

"Because she isn't snoring."

Could she stand another person being that close? Could she even *let* them? How was she supposed to know, if she never had any experience in that area? Could she picture herself making compromises, learning to live with some nebulous somebody's flaws and expectations? What if they changed? What if they woke up one day and decided they didn't love her?

"Wow, as if siya hindi din snorer."

Jo Yihwan could love her, of course. He'd said it on various live events and shows, at the end of every concert, and that hadn't changed. Saranghae! But that was delusion, and delusion was easy. Delusion was fun, and hurt nobody, certainly not her. In delusion she happily stayed. Amen.

"Her eyes are open!"

"Mabel, she's slept with her eyes open before."

"I'm not asleep," Mara announced, turning her head away from where it was resting against the car window to glare at her youngest sister, stuffed in the back row of the Honda beside her. "I'm dizzy."

"I told you, you should have sit up front na lang," a voice piped up from the front passenger seat. David, the groom, in a Barong Tagalog that could have used one more session with the sastre. "You're always dizzy pa naman in the car."

"Well, we can't exactly pull over and swap seats now, can we?" Mara shot back, her headache getting in the way of her usually pleasing personality. Ha-ha.

"In this traffic, it's actually a possibility." Mabel, shifting in her seat beside Mara, looked out the window on her side of the car and sighed at the terrible Tagaytay traffic. It was already pretty bad up here on a normal weekend—their family knew well to stay away. But a weekend just after the holidays? Absolute hell. Bad choices made all around.

Not that Mara was going to say that out loud. This was Marina's wedding day! A determined Marina was a Marina that got what she wanted, and so, a wedding the week after New Year's in Tagaytay with all the traffic.

"Are we there yet? I need to pee," announced the bride

from the middle row, solely occupied by her, her bouquet and the train of her bespoke Heleyna gown. The middle Barretto sister was gorgeous. She always was. But even more so today, on her wedding day, all glowing skin and softly curled hair. Even after a night of very little sleep, running on adrenaline and, well…love, Marina looked as beautiful as ever. "Ate, can we pee?"

Mara had this moment earlier at the church, of seeing her little sister walk down the aisle, her face luminous and stunning. A woman in love. It suited her well. Mara remembered beaming with pride, fighting back tears and thinking that this was truly, truly worth it.

"Fuck, I really need to pee."

"Ate Marina, you have to stop saying that, because now *I* need to pee."

So here they were, ten minutes later, in a bathroom of a Starbucks. Mara was hunched over Marina slightly, holding up her baby sister's volumes of skirt, as well as the hem of her own burnt orange dress. Ah, maid of honor duties.

"Do you hate me?" Marina looked up at Mara with her large, sweet eyes, mid-pee. Her family always joked that it was impossible to refuse Marina anything with those eyes. Marina had a big three astrology placement of Cancer Sun, Libra Moon and Gemini rising, which made her the most in touch with feelings among the earth and fire sign Barrettos. Her face was all worry and innocence, and totally unfazed that this conversation—which they probably should have had months ago—was happening now, of all times. Of all places. Hay, air signs.

"Would I be doing this if I hated you?" Mara, with two earth signs (Capricorn Sun, Virgo Moon) and a rising fire sign (Scorpio, heh) asked. Her thighs were cramping, because she was still in heels and standing at a very awkward angle. She was trying to find her words, which even in less stressful situations wasn't easy.

"You're avoiding the question," Marina scolded her lightly, ignoring the frosty bite in Mara's tone.

"Eh." Mara shrugged. "Alam mo na 'yan, Marina."

"Are you mad that I got married before you did? Are you mad that I didn't tell you first? What are your feelings about it?"

"Marina." Mara shifted her hold on both their dresses, feeling her back start to protest. She was pointedly avoiding her sister's gaze. "I don't—"

"I know it hasn't been easy for you, all of this."

"What do you mean?"

"Oh, come on." Marina rolled her eyes in a way that would have made Mara proud if it wasn't directed at her. "Every person who found out I was engaged congratulated me then asked you if you're okay to be...nalipasan."

Mara wrinkled her nose in distaste. *Passed over*, which sounded so bland compared to how the Filipino word hit. Nalipasan sounded so harsh, like something terrible had happened to her. Nasaktan—hurt—was formed the same way, different root words with the same prefixes and suffixes (English major ka, girl?) to mean that something had happened to her. Something that wasn't good, when in fact it was just... it was what it was.

Mara squirmed uncomfortably. Surely Marina had bigger things to mentally break down than Mara's messy swirl of unexamined emotions. Mara knew she could say exactly what her sister wanted to hear—*I'm fine, I'm okay. I'm so happy for you it makes me want to burst into tears*—and Mara wouldn't be a liar, because it was all true.

But the funny thing about being human was that two things that sounded contradictory could both be completely true. That as much as Mara was happy for Marina, there was a little box locked tight in the back of her head, one she'd labeled "My Formerly Delusional Feelings for David—DO NOT EXAMINE."

Because David had been Mara's friend first. Her office mate, whom she bonded with over work calls during the pandemic while they navigated marketing makeup to a world that didn't need it. Who she got even closer to when work from home sadly ended, who encouraged her to open Wildflower. Owned 10 percent of it, in fact, because David was the kind of guy who put his money where his mouth was.

David was Marina's husband now. And it had nothing to do with Mara at all.

"I could never be mad at you," she said to her sister now. "Nalipasan is just a word. People will always have words. If it's not me being unmarried, it's me being fat, it's me being in a job they don't understand. And I don't need to listen to them, because they're not important to me. You are. And Mabel, and Mom and Dad."

"And David."

"Yes." And her teeth were only a little bit gritted when she said that. "David now, too. Alam mo na yan, Marina."

Two facts. Seemingly contradictory. Both equally true. One, that she loved that her sister was marrying someone Mara thought was great. Two, that Mara was not quite over that she thought David had been in love with *her*.

"Okay." Marina seemed satisfied. She stretched and reached behind her to flush the toilet. "I just want you to be happy, too, Ate. Whatever that looks like for you."

"Are you sure you want me to be happy, or do you just pity me?" Mara asked, genuinely curious. But when Marina winced in response, she knew her tone came out too harsh. Too sharp. She said too much, and it wasn't what Marina wanted to hear. Mara decided to backtrack. "Marina. Please don't focus on me. You worked too hard on today to feel guilty for being happy. And it's good to feel happy."

"But—"

"No buts," Mara insisted, standing back up and holding out her free hand to grip her sister's. Reassuring Marina that things were okay was territory she knew well, and one she could guide her little sister through. Comfort zones were Mara's favorite place to be.

They made their way to the sinks to wash their hands. "No buts. Just like you."

"Gaga!" Marina exclaimed, giggling as she flicked water in her sister's direction. Mara squealed in surprise.

"Hala!" Mara exclaimed back, retaliating after she washed her own hands.

"Hoy, hoy, hoy, what's happening here?" Mabel asked as

Marina opened the door with a flourish. Mara spotted David at the counter retrieving their orders. She was very much looking forward to her peppermint mocha. "Having a moment without me?"

"Married women are so scary," Mara announced, moving out of the way for Mabel to wash her hands. "Mabel, take your Ate to the car. You can chismis with her while you wait for me."

"Why, what are you doing?"

"I need to pee, too."

She didn't really. Mara just wanted a second to catch her breath. It wasn't easy, running around in heels and a dress cinched to her waist. She looked at herself in the mirror. Her hair was intact, as was her dress and her lipstick. Nothing out of place, everything as she preferred. The hair was a little too stiff for her liking, but her makeup made her look like a blushing, happy maid of honor. She looked pretty, she thought. Gorgeous, even.

She didn't *look* like someone who was passed over. But the feeling was there, like a loose thread she had yet to cut off of a crochet project.

Mara took a deep breath, taking in Marina's worries, her fears, her guilt, and breathed them out. She refused to hold on to any of that right now. And with a smile on her face, she headed back to the car. David had graciously decided to put all of Marina's skirts on his lap and let Mara take the front seat.

"Sipsip," Mara teased him as he handed her iced coffee over. One pump mocha, three shots peppermint, just as she liked. David was a sweet guy that way.

"You're welcome, bestie." He winked back at her before letting Marina rest her head on his shoulder. They really were sweet together. "LOL, your face showed up on my feed again."

"Are you scrolling social media on your wedding day?" Mara asked tersely, as Mabel started laughing in the back seat.

"Oh my god, it never gets old." She chortled, as David presumably sent the goddamn meme to their group chat ("Lady Whistledown Chika Room"). Mara didn't even need to know what the meme looked like—she'd seen it on her feed, in her inbox, had it printed out and taped to her office door.

It was just a photo. A photo one of David's friends (ugh) randomly took of her and posted on his stories. They had been drinking when he said something idiotic, and Mara glared at him like he was gum under her shoe while he had his camera pointed at her.

But the way the internet worked, Mara's scowl had been terrifying enough to turn into a universal photo that stood in for threatening bodily harm and/or emotional damage to anyone who saw it. It became an eldest Asian daughter meme. An "Oh you think you have it hard? Try being the eldest daughter in an Asian household" kind of thing.

On the bright side, she noticed people were a little more hesitant to mess with her after that. But on the not-so-bright side, she didn't know what people were doing with a photo of her face.

One of her many, many goals for tonight's festivities was to hunt down the member of the groom's wedding party (he had been in charge of the wedding cord, how appropriate to wring his neck with) who had managed to evade her thus far and shove something up one of his orifices. She had not decided which one yet.

Jay Montinola, Secondary Sponsor for the Wedding Cord. Oooh, just the sound of his name made her blood boil like the fires of Tartarus.

"Ate, do you think we can stop by McDo or something?" Marina asked as their car pulled away from the coffee shop. "I'm starving."

They finally made it to Luisa's, one brief fast-food stop later. The bride and groom were promptly whisked away for touch-ups and more photos, and the bridesmaid and maid of honor were left to their own devices.

Luisa's was the premiere garden venue in Tagaytay. Best for laid back, but still formal weddings, which meant most weddings. Of all of Mara's clients, one out of three chose this place as their reception venue, for good reason. It was always worth it to attend, being such a gorgeous venue, and (mostly) because the food was *divine*.

"Anak ng kabayo," Mabel hissed as she somehow managed to clamber out of the Honda. "Ang lamig. I need the strong arms of a man to provide help. Sexy help."

"Raise your standards." Mara laughed as she wrapped her arms around her sister's bare shoulders. It did little to ward off the cold, but it was better than the six yards of organza they were wearing between them. Tagaytay in January meant piercingly cold winds or still, misty fog, and there was no happy middle. Neither were ideal formal attire conditions. "Don't worry, Mabel. All we have to do is go to the venue, find Des to change our shoes, then we will enjoy ice cream and beer until we have to have dinner. Good plan?"

"Good plan," Mabel agreed. "Ate, your skin is colder than mine," she complained as the sisters shuffled toward the casita pavilion, the holding area for the guests until the reception later that evening. "And my feet hurt."

"What are feet?" Mara deadpanned to her sister. "Also of course my skin is cold, I'm a cold-blooded—"

"H-oh!" The cheerful voice of the wedding coordinator cut Mara off as they arrived at the registration area. Desiree had come highly recommended by her clients and, in fairness, was doing a great job. Mostly because Des very quickly understood that the person who knew what the bride truly wanted was the maid of honor. "Ladies, I have your sandals. Um, ma'am."

"Des, please stop calling me ma'am." Mara sighed. "I'm not that scary."

"Nah, Ate. You're scary," Mabel reminded her, grabbing her paper bag from Des. Mara opened her mouth to protest, but Mabel was quicker. "Of course we all know it's what's best, and you're almost always right."

"As you guys should."

"Still scary, though. Meme-worthy kind of scary." It took her sister two seconds to switch out her shoes for sandals, and she zipped back into the venue before Mara could say anything.

"A meme? Oh my god. That's why your face was so familiar." Des gasped, and Mara had to hand it to her. Marina's wedding planner didn't miss a trick. "You're the eldest Asian daughter."

Great. So, new plan. Mara was going to change shoes, find David's friend (Jay Montinola, cord sponsor, bane of her existence), glare at him with the fire of the deepest pits of hell until he spontaneously combusted into fine dust, and then get ice cream.

Good plan.

Two

Somewhere in the parking lot of Luisa's, Jay Montinola sneezed so hard he tripped on his own two feet. The sneeze was loud enough that he caught the attention of some of the other guests making their way to the ballroom—sorry, the casita where they were supposed to wait *before* they got to enter the ballroom—at the designated reception venue for #DavidPutsMaringOnIt. The struggle for clever hashtags was too real.

Close by, he heard a gasp.

"Oh my god, isn't that—"

"Girl, go up to him! I swear the kiss thing is real. Remember Jam got married last year, just because she accidentally kissed him during mass?"

"I'm not *that* desperate."

"Even if it means finding *the One*?"

"That was a huge sneeze," Mon Mendoza, groomsman number six and wedding lector, commented beside Jay, falling into step between him and the gossipy wedding guests as they continued to walk down the slope of the large parking lot. "Someone's thinking of you."

"Me?" he said incredulously, but laughed anyway. "God, that sounds ominous."

"Quick, think of a number between one and twenty-eight!" Scott Sabio—also a groomsman but at a higher billing as he was in charge of the array—chimed in, walking behind them. Jay didn't miss his friend closing ranks, hands in his pockets and looking for all the world like a lord surveying his land. He held in the urge to give them both hugs and smiled instead, playing along.

"Aren't there only twenty-six letters in the alphabet?"

"Duh, we're including ñ and ng. It's only proper."

"I want tacos," Jay announced suddenly, just as their little trio finally arrived in the ballroom. As crowded as the room had become, it was easier to blend in like this. Most of the guests were already at the pre-reception venue, and they were lucky enough to find seats toward the back, in the covered veranda. "Do you think there will be tacos?"

"It's Luisa's—they're definitely going to have tacos. David wouldn't *not* get tacos. Wouldn't not? Is that grammatically correct?"

"It's a double negative," Mon explained. "Grammatically correct, but sounds like you're obfuscating your words."

"Obfuscate?" Jay echoed in a high-pitched voice, teasing. Mon, cool as ever, simply raised a brow at him.

"We're going to be here for a while yet, Jay," Scott chortled, crossing one leg over the other and flipping his hair. A couple of people turned their heads, because it was hard to miss seeing a handsome man flip his hair, but Scott didn't seem to notice. "We can talk about you being back from Hong Kong."

"I've been back for four years! Pose," Jay pointed out, holding up his camera and snapping a casual photo of Scott. Then another. And another. Scott, being Scott, changed up his poses every time. Even pretended to hold a drink that he definitely didn't have.

"Yes, but we lost almost three of them to the stupid pandemic. So you're like a fresh balikbayan!" Scott enthused, making Jay laugh. He'd spent most of his post-college life in wealth management at a private bank in Hong Kong. He came home for the Lunar New Year one year, in 2020, and then… he couldn't go back. Then "couldn't" turned into "didn't really much want to."

"That's one way to look at it," he agreed. "Although I do miss having balikbayan money. For this wedding, I'm down, what, one thousand pesos in toll fees, two thousand on gas, two thousand more for a wedding gift?"

"You're only giving them two thousand as a wedding gift?" Mon, who was sitting beside Jay, wrinkled his nose in distaste. "Don't you work in finance?"

"Consulting now, actually. And now we're stuck here for the next several hours because we like David *that* much."

"Didn't David let you cheat off of him on the math final in senior year?"

"He did. And yet I have no tacos." He shot three more photos of Scott, who was looking dangerously into the lens of the camera. What a goofball. "Smile, Scott. I can't sell these photos on OnlyFans if you're not smiling."

"Oh, *please*. Fans appreciate variety." He posed again. "Oh my god, Jay. Stop." It became increasingly obvious to anyone who was watching the two that Scott actually did not want Jay to stop and was posing quite handsomely with every snap. "Also, good to know your being kuripot hasn't changed."

"*Makwenta* might be the better word." Mon's little dimples popped up in his amusement. "Someone who keeps score. Jay's not a penny pincher."

"Gago." Jay chuckled, lowering his camera and shaking his head. Reviewing the images made him laugh, because it was Scott, and it was impossible to take a bad photo of him, especially when he was in a barong that fit him perfectly, in a venue that screamed "casual fancy" behind him. He was shooting in black and white today, playing with lighting, capturing casual and ceremonial moments without taking away from the formalities of the wedding. It had taken him forever to settle on which camera to shoot with, but this was a good choice.

Scott held out his hands in a "gimme" gesture, and Jay handed him the camera to review the photos.

"Ooh. I do look good. If you're putting that up, I want a cut. Ten percent."

"You're lowballing yourself. Forty." Sure, most of his photos of this joyous occasion were now of Scott fooling around with the decor and foliage, but it still suited. The beauty of bringing around a camera just for fun was that you could take stupid pictures of groomsmen while waiting for the taco stand at the pre-reception merienda to open up.

You can also hide from certain people. Jay looked around the ballroom quickly, scanning the room for a flash of burnt orange fabric, waiting for a chill to run down his spine at the sight of a certain seething someone. Nothing? Nothing? Excellent.

See, he was not, as David said, a "scaredy-cat." Because scaredy-cats would have said no to being a secondary sponsor of the wedding in fear of the maid of honor. (Jay had done an excellent job looping a cord around David's neck at the church, which he thought was appropriate for the life his friend was choosing.) Scaredy-cats would have booked it back to Manila the second the wedding was over, duty fulfilled. But Jay was not a scaredy-cat. He was a mature thirty-five-year-old adult, taking stupid photos of his hot friends.

"Or better yet," Jay began, but he and Scott were clearly of the same singular brain cell and the both of them said, "Sixty-nine," at the same time.

"Four. That's how old the two of you are." Mon chuckled.

"Three, that's the number of hours we're still stuck here." Scott groaned, drooping backward into his chair and pretending to melt into it. "Five. The number of hours I slept last night."

"That's not too bad...?" Mon pointed out.

"I need seven hours of beauty sleep, Moning. You know this."

"Bored, that's what we are," Jay said, holding up a little V with his thumb and index finger in a pogi pose as Scott took his photo. "But still looking good."

"I've been smiling and taking pictures for the wedding photographers for several hours. My face is glued like this permanently now, and I can't sue for emotional damage because I agreed to be David's groomsman," Scott complained. "This is what happens when I'm hired for my face card."

"It's a good face." Jay shrugged, taking his camera back to take more photos. On a scale of one to ten, how bored were they? "So if you're the visuals of the wedding party, what does that make Mon?"

"Power forward," Mon said, now cradling a beer in one hand and looking at his phone.

"Is that soccer or basketball?" Jay asked, frowning. "I don't do sports."

"The photographers asked more than once if Scott was the groom," Mon added, and Scott groaned. Mon was always the picture of calm and stability, and his current pose showed it off. Jay took a couple of photos. "David thought it was hilarious."

"Marina and her sisters, not so much." Scott winced, and Jay failed to fight the slightly terrified laugh that burst from out of his throat. He fumbled with his camera to pretend the sound he made was because of a camera thing. But Scott and Mon had known him since high school. It wasn't easy to hide anything from them, which he added to the list of things that sucked about being at this wedding in particular. "Huh. Moning, you were right."

"I told you." The tone of Mon's voice had not changed at

all, barely looking up from his phone. "Jay's terrified of one of Marina's sisters. But I don't know which."

"I'm not—"

"Is that why you aren't a groomsman?" Scott asked, and his ears practically perked up at the possibility of chismis. "Hala, hala. Demoted to cord sponsor despite being the one closest to David."

"Did you guys notice the flower arrangements have a little sprig of purple?" he asked suddenly, pretending to be very distracted by the abundance in flowers in the reception. Sometimes changing the topic worked wonders on his friends. "It wasn't in the invitation, and it's not in the theme color. I wonder why."

"Maybe you should ask Marina." Oooh, Scott was *pushing* his buttons. Jamming his finger into them repeatedly like a naughty child who was told not to. Jay narrowed his eyes at his friend, but Scott was too busy pressing imaginary buttons to pay him any attention. "Or wait, isn't her Ate a florist? Is that why she looked familiar?"

"I was thinking she looked familiar, too," Mon agreed. "Jay? Thoughts?"

"I have no thoughts. David didn't say why I wasn't a groomsman?" Jay wondered out loud, deflecting, because he absolutely knew *why* Mara Barretto's face was familiar, but he was never, ever going to tell his friends. Guilt was a meal that kept you full, like when you force fed yourself amaplaya because it was literally the only thing on the table. Blergh. "He's usually chismoso about these things."

"He said it would make sure you were free to take your

photographs," Mon said, because Mon was also secretly a chismoso about these things. "And while I think you're an amazing photographer—"

"I'm not a photographer." Jay made a noise that was half laughter, half scoff, waving his friend away. He wasn't delusional enough to think that he was better than the people literally paid to photograph David and Marina's wedding. He held up his little digicam. This particular Fujifilm was not the top of the line, but it was reliable, and on sale when he bought it. "It's a point and shoot. All you have to do is point, and shoot. Not exactly a skill issue."

"Tell that to professionals, man." Mon laughed, still without looking up from his phone. "But I think there's something you're not telling me and Scott, and as your friends, we just want to make sure everything's okay between you and David."

"Oh, David and I are fine," Jay assured Mon, which wasn't a lie. He and David *were* fine. He and David even laughed at the church when Jay made a joke about having a phone charger at the ready because, ha-ha, *cord* sponsor.

"So it's Marina you have a problem with."

"Jay, you aren't paying attention to me," Scott, the thirty-plus year-old man, *whined*. There was something about hanging out with his high school friends that brought out their younger selves—they still liked to wheedle each other and tease mercilessly. It was childish, but nostalgia hit Jay hard whenever they were together. He missed it.

"Oh my, I would never ignore my talent! Please, sir, pose by the ice cream cart," he said, as he and his friend shuffled over to the ice cream stand near the seating area. One hour down, one more to go. But what else were guests supposed to do in between the 3:00 p.m. ceremony and the 7:00 p.m. reception start? Scott was being petulant, insisting he would look better by the window. "I don't know how Ava stands you."

"My girlfriend loves me. But I love her more, and standing each other is the least that we do," Scott said proudly, his already handsome face almost aglow with the love of someone Jay thought was a cool person. It mystified him, how easy it was for his friend to say it out loud. Even David had just done it, in front of God and all the witnesses, and there had been zero hesitation in his voice when he made his vows. Not only was he willing to spend an ungodly amount of money to say it out loud (Luisa's wedding was *expensive*, and that was without renting out a second ballroom as a holding room), he was willing to stake his name, his life, his reputation on it. Because wasn't that the point of all of them being invited?

Terrifying. There were no guarantees in love, even less in marriage. More so in a country that had no divorce law.

"I could never," Jay said out loud, keeping the camera up and seeing Scott's change from sentimental softness to surprise, then amusement, all through the lens of his camera. "Sorry. I'm happy for you, really, all that standing. Woo, go team ScAva."

"That is a terrible couple name. It sounds like a skin disease." Scott winced.

"You know, Jay," Mon piped up from where he was still sitting like an old Dad watching his kids play in the pool. "For someone so good at capturing human emotions with a camera, you get very awkward when feelings are brought up."

"Hey, hey, *hey*." The need to defend himself rose quick and hot. He could stand to be berated for being terrified of a woman he barely knew, but not for being emotionally unavailable. Because he was *here*, wasn't he? "Just because I'm not in a stable, long-term relationship like you guys, doesn't mean I'm—"

"You asked if David had a cold when he was sniffing at the altar," Mon pointed out.

"The pandemic isn't over, I was being cautious."

"You made little beep boop noises when he kissed Marina in front of everyone at the church," Scott added.

"I was trying to be entertaining!"

"You haven't been in a serious relationship since Selena."

"Okay, yes," was all he said, frowning at his friends to get them to stop. He wasn't in the mood to revisit that, especially not right now. "And because it was Selena, you know why I don't want to be in a serious relationship. Plus, I'm between here and Hong Kong, I don't really see myself settling down anywhere anytime soon. And I have other priorities, you guys know that."

Her name was Luna, she was nearly four now, and the love of his life. Unfortunately for Jay's nightlife, his niece had an early bedtime, and according to his sister, "can't party," which Jay thought was a real shame because Luna had inherited her ninong's dance skills. But Mom trumped Ninong every time, and Jay was going to have to settle for that.

He smiled when Scott and Mon studied him with what he could only describe as concern. It was sweet of them, worrying about him, but Jay was fine. "Also I still date. I date *quite* a lot, thanks. I've seen the insides of more condom—"

"Ew." Scott wrinkled his nose.

"*Condominum* units than most real estate agents. The market for condominiums is wild, guys. Apparently the market is hot and I'm losing money because I'm not making it," he said quickly. But there was absolutely no shame in his voice. He liked going out, liked meeting new people, and making them feel special. He actually preferred flitting from place to place. It was exciting, and fun, even when his back hurt the next day because he was thirty-five and decrepit. "But it's too near Luna's school, I would never give it up."

"We're talking about emotional vulnerability, not sex," Mon reminded him. "Not the same thing."

"Also, Luna goes to school now?" Scott gasped. "But she's a baby!"

"It's pre-school, so everyone is a baby." Jay chuckled. "But I'm fine. You guys are great at making other people happy, it's just not me."

Jay didn't get to see Mon and Scott as often as they saw each other—the two of them had gone on to study in the same university, had their own barkada without him, saw each other often because of work—Jay had been in Hong Kong for the longest time, and was only starting to get more time for friends since coming back. He'd missed a lot of random dinners out, coffee invitations and big trips out of the country because of work, because of family. But he was there when they asked him to be. He felt guilty sometimes about being a bare minimum friend, but he made his commitments. His friends understood that.

"Speaking of serious relationships," he said, ordering himself a cone of barako ice cream. It would have to do, for now. "Where are your better halves?"

Mon and Scott gave each other looks, a silent communication done easily by those who have known each other for as long as they had. And Jay, being their friend for about the same amount of time, could understand every word. "Is he deflecting?"

"Yes."

"Should we let him?"

"Yes. Because we like him. Also do you think I look good in this barong?"

"We didn't get plus ones, actually," Scott said, chuckling after Mon rolled his eyes at his unspoken question. Scott had ordered ice cream, too, and was taking a huge chomp off of the side of his quezo real mountain like the chaos demon that he was. "So Ava took her cousin Tori to this new degustation—"

"Degu-what?"

"Tasting menu," he explained, "in Silang. They went to a tasing menu place without me. The guy who makes a living off of food videos. They are sending photos, and it is taking everything in me not to shove this entire ice cream cone into my mouth and follow them."

"The food here in Luisa's is good, too, though," Jay pointed out, but Scott answered him with a pout that was so pitiful that he actually wanted to take his words back. "So they say."

Scott was everyone's favorite foodie influencer, after all,

and it was rare for him to be so excited about something in the Philippine food scene, saturated as it was. His girlfriend Ava's plans had two things that were sure to make a man like Scott Sabio suffer—not being included in something, and not being included in something food-related. It was devious and hilarious, which was one of the reasons why Jay thought Ava was a perfect match for his friend.

"If it helps, I didn't get a plus-one, either," Mon announced. "Olivia's in LA anyway."

It was a flex for Mon to say things like that so casually. It came with the territory of dating *the* Olivia Angeles, the most famous Pinoy in Hollywood. Since the SAG and the WGA strikes ended, Hollywood was back in full swing, and Olivia's schedule was booked with meetings, shoots and re-shoots, constantly flying back and forth. Jay wondered how Mon could stand to be half a world away from the person he loved. He hadn't had much of a chance to see Mon and Olivia together—Jay hadn't actually met her yet—but a Mon in love was a happy Mon, and good for him.

"Did you hear what David said when you told him that?" Scott chortled, shaking his head in disbelief. "God, I love the guy but sometimes he can be dense as… Mon, help me out."

"Osmium is the densest naturally occurring element in the world," Mon supplied. "But yeah, I heard it. Something about Mara not liking it if Olivia showed up and upstaged Marina. He said it when he was introducing me to Marina's parents."

Jay winced, because *oh* David. He was a good guy. A really nice one, actually. But he tended to absolutely not consider anything whenever he opened his mouth, which had gotten him into a lot of trouble in the past. Like, for example, turning a photo Jay took into a meme and posting it everywhere online.

"Yeah that was really tactless of him," Mon said. "Marina's Ate is a bit…"

"Scary?" Scott asked, and Jay couldn't help himself. He made a noise. In general, Jay made a lot of noise, he was a noisy guy. But the sound that came out of his mouth was partway between a laugh and an agonized whine. Because it was actually pretty funny for his friends to be *so close* to his reasons for not being a groomsman, and yet so far. "What the hell was *that*?"

"What was what?" Okay, his voice was a little too high-pitched and nervous. He cleared his throat, then stumbled on his way to sitting down on the lounger next to Mon. "What was what?" He had the feeling of being caught, but without knowing what for. Not the first time it happened to him, really.

"That little Jay noise you made," Mon said, tilting his head in confusion. Across them, Scott gasped and pointed.

"You're scared of Marina's Ate."

"Okay, that's—" he began, but really, what was the point? "Yes. Fine, fine, yes. I'm scared of Mara. In fact we are sitting here, at the very hidden corner of the entire ballroom, because I do not want her to see me."

"Why? What did she do?" Scott asked. Jay felt like he was bracing for a punch in the stomach, because it wasn't anything that *she* had done, it was all him. Him and an enterprising idiot on the internet who thought the image of Mara

Barretto scowling was funny enough to share with the rest of the world. That idiot being David. But Jay was never going to say *that* out loud. "Oh god. What did *you* do?"

"Well…" Jay winced again.

"Jaysohn Montinola. I am this close to karate chopping your ice cream out of your hand." Scott held up said karate chopping hand, and Jay curled his body over his ice cream to protect it. Oh god. This wasn't going to be fun.

"I may have," he started slowly, "taken a really bad photo of Mara when we went out one time. I was just trying to capture the moment, be present, you know? And then she got really annoyed with me, and I took a photo of her, and that photo turned into a meme, and…"

"Oh my god," Scott gasped. Mon's confused blinking was the perfect companion to his disbelief. "Of course. That photo was everywhere. The eldest Asian Ate. Oh my god. It's Mara Barretto?"

"Wait," Mon said. "You went out with Marina's sister?"

"Noooo," Jay singsonged. "I went out with Marina. David set us up. This was like, a year ago."

"So," Mon concluded, because he was a terribly smart guy, "you're the last guy Marina dated before—"

"Before she decided she would rather fall in love with David instead, yes," Jay admitted, and as much as he was determined not to be in a long-term relationship anytime soon, it still stung to say it out loud, of course. It always did. But you learned to smile, be happy for them and move on. It was easier that way. "David thought she and I would suit each other, which is hilarious, now that I think about it. So the four of us went to that gin bar in Quezon City—"

"With the tea-based gins. Ooh, I love that place." Scott nodded his approval. "The secret bar in Nomnom Commons has a more unique selection, but you can't beat QC for chill vibes."

"—and that's when I took the picture. I was taking a picture of our drinks, and I said something about the female equivalent of a quarter-life crisis is quitting their corporate job and starting a small business."

Both Mon and Scott's faces were hilarious. They were the same horrified faces they made, Jay realized, when David collided with another player playing basketball and broke his nose in high school. Which was fair, because this was about the same level of "what the fuck."

And, he admitted, that was probably the most douchey thing he'd said in a long time. He hadn't even known Mara ran Wildflower at that point. His finger had slipped on the shutter button just as she had glared at him like a worm to crush under her boot (which, fair). Then Marina fell in love with David, he wasn't asked to be a groomsman, and that's how this story happily ended.

"Your fears are totally justified," Mon said. "Because that was terrible. Cancelable. Jesus, Jay. Marina also worships the ground her Ate walks on, and David invested in Mara's flower business."

"Have you apologized to her?" Scott asked. And really, that was such an obvious answer, right? Find Mara, put his tail between his legs and apologize.

But the thing was, Jay didn't know if Mara wanted this brought up again. Internet trends came and went quick, and this was disappearing just as fast as the next. Maybe she just wanted to move on?

"Ummmmm."

"Wow. It's a miracle you were still invited to the wedding."

"Of course I was still invited, I was the last guy Marina dated before she found The One." Jay snorted, licking off his ice cream in slight agitation. Marina and David were not the first people to invite him to their wedding because he had inadvertently pushed them toward each other, and he knew the drill. He got invited to witness their love because he made it happen. Or, if you believed the urban legend, his kiss did. "Like that girl I accidentally kissed during the Sign of Peace part one Sinbang Gabi."

"What?"

"It was 4:00 a.m.! I was tired! Her Lola was a great dancer."

Okay, so in the case of him and Mara Barretto, he was definitely the asshole. Finding her and apologizing was definitely the right thing to do. If only to a) clear the air between them and b) set a good example for his niece because he was not going to be a bad ninong. Canceled people usually wrote, "I'm sorry if you were offended" notes on their phone, posted them on social media and hoped for the best. Jay knew he could be a better person than that.

"I'm going to go somewhere else so you guys can talk about me," he said, standing amid Mon and Scott's vehement protests. He personally never subscribed to the urban legend that surrounded him, but he did work with numbers a lot. His record (so far) did not lie. Ten to none, every girl he kissed would marry the person they dated after him.

Jay refused to face what was behind the numbers, even when wedding guests from Tagaytay to Tawi-Tawi talked about the incredible magic of his kiss. He thought of Mara again, at the anger that flashed in her eyes and made his entire soul shiver. Yeah, he definitely didn't deserve to be invited to this wedding.

"Or you could—"

"Apologize." He sighed, because god only knew if Mara would even listen. But she deserved an apology, even if he didn't deserve acceptance. Jay was just going to build up to it muna. "If you don't see me at the reception…"

"We'll tell Luna her ninong died trying to do the right thing," Mon assured him.

"We'll tell Ate Irene that you died because you were an idiot." Scott nodded. "Go, go."

Three

Growing up, Mara *loved* watching princess movies. *The Swan Princess* in particular was her favorite. She learned at a very young age that falling in love was done when you were wearing a beautiful dress. It made sense because a beautiful dress made you feel beautiful, and how could a prince not see that?

In her younger days, Mara loved to pretend that she was the princess. She liked to throw her mother's yellow sweater over her head (because the princess was blonde, of course she was), and tied ribbons up the arms of her mother's bathrobes to simulate Princess Odette's puffy sleeves. She would sing the songs word-perfect, skipping through the house, twirling and waiting for the day someone would make a vow of everlasting love to her.

What else *was* there?

Years later, many of those concepts were unpacked, of course. When all she saw were thin, blonde and blue-eyed princesses, she changed the channel. She found more princesses to watch—more Filipinas, Black women, other Asians and Latinx people to inspire her. Vows of love would come after a lot more trials than facing an evil wizard or a spell that turned you into a swan in the daytime. Vows were tested on a daily basis when the person you chose failed to meet some expectation you didn't express.

But the power of wearing a pretty garment and feeling beautiful? That was never going to get old.

But it would be nice if someone said it to her, right? *You look beautiful. You look like someone to love. I will do my hardest never to disappoint you.*

Sadly, the fantasies remained fantasies. The closest Mara got to *The Swan Princess* was with one client who wanted to re-create the dress from the movie. Complete with puffy sleeves and blond hair.

"Thanks for the sandals," she said to the wedding coordinator, who stood beside her and off to the side of the ballroom. Des had just explained that the tacos were still being made and would be served with the other after-party food following the reception. Disappointing, but late tacos were better than no tacos at all. "You know you didn't have to help me take off my heels."

"I can tell when a person in a gown isn't totally comfortable in heels," she said, and Mara had to agree. Heels, she decided, were the worst part about wearing a dress. "And it can't be easy, with your…um." Des very pointedly eyed Mara's body. Her arms, her legs.

"My boobs? My stomach?" Mara asked, daring Des to say it out loud. It wasn't exactly rocket science, connecting her discomfort to her weight. But even though that was applicable to her, it was not something to just be assumed. "Thanks for the consideration, I guess."

"I didn't—I mean, wasn't—"

"Relax, Des. It really was hard. My feet thank you. And I did appreciate your help," she said, and the wedding planner sighed with something that sounded much like relief. "Are we still on track to start the reception at seven?"

"The Wildflower staff is just about to finish up, and the sound system is being tested as we speak," Des said, nodding and peeking at the clipboard in her hand. "I'm checking on your sister after this, and if we can find your parents before six, we should have enough time for family portraits and head in."

"Find my parents?" Mara echoed, taken by surprise. "You mean they aren't here yet?" She swept her eyes across the venue and, sure enough, found the ballroom absent of her father's salt-and-pepper hair and her mother's scarlet red dress.

Her parents had left the church a full hour before Mara and Mabel could join them. The plan had originally been for the unmarried Barrettos and their parents to head to the venue together. Mara had briefed her parents of that plan during the despedida de soltera. But no, Mara and Mabel were left behind, and had to hitch with David and Marina in the bridal car, and now her parents were not even at the venue yet.

"I'm going to see to the bride," Des said, smiling sheepishly. "You can let any of the staff know if we can get an ETA on the father and mother of the bride."

Mara nodded wordlessly, but after a moment remembered why she wanted to talk to Des in the first place. "Please make sure Marina and David get dinner. Marina gets mad when she's hungry, and David has acid issues. Can't miss a meal."

"Got it!" Des shouted over her shoulder before she disappeared to wherever Marina and David were. "You really should get some kind of award. Best Maid of Honor."

"Ate Doing Bare Minimum to Get Everyone Together?" Mara joked to herself. Her mother picked up her call on the third ring, seemingly unconcerned that they were currently MIA.

"Oh, honey, we went to Sonya's Garden!" her mother exclaimed like it was just another Saturday at the mall, and not a wedding in the middle of January. "Your dad had to meet with Alden, and I remembered how much you liked the Spanish bread."

"You went to a *meeting* on Marina's wedding day?" Mara asked with disbelief, because for all the scenarios she anticipated from her parents, disappearing to the complete opposite end of Tagaytay for a business meeting was not one of them.

"Don't be mad na, anak. You can have Spanish bread for breakfast tomorrow at the hotel."

"I'm heading back to Manila tonight, remember?" Mara asked, but maybe her mother didn't remember, which she really should be used to. Both Martin and Jasmine Barretto had just entered their sixties, holding hands and diving into the deep end of being lovable and unreasonable at the same time.

Mara wondered if age really was the determining factor of this role reversal, where it felt like she was parenting *them* when she was only just learning to pick up after herself. Or maybe her parents had always been as free-wheeling and "ba-

hala na" as two boomers could be, until she was the one controlling their schedules, appointments, meds, because *she* was
the one who needed stability.

"Cheese hopia, then."

"Are you guys coming back now?" Mara asked, sighing.
"It takes a while to get from there to Luisa's."

"Oh, we're staying here a bit longer. Your dad's not done
with his meeting, and I wanted a bit of merienda before the
reception."

Mara's dad was a fan of a neatly tied afternoon. If he could
stuff ten things to do in one outing, that was his favorite kind
of day. Which was totally fine. Days like those were needed
sometimes. But any *other* afternoon would have made more
sense than this one. Boundaries, people!

"There's food here," Mara pointed out, gesturing to the
entire veranda designated for serving snacks and drinks until
dinner. "Marina specifically requested food for Papa."

"Yes, but we wanted Spanish bread from Sonya's." Mara
sighed and rolled the growing tension out of her neck. "Did
you really expect all the guests to just wait around at the
venue until seven?"

"Yes, which is why Marina and David paid extra for ice
cream and beer!"

"Hay nako, I can picture your angry face na." And Mara
could very clearly picture her mother's pouting face through
the phone. She sounded disappointed, which was always shitty
to be on the receiving end of. "Like in that picture everyone
shares in group chats."

"Please let's stop talking about my internet infamy." This

was not the first time Mara had asked her family to stop bringing it up. "Just be here by six, please? The photographers want to do one more session with the family before the reception."

"Photographers! As if they're in charge of the wedding!" Her father scoffed in the background. "I didn't like the way they hovered around the venue. They weren't even dressed up! It ruined things."

"They're just doing their job, Papa. Also, Marina really likes their SDEs."

"Is that a marketing term?" her mother asked. "Super Duper Endowment thingy?"

"What? Same-day edit. It's a—well, you'll see later." Mara sighed, chuckling at her Mom's assumed acronym. "Basta. There are things happening here. And a schedule that Marina and David both want. Please, let's all cooperate na lang."

"Okay, okay. We will see you later, anak," her mom cooed, another tactic to try to get her to shout less. It worked most of the time. "Try to have fun! It's *Marina's* wedding day, after all."

Mara pulled the phone away from her ear and mouthed, "Wow." Okay. It was time to hang up, because Mara was not ready for her mom to tell her to back off. But who else was going to worry about these little things that mattered, if not Mara? Better her than Marina, especially today.

Mara tucked her phone back into her tiny purse. Mentally she ticked off a little box next to "locate parents" in the list of things she needed to deal with. Most days that list was so long that the only way her brain didn't explode trying to keep track of it was by writing it down. Today, though, the rest of the list was suddenly, oddly, not so important. Maybe she *should* start trying to enjoy today.

Worst day for a delay on Luisa's tacos.

The casita extension of Luisa's was reminiscent of a rich relative's living room, if said rich relative had a living room the size of a ballroom in the middle of the Tagaytay mountainside. Luisa's was one of those upper-middle-class places that radiated chic, classy and elegant Pinoy tastes, usually run by chic, classy and elegant upper-class Pinoy families. The kind of families that were über-rich, but you didn't actually know why.

The ballroom was furnished with antiques so fancy that Marina only knew them by their Spanish names—estantes, bastonero, mesita. Impractical in a modern home, but oh-so-elegant in a formal setting like this. The swirling patterns on the floor were the work of one family in Ermita that had been making patterned concrete floor tiles since the Spanish colonial period.

All the entry and exit points of the ballroom were built under decorated arches, and the bar tables in matte green glass added a special modern touch, matching the pots of several houseplants growing happily in the empty corners. In the background, the string quartet was playing Stevie Nicks's "Crystal" as Mara walked by, making everything dreamy and romantic while the wind wafted cold air through the space.

She paused in front of the mesita that greeted all the guests by the entrance, the centerpiece of the smaller ballroom. She had personally made the large arrangement and placed it on the table herself in an antique vase of deep red Murano glass.

Marina wanted all red, warmth and fire, and so Mara complied. "Fall vibes, Ate, I want Fall Vibes!" She chose deep orange birds of paradise to cascade down from the top and rich red chrysanthemums and ranunculus with bursts of orange stargazers. She chose dyed foxtails and eucalyptus, selecting wispier leaves that faded in the background of all the reds and oranges. Mara had arranged this particular piece on their dining room table, with Marina exclaiming appreciatively in the background.

But she didn't remember the photographs placed on the table, printed and framed like they were entering Marina and David's living room. It was a nice touch.

She recognized half the photos of course. She was in a lot of them, or had taken the others. The timeline of Marina growing up was something she was only too familiar with, gaps of time between the photos filled in by her own memories. There were a few baby photos, them on trips together, David with his family, their friends…and one photo that Mara had never seen before.

It was a photo from the night she went to that gin bar with Marina, David and Jay. The fateful night when Jay had taken her photo and sold her to the internet. But she'd never seen *this* photo before. Clearly Jay had also taken it—it was from the same angle as the meme photo. In this photo, David was speaking to Marina, the smile on his face showing he was unmistakably in love while she laughed at whatever he said.

Meanwhile Mara was sitting next to her sister, looking completely away from the camera, totally unaware of what was happening right in front of her.

Hot embarrassment warmed her cheeks. Had she really been that stupid? This was the night David told her he was in love, and Mara had stupidly assumed that he had been talking about her. Silly of her, thinking that it had to be her because he asked her to eat out with him all the time, because she shared things with him that not even Mabel or Marina knew. Because he drove her home, because he said she looked pretty. It certainly couldn't be Marina, he'd just set her up with his friend!

She really didn't know if that memory on full display, or Jay turning her face into a joke, was the highlight of that particular evening.

Mara cleared her throat, hoping it would help push down the bitter taste on her tongue. She began to step away, already making up an excuse about needing to check on the flowers. Screw the beer and ice cream, she just needed to get away from this wedding for a minute. But the road to being alone was laid with weddings guests and relatives who needed to talk to her.

"Hija, this arrangement is lovely, can we take it home?"

"Marina is so lucky her Ate has a flower shop, so convenient!"

"You look good ha, are you dieting?"

"Naku Mara, make sure you stay away from the ice cream booth. All those flavors, too sinful."

Those comments were fine. Those she could handle because she got them a lot, fat phobia included. What made her grind her teeth and wish for a wormhole to jump into were the ones that clawed on the feelings she was trying not to pay attention to, such as:

"It's just so modern, no? Marina getting married first?"

"Naku, you should hurry up and get married before it's too late, Mara!"

"You're *still* single? A diet might help with that. Have you spoken to an endocrinologist? I've heard wonderful things about this weight loss pill for diabetics…"

Good god, save her.

Or, since Mara was single, she was going to save herself.

She was her parents' daughter, after all. And while the elder Barrettos had zero boundaries, Mara's were sixty feet tall. So she smiled to all the comments, nodded at all the words, and said she was going to the bar to get a beer. Which she did, taking a deep sip of the craft beer on tap. It helped. "Mara, dear!" exclaimed a voice. Mara looked up and saw her Tita Claudine, breezing through the crowd in her deep red gown, the same shade as all the other ninangs. Tita Claudine was her father's eldest sister, her favorite tita. In her dream weddings, she always had Tita Claudine as her ninang, but that honor went to Marina today.

Which was fine. Tita Claudine was *everyone's* ninang. "Look at you! I thought you said you were going to tell Marina that orange wasn't your color."

"It's not my color, but it's hers." Mara put a hand on her chest to keep the dress from shifting as she took a deep breath. Her top's boning was shaped like a corset, held up by a long zipper instead of a button to "give shape" and very little breathing room. "And thanks for the compliment, Tita. Very nice."

"I didn't say you didn't look lovely. You look like a happy marigold. With glasses."

"You could just call me pretty." Mara sighed, but she was going to take "happy marigold." Sure, why not.

"I wonder what *your* happiness is going to look like," Tita Claudine mused, wrapping an arm around Mara's and squeezing fondly.

"Not Luisa's, I don't think." She cast a look around the place. As much as she loved the venue's rich society decor, it was already Marina's, and it would be for as long as Luisa's stood. Plus Tagaytay traffic was really bad. It was asking a *lot* out of everyone just to come. "This is Marina's place now."

"I didn't mean your wedding, Mar." Tita Claudine interrupted her thoughts. "We all get to choose our path in life. It doesn't always end at the altar."

She knew that, and knew it well. In fact, she spent most of her twenties learning that she had the privilege to make a choice. Studying why she wasn't required to get married, that the world was trending away from marriage and kids because society wasn't fair to women (and to a lot of people). Meeting people who made different choices, and were happier for it.

"I never married," Tita Claudine pointed out. "I chose that, and I like it for me. Now I can flirt harmlessly with other wedding guests because it's fun. I'm just having fun. Happy with my choices. Are you?"

What a question. And trust Tita Claudine to be the one to ask out of nowhere. And maybe it was the environment, or the dress, or just Mara's feelings bubbling to the surface. But she knew she had something to say.

"I think for me to make a choice, I would need to be presented with the options," Mara said slowly, carefully. "And for me to say I choose to be single without finding out for myself what not being single is like—seems unfair," Mara announced suddenly, biting her bottom lip as if taking the answer back. Too personal. Too vulnerable, especially for a day that wasn't hers. Too late now. "If I stay single it's because I preferred it, not because nobody wanted me."

Tita Claudine tilted her head curiously at Mara, and she had a strange feeling like she'd said the wrong answer to a teacher's question. But before she could say anything back, someone had ambled over to them with an unmistakable swagger.

"Aha! Mara, there you are." Tito Bong, her father's youngest brother, tipped his fedora at them. Mara knew that Tito Bong had agonized over that hat choice for at least a week. The Barretto siblings were always well dressed and loved to impress. Even Mara's father had especially commissioned a beautifully embroidered piña cloth barong from Laguna—a four-hour drive back and forth.

Tito Bong was holding a bottle of craft beer in one hand, and a bright red envelope with gold Chinese lettering in the other. He held up the envelope to her. "Here."

"Here?" Mara echoed, confused by the appearance of the ang pao. It was a pretty thick envelope, too. "For Marina?"

"For you," Tito Bong said, which only confused Mara further. "For the wedding."

"I'm not the one that got married…?"

"Bongs naman, fix the meanings of this!" Tita Claudine rolled her eyes at her baby brother, making Mara laugh. Yep, the drama was inherited from one side of the family, and one side of the family only.

Tita Claudine gently took Mara's wrist, the same one that was still holding on to the surprisingly thick envelope. "Mara. I'm sure you heard this na, but there's a tradition that when the younger sibling marries before the oldest, the oldest gets a gift from the younger. It's usually gold."

"That's a tradition?" Mara asked, the first time she'd heard this. Although maybe someone had mentioned it in passing? It wasn't entirely unfamiliar. "Is that sukob?"

Tito Bong and Tita Claudine looked at each other, confusion and surprise evident in their eyes. Unfortunately neither sibling seemed to have the answer and wordlessly shrugged at each other. Basta, it was a thing, so it was going to be a thing that they honored. Tradition!

"Sukob is when siblings get married in the same year. That's malas," Tita Claudine explained, tutting her lips and whispering, as if talking about sukob at a wedding was bad luck in and of itself. "It's also a Kris Aquino movie. It was ok lang."

"Ate," Bong said behind her, holding his beer away from his body. "The point. It's way over here with my craft beer."

"Yes, the point," Tita Claudine huffed, making sure to direct a glare at Tito Bong before giving Mara a warm, gentle look. "The point is, Mara. Nalipasan ka."

Jusko, would she ever escape that fucking word? "And…?"

"And so, money." Tita Claudine pressed the envelope into her hands. "It's a luck thing. Marina got hers, passed it on to you, and as her new ninang and ninong sa kasal, we added to it."

Mara had no idea what to feel as she held the surprisingly thick envelope in her hands. On one hand, free money. On the other hand, just because they said it wasn't a consolation prize, didn't mean it didn't feel like one. As if she lost out on something, because her baby sister had gotten married first.

But then again. Free money.

"Use it for something fun," Tita Claudine urged her, "or something really, really stupid."

Japan was lovely in the spring. As was Seoul in the fall. Or she could buy new underwear in Melbourne, since her size didn't exist in Asia. New underwear was always nice.

"Just don't use it on food," Tito Bong said, rubbing his larger stomach. "Collectively our family's done enough damage to buffets from Manila to Tagaytay."

Mara was a good daughter and a fucking awesome niece because she knew that Tito Bong was aware that his little comment was absolutely uncalled for. And while millennials and Gen Z kids acknowledged they had shit to unpack when it came to their body image, it was way harder trying to convince the boomers of that.

So she smiled at her tito (pitying him a little that at his age, he was still so unhappy with himself that he needed to bring her into his self-hate) and excused herself to head to the reception area, saying she needed to check on the flowers.

This Barbie needed a fucking break.

Four

Making her great escape to the ballroom felt like a gasp of air after breaking the surface of water. There really wasn't any need to check on the flowers—she trusted her team and received updates on their work chat throughout the day. But it was an excuse to escape, and Mara was going to grab that excuse by the horns and wrestle with it if she had to. Besides, updates were one thing. Actually walking into a completed setup for the first time was another. It always took her breath away, seeing a vision come to life and the comfort it provided to a room.

And not to brag, but Mara had really outdone herself with this one.

Marina had requested red for her intimate Tagaytay wedding. Just one hundred guests, on a weekday. She wanted a red that invoked love and romance, the kind that they saw in movies with ending scenes in rooms like this. And because Game of Thrones had ruined red for weddings (among other things) forever, Mara and Marina compromised and fully leaned into Fall vibes. Nothing that would clash with the main ballroom's elegant decor.

On days where the ballroom wasn't filled with wedding guests, it was a restaurant. It didn't need much in terms of adornment, honestly. There were chandeliers hanging from the ceiling, white beams adorned with crown molding, black-and-white patterned floors. The couple's table was set against a wall of mercury glass mirrors, the tables for the parents, ninongs and ninangs across, guests surrounding them. With details like this, one had to be subtle or go balls to the walls with their concept, and Wildflower was all about the balls to the walls. Just like that one time, when the PBA hosted a reception, and Mara used old basketballs to put flowers up on the walls.

Anyway. The Marina-David nuptials had dozens of burgundy red roses on the tables, matched with birds of paradise, peonies and dahlias of varying shades of red, orange and pale peach. The place screamed autumn romance, with the dried, dyed flowers filling the emptier spaces. Mara approached the arrangement at the couple's table, rearranging some of the blooms. Even as she straightened up some of the flowers, she couldn't help but think about the money burning a hole in her pocket. She'd peeked at the envelope earlier. There was enough for a plane ticket abroad, a trip to Boracay, a night at a swanky hotel.

It's Marina giving you luck, she remembered Tita Claudine said. What was Mara supposed to do with that luck?

Go away. The idea was tempting. Too tempting, really.

"Mmm."

Uh, that wasn't her. She wrinkled her nose at the sound. It was a little…um, enthusiastic.

"Oooh!"

Maybe a wedding guest.

"Mmmmmmmm."

Mara pretended she hadn't heard that and decided now was the perfect opportunity to post some stories of the event. Wildflower's social media was a beast that needed to be constantly fed with content. She took a few photos before choosing a sweeping shot of the venue, carefully crafting a caption that was sentimental but not overly so—*Flowers for a family affair. Our favorite kind of special event*—and hit Post.

"Oh, shit that's… Mmm."

It had not been hard for Mara to fall in love with flowers. Her grandmother had a garden in what was now the Barretto family home, and Mara grew up around a small grove of orchids, rows of buttercups, making chains of santan flowers every afternoon. She made wishes on weeds and played with makahiya plants.

"Mmmm."

That she rediscovered this love in her thirties, made a living out of it, was a gift, one she was happy to receive. It felt like a full circle moment, being able to use the flowers she first saw in her Lola's gardens in Marina's wedding arrangements.

"Mmmmmmmm."

What *was* that? Mara's phone almost immediately buzzed as likes came in, more so when she reposted it on her stories.

She must have posted at an optimal time, although who even knew when that was anymore, right?

"Shit. Oh shit."

Still ignoring whatever that was, she started tapping replies to some of the messages, sending hearts and likes, trying her hardest to ignore the sound. She made sure her phone was on max volume, so whoever it was wouldn't miss that there was someone else in the room, who could hear...whatever it was they were doing.

"Ah, fuck, that's good."

"Hoy naman! Can you take that somewhere else?" she snapped, whirling around, ready to admonish whoever decided that hooking up in a seemingly unused ballroom was a good idea. *Please don't let it be Tita Claudine...*

What she saw, instead, was a single person. The one guy wearing a tux to a barong wedding, holding a platito of illicit soft tacos, with one halfway to his mouth. Mara felt a jolt of surprise shoot through her body even as Jay Montinola stared at her with his own shocked, wide-eyed surprise.

The annoying thing about Jay was that it was *almost* impossible to hate him because he was just so goddamn *nice*. He smiled at everyone, knew how to be meek and sheepish. He personified every expression he made. Laughed at jokes so hard the corners of his eyes crinkled. Filled quiet moments with little sound effects (Mara was pretty sure she heard him make "beep-boop" noises when Marina and David kissed in front of the church). And he did this thing where he leaned in close while actively listening to you speak.

At the time she met him, it made her think he would be

good for Marina, because he seemed like a guy who found life interesting and fun. He brought up memories and stories at that one dinner that his friend David had long forgotten, ones that made him laugh and call Jay, "The best."

But the operative word here was *almost*, because Mara had every reason to glare at him now. He'd been thoughtless and posted her unflattering photo for the public to see, without even having the decency of tagging her. And even worse, he never tried to find her, to explain himself, to tell her what happened. Now his cartoon-like freeze was just annoying, and she felt a very urgent need to snap at him even more. Snatch the tacos right out of his hands.

While he couldn't take back what the internet had claimed, she could make him squirm. And that would be enough, because while Mara was a reasonable woman, she was also a petty bitch.

"You," she said, her voice cool as ice as she straightened her back and stared down at him like a piece of gum under her sandal.

"Me?" he asked, sounding confused and innocent with the taco still halfway to his mouth.

"Yes! You!" she exclaimed, and she was aware she was screeching, just a little, but all she could see was red. "Go away!"

"I'm still eating!" he said back, and lo and behold, he still had a taco on his plate, and he swallowed the bite. The silence was awkward and weird. "Um…taco?"

"It's Mara, actually." She realized her mistake quickly, and she flinched when he opened his mouth to correct her, then immediately took it back when she glared again. Damn it! "Arrgh! Where did you get tacos? I know for a fact they're not serving those until after the reception. Also, you're not supposed to be in here!"

"Well, I was on my way out of the other ballroom when I got lost and ended up in the kitchen. The staff took pity on me and gave me a test batch." It sounded so plausible, but Mara wasn't inclined to feel generous at the moment. "Okay fine, maybe I asked. Begged. Cried."

"Bribed?"

"Oh, not bribed. I'll leave that to the politicians," he said, nodding. Then he adopted a Kris Aquino game show host voice and said, "Pilipinas, tang ina talaga!"

"Thanks, BBM." Her voice dripped with sarcasm, because what had that man ever done for the country? Nothing. At least on that, they could agree.

"Amen," he said, raising the taco to the empty air before he took a bite. Mara watched him, and he looked like he was in the absolute throes of ecstasy. Damn, it looked really good, and ice cream was yummy, but it wasn't any kind of decent merienda. Jay noticed her watching and stopped mid-chew. "Are you sure you don't want any? You seem fixated on—"

"I'm not fixated on the tacos. I'm trying to intimidate you." Mara stepped closer to Jay, which was unfair because he was taller than her. Most people were, but she never let that stop her before. "You're the worst, Jay Montinola."

It did give her some satisfaction, however, to see him swallow his food like he hadn't savored it at all. That his shoulders were practically up to his ears. That his eyes were fixed on her, and she was close enough to catch that he was wearing cologne. He smelled nice. Damn it!

"You remember my name," he noted, and the fucker had the audacity to laugh! Like he couldn't believe this was their life. Well, strap in, buddy. Mara had no plans of letting him slide. "That does not bode well for me."

"Why were you trying to leave the other ballroom?" she asked. And if she was frustrated, she was very determined not to show him. "The other ballroom has everything you could need while waiting for the reception. Seating. Food. Beer."

"Not tacos." He snorted. Mara glared at him again, and all he could add to that statement was, "I left, because…"

"Because?" she prompted, tilting her head so he knew that whatever answer he was going to give her was not going to be satisfactory.

"Because, Mara. I was looking for you," he said. Which, god*damn* it, was a good answer. "I was looking for you, because I am the worst."

"I already said that."

"And I'm agreeing with you." He lowered the now empty plate of tacos, wiping his mouth with a napkin he'd tucked underneath, then putting the soiled napkin in his pocket. "I wanted to find you and apologize. For the photo and for what I said. It was shitty of me."

Mara took a step back, because suddenly she was too close, and it was hard to breathe when he was looking at her with such earnest contrition. She swallowed a lump in her throat, felt her hands fall from her sides. Of all the things she expected Jay Montinola to be—jerky, unapologetic, smug—she hadn't expected contrite.

Why would she expect any of those things about a guy she met one night a year ago?

"I see," was all she managed to say to that. "You're...apologizing. And sweating."

"You make me nervous."

"Oh." Never let it be said that Mara Jane Barretto was ever caught off guard without something to say. She had words. Not a lot of words sometimes, but words. *Oh* was a word, right?

"Also I want to apologize that it took me this long to talk to you about it. I didn't know if you want to unearth all of this, but honestly, I just didn't want to deal with it. I was ready to accept that you just hated me. But that's ridiculous, and such a waste of energy on both our parts."

Jay scratched the back of his head, and god, even that looked apologetic. Like a menswear magazine cover pose, as if to say to the viewer, "Oh my god, I'm sorry, are you affected by my face?" To which the answer was always, *yes*. Mara in particular was caught off guard by the action, and yes, that was the sound of her brain short-circuiting.

"I would like to be the kind of person that tries to do better. So I went looking for you. And I found—"

"Tacos."

"You, Mara. I found you. And now, you can do whatever you want with me." He held his arms out to her in helpless surrender. "I deserve the worst."

And she was not sure what it was. Maybe it was the faint

scent of flowers in the room, the cool Tagaytay air making her feel out of her own body. Maybe it was Jay's earnest words, and the chilling of her own anger. But when he looked at her and willed her to do her worst, she could...picture things. Things that came in flashes, that made her cheeks heat and her heart skip a beat. She could picture him underneath her, him smiling as she gasped, exchanging rough kisses, heartily consented touches in places only Mara herself had touched.

Tang ina? Mara had to physically shake her head to shake the images away, flouncing off and walking to the presidential table, which suddenly needed some rearrangement. *What the fuck?*

What she hadn't counted on—and had forgotten to notice—was that Jay Montinola was fucking handsome. As if his mother had taken his baby self by the ankle and dipped him into a magical pool of gwapo. He had a sharp jawline and a fine nose under his longish hair. His crinkle-eyed smile was sweet, and it was the kind that made you want to smile back (she didn't, because she had *willpower*). And she hadn't really looked at him before, because she simply knew him as Marina's date. But he wasn't Marina's date anymore, was he?

"You okay, Mara?"

Stop, she told herself, shaking her head to rid herself of those thoughts. *You're just feeling sorry for yourself. Do not focus on Jay Montinola.*

"I'm fine, just—" *Flustered as fuck.* "I need to finish this."

She whirled around and walked to the presidential table. It was set for twelve—for their parents, David's parents and the rest for the principal sponsors and their plus-ones. Theirs had to be the grandest setup, and Mara thought the current arrangements were a little too clustered at the center. No problem.

"Can I take photos?" Jay asked, holding up a little camera in his hand. Mara narrowed her eyes at him, as if she could suss out his true intentions. "For Marina and David. Too soon? Fine, too soon—"

"It's fine. Not too soon." Mara shrugged, because she was cool. She was *totally* cool. She had been attracted to people before, of course. It happened to her a lot through screens, through words. But this close it was always harder, because she wasn't used to it. Was already thinking of all the reasons why she had to tamp it down, put it away.

Why, again?

"Can I ask why the purple?" Jay asked suddenly. He was as focused on his camera as she was on her flowers.

"Hmm?" Mara asked, and it was her turn to be surprised and innocent.

"The purple flowers," Jay repeated, pouting his lips to point in the direction of the purple statice flowers. "In a sea of red and orange, there was purple. I was just wondering if it was her favorite color, or...?"

Mara shifted uncomfortably where she stood, and it wasn't because of her flatter shoes. She was trying to decide how much she was going to say, how much of herself she would reveal to Jay. She already felt like he knew too much about her, and this was the longest conversation they'd ever had.

"You dated her for three months, and she didn't tell you her favorite color was autumn?" Mara teased instead, and Jay laughed. There went the eye crinkles. And also, as proof of his sweet-boy vibes, his mouth actually formed a heart when he laughed. How adorable was that? Mara had only seen it in anime. But there he was, a man in real life giving her a heart-shaped smile.

"We really weren't meant to be, I guess." He shrugged like it was no big deal. Good for him. Because Marina probably ended things with him properly. There had actually been something mutual, consensual and out on the table for them both. "Ok lang. I'm not really a relationship kind of guy. Feelings are not my thing."

"Ha? If I recall correctly, David called you a serial monogamist. It was your selling point."

"David's in marketing. He will say a lot of things to get the deal." Jay snorted. "Also serial monogamist means I date a lot. And I do. I like dating, and I date one person at a time. But let's just say, I'm not the kind of guy people fall in love with."

Mara highly doubted that, but she said nothing. It reminded her of all the times a thinner friend would complain to her—a US size 22 who can't even buy underwear in this country— that they were getting fat now. That their clothes didn't fit. And she would hum and say something vaguely like, "There, there, poor thing."

"Isn't it funny how much meaning we attach to flowers?" he asked her suddenly, his gaze focused on the blooms that she was rearranging. "It's a plant. It's a dead plant, essentially. Meant to wither and fade away. They don't last very long, and they aren't meant to."

"Sometimes they do. This one dries out really nicely," Mara

said. She'd made these arguments before to various customers. Why this flower? Why spend money on something this cheap? And out of theme! "And a specific, single bloom may not last forever, but you always find the statice in the grocery, in an everyday arrangement. I wanted Marina to know that it's not so stately and serious, marrying someone you love."

Ha. He had nothing to say to that.

"I added the purple," Mara announced. And she suddenly felt defensive of her admittedly sentimental choices. "For very selfish reasons."

Their eyes met across the presidential table. He had nice eyes, shaped into points on the sides. Serious but so expressive. His eyes were looking at her face now, moving, trailing down to her lips. Mara pressed her lips together, her throat suddenly feeling dry. "They hid their feelings for each other for a long time, as you and I well know."

A bitter pill to swallow, but she was used to that now. She and Jay exchanged wan smiles. The smiles of two people who had been completely fooled.

"I thought it would remain unseen and unnoticed." She shrugged like she hadn't kept that little secret to herself. She hadn't told anyone about it, mostly because nobody asked. It was freeing, to be able to say it out loud. "They felt that way about each other for so long that they just let it grow and turn into...this. A color that doesn't quite stand out, that doesn't quite fit in, but has been there all along. In a selfish way I wanted to commemorate the way they hid their feelings."

There was now silence between them, and Mara's stomach

twisted. She'd said too much. Jay wouldn't understand. She felt a little raw and exposed, even with the little she'd said.

"They're just flowers, and like you said, they don't last," she said quickly, because she'd gone back and forth about this silly, insignificant, even petty little thing. "But they have meaning to the ones who chose them."

"Hay. I keep making you upset." He sighed, shaking his head. Mara couldn't tell if it was genuine disappointment. "My mouth goes places my brain can't control."

He held up the camera again and caught her blink at him in confusion, her heart flipping around in her chest as butterflies swirled a storm inside her. "But this is sweet, Mara. Doing this for them."

"I just told you I called them selfish in flowers." She laughed bitterly.

"Doesn't mean you don't love them. You were hurt, and you wanted it to be acknowledged in a way that mattered to you," Jay pointed out. "The way I see it, there are worse things to do than to say you were hurt in flowers. Now smile, beautiful."

"Flatterer." She raised a brow at him and let him take another photo.

"Hey, I mean it!" Jay said, frowning as he lowered the camera. "You are beautiful. Today you look like a princess. I said that out loud, when I saw you at the church this morning. Which was how I remembered that you hated me."

"I don't hate you." She dismissed the thought with a snort. "I hate what you did. And that you didn't apologize."

"Well, I did na."

"You didn't, actually," Mara clarified while resuming her tasks. Spreading the flowers out to the farther edges of the tables, accepting the shears one of the staff offered her. In her peripheral vision, Jay sauntered (sauntered!) over to the presidential table, a hand on the back of the chair across where she was quickly pulling deep red anthuriums and carnations from the center arrangement, evening out the whole display.

"I didn't what?" he asked as Mara gave the shears back and told the staff what a good job they did.

"Apologize to me," she said, looking up from her work. "You said you wanted to apologize. But I didn't hear a single 'sorry' from you."

"I groveled!"

"Did you, though?" Mara asked, her voice dripping with sarcasm. "An apology must be sincere, and from the bottom of your heart, if you have one. All I got was a half-hearted offer for tacos, and an acknowledgment of you being a jerk. You said you wanted to apologize, but I don't think you actually said it. And I think I deserve a little more than a few words and zero sorrys from the guy who made me feel small. When I'm the least small person in the room."

They stared at each other across a chasm of flowers. Mara held on to her pride and dignity as Jay seemed to be trying to read her. He did not look like he was successful. "Has anyone told you that you're—"

"A bitch?"

"I was going to say scary," he said, slipping his camera into his jacket pocket. "But let's drop it. You want an apology. Something big, and sincere. From my heart. My heart?"

"Yes, your heart." Mara chuckled. He was cute. She appreciated cute. "You have one of those, Mr. Feelings-Are-Not-My-Thing?"

"Hey! I have a heart." His voice was sharp, a little scary. He held up a finger in warning, and Mara jumped in surprise. Oh, Jay could get intense, really quick. "Maybe. No. I can do this. I'm good at this."

"I'm sure." She resumed her work. Made it sound like she didn't think he was good at this at all. "I'm sure all the girls love it when you make an apology."

"They do, actually!" His voice went slightly high-pitched as he came on the defensive. No so intense anymore, silly? He was squirming, and, ha-ha, mission accomplished. He was pacing in front of her, back and forth across the presidential table, and she could practically hear the gears in his head whirring. "But it usually ends, well, not at a wedding reception, that's for sure."

Mara laughed. "Has anyone told you that you're a—"

"Ladies' man?"

"I was going to say chick boy, but I guess that means the same thing." She pulled a lone crimson anthurium from the arrangement in front of her. She waved it at Jay, who stopped pacing. "Well?"

He grinned. It was the grin of someone who knew he was about to make Mara eat out of the palm of his hand. That one grin was enough to make her stomach flip, her hands hold tighter to the flower in her hand. With a grin like that, it was no wonder David suddenly had to tell Marina he loved her. A rival like Jay was hard to beat.

"Mara Janine—"

"Mara *Jane*."

"Mara Jane Barretto," he said, walking around the table so he could stand in front of her. And a fine man in a fine tux— even a man that annoyed her to her core ten minutes ago— was always going to take her breath away, especially when all that dramatic energy was directed her way. He paused, like he was considering something. "Can I hold your hand?"

"Do you think I can be swayed by a little romancing?" What could she say? As someone who had never experienced being romanced, this was overwhelming, but also (to her) very, very funny.

"Is it working?" He took her hand, still grinning. His fingers were longer than hers, his fingertips cool against hers. Mara pressed the flower over her mouth to contain her giggles, because he would be able to tell that she was feeling all the kilig. And it was not supposed to be this easy.

"I'm listening," she said instead.

He squeezed her hand. A storm of butterflies rushed through her entire body, but she ignored them. Jay used his free hand to unbutton the front of his tux. *Um?*

"Mara Jane Barretto," he repeated as he got down on one knee, in the middle of the wedding reception, with an audience of absolutely no other people, surrounded by flowers and mirrors and music in the background. MUNA's cover of Britney Spears's "Sometimes" played, which she had to admit was pretty perfect.

"I am so sorry that I posted that photo without your consent. From now on the only photos I will take are of you and your radiant beauty." She wrinkled her nose in distaste. And to be fair, he picked up on that right away. "Too thick?"

"A little thick."

"Well, I'm not taking it back. You are very beautiful, Mara. And I really am sorry about what I said, too. Clearly, you're brilliant at what you do. Everyone can see it. And I was an idiot that I didn't look hard enough."

The words were soft, spoken only to her. Mara squeezed his hand back just to make sure she was still upright. This was so *silly*. And yet it made her laugh, made her feel bubbly and light.

"I'm sorry," he concluded. "And I mean that more than GMA did."

Mara rolled her eyes, but she found this amusing enough. Jay hopped up from where he was kneeling. It was so quick, too quick really, that Mara jumped back in surprise. Jay's quick reflexes remained, though, and he caught her easily, pulling her up by the waist to press against his body. He nearly lost his own balance, so he used his other hand to steady himself against her. Mara gasped, and Jay's eyes widened in shock.

Too close, too intimate. Too fast. Mara didn't like it, even if her heart was hammering in her chest. Was she sweating? She didn't want to be sweating. She needed this to stop, they'd taken it too far, she didn't—

"Mara?"

"Apology accepted," she said quickly, looking away. "Let me go."

"ATE MARA!" That was Mabel standing by the threshold of the ballroom, her eyes wide with shock and confusion. "Ano 'to? Hath a miracle occurred? Should I call the Vatican?"

"Mabel!" Mara took ten steps away from Jay and toward her youngest sister. She noticed Jay's hands were suddenly in his pockets and that he was now finding the chandeliers the most interesting thing in the room. So interesting that he had a blush spreading across his cheeks.

Oh god, she was *fucked*. Mabel was always terrible at keeping secrets, and Mara had about five minutes before Marina found out about this. No amount of threat, bribe or flattery would stop Mabel Barretto when she had a secret.

Mara looped her arm around her sister's and started to pull her away from the ballroom. "Were you looking for me for the family photos? We should go. Wouldn't want to miss that."

"I should head back to the other room," Jay announced suddenly. "My friends will be waiting. Bye, Mara."

"Jay." Mara gave him the most curt of nods before she left the room. A tightness in her chest eased as he left. God. That was…something. She'd never had anyone… And the way he looked at her was…

"Jay? Like Jay the guy you met at that gin bar?" Mabel gasped, craning her neck back at the ballroom, where Jay was probably watching them leave the room and asking himself what the fuck he'd almost done. "Didn't he date Ate Marina? Don't you hate him?"

"We…sorted things out."

"I bet you fuckin' did."

"Mabel Janina!" Mara hissed, as the sisters made it to the restaurant's salon, a gorgeous backdrop of deep green wallpaper for the family photos. Marina was already there, her reception dress being fussed over by the stylists and the assistants. Farther into the room, David was with his family, taking their family portraits. "He apologized to me, that's all! Do *not* tell Marina, I swear to god—"

"Ate, I've apologized to people I'm actually close with, and we never looked at each other like *that*."

"Like what?"

"Like zippers had ceased to exist."

"Whose zippers ceased to exist?" Marina asked. Her eyes sparkled with curious delight as the crowd of staff dissipated and her sisters joined her. "Ate, you look flushed."

"Nobody's zippers ceased to exist!" Mara said. "Oh my go—"

"Ate is flushed because I caught her flirting with Jay!" Mabel said. Secret spilled in less than a minute. Mabel's record was getting worse. Mara groaned and wondered aloud if anyone remembered the time Mara told not a single soul that Mabel's underwear was held up by a safety pin at the rehearsal dinner, but her sisters ignored her. Sad! "I saw them making kilig eyes at each other in the ballroom. Also he was on one knee for her."

"Mabel!"

"Jay Montinola?" Marina shrieked, like it was the best thing she'd heard the entire day, and it was *her* wedding day. She pounced on Mara, shaking her arm, and she stumbled back in shock. "Oh my god, Ate, *yes*. This is a great idea! Did you kiss him?"

"No!" That was Mara.

"Yes!" That was Mabel.

"Are we talking about kissing Jay?" David asked, coming up to them as he pressed his cheeks down to relax his muscles. Great. The peanut gallery was complete. Mara was having a fantastic time. "His kiss is foolproof. Ten to zero, I think his stats are, after today."

"Stats?" Mara asked. "Dude, gross. You keep *stats?*"

"They don't. He's talking about—" Marina cut herself off and turned to David. "Babe, I wasn't talking about his curse."

"Curse, he's cursed?" Mabel gasped dramatically. A camera flash came off without warning and threw Mara even more off kilter.

"Hi, can you warn us before you do that?" She glared at the photographer, who smiled sheepishly and muttered an apology about how they were just taking test shots. Meanwhile, David, Marina and Mabel were all talking over each other. Which meant that David was clearly bonding with her sisters, but, oh my god, she could not get a straight answer from any of them.

"TIME FIRST!" Mara commanded the entire room with a shout so loud, even the photographers stopped in the middle of their task. She shook her head at them, prompting them to resume their work, before she turned to her brother-in-law and sisters, still holding on to the anthurium. "What the fuck are you guys talking about?"

"So there's a thing that happens," David began. "A curse."

"It is a curse, but it's really more a curse for Jay. Not for the people who kiss him," Marina added, also unhelpfully. "Obviously, they end up just fine."

"Marina," Mara groaned. "From the beginning."

"Okay, remember when my car broke down in the middle of C-5, and I realized that I loved David when he was the first person I called?" Marina asked her. Mara nodded, having heard this particular story recounted several times. In fact, she heard that story just today when Marina read her vows in front of the church.

David had commuted like a bat out of hell from Makati when Marina called (well, as fast as a bat could commute in Metro Manila, which still took a while). There really wasn't much he could do to help aside from sit with her in the broken car while it was dragged via wrecker from Taguig to Rizal on a Friday night. The proximity led to them admitting their feelings for each other, and the rest was history. "I had just come from a date with Jay, where we'd kissed for the first time."

"And you remember when Selena Guerro got engaged, she had this whole post about the ex that was her good luck charm?" David asked. And again, yes, Mara remembered because even she who wasn't into local celebrity gossip had heard about it. Had read the post and commented how odd it was to credit your latest relationship to your ex. "Guess who."

"Wait," Mabel said, shaking her head in confusion. In her mind, the pieces arranged themselves into a simple answer. Not the most logical, but perhaps the most simple. Occam and his razor rejoiced. "Are you saying he's like...a last kiss guy?"

"*The* last kiss guy." David nodded. "If you want to find the one, if you want to marry the love of your life, even if you've never *had* a love of your life, you kiss Jay Montinola. A hundred percent, the next person you meet, you marry."

"We're here!" A familiar voice filled the room, as Mara, Marina and Mabel's parents burst into the salon in a flurry of formal wear, their driver carrying a tote bag full of Sonya's Garden treats behind them. It would have been hilarious in slow motion. "Time for family photos!"

I'm not the kind of guy people fall in love with. Jay said as much to her in the ballroom. And as Mara smiled for family photos, squeezed closer together and followed prompts of, "wacky, wacky," she wondered if kissing Jay Montinola *was* actually a curse. To her it sounded more like an opportunity.

But she didn't think she could kiss Jay. Not this time.

Five

So. That happened. Jay had gotten himself into sticky situations before—the kind he would never repeat to his niece. Not now, not ever. But tonight was the kind of sticky that wrapped around your heart and made it feel like you'd done something wrong. When in fact, he hadn't.

He was a go-with-the-flow, bahala-na-si-Batman kind of guy. He didn't mind being told what to do. But yeah, if there was a bingo card for how Marina and David's wedding reception was going to go, kissing the maid of honor definitely wasn't on his list.

Because he almost had. Had come *really* close. They were already there, his balance just intact and Mara in his arms. And she was gorgeous. Her soft, warm skin and plump cheeks were flushed red. He could smell her perfume, something floral and sweet—but not overly so, like a second skin. He would have asked her if he could kiss her. She could have said yes. If she said yes, then Jaysohn Montinola would have kissed the fuck out of Mara Jane Barretto.

But alas, he did not. And he knew at that moment he'd done something wrong, because Mara had seemed flushed and upset. Now here he was, the human disaster relegated to the back tables with Mon and Scott, wondering what he'd done.

The dinner had been exquisite. Maybe. He couldn't seem to recall specifics, just a vague sensation of being pleasantly full. He remembered there was a steak. Foie gras, perhaps, and Scott commenting in the background on how it didn't quite go together. But it was still good.

Jay could be shown three dishes and asked to correctly identify which ones he ate tonight, and he would not be able to guess a single one. How can one leave a fancy restaurant after a free meal and still not know if the food was good or not? How very un-Pinoy of him.

Usually, this meant that his brain was preoccupied with other things—work he needed to do, a fun thing he could do with Luna, a dance he wanted to learn. But not tonight. Tonight, he was fully distracted by a kiss that never happened.

Why, though? Missed connections had happened to him before. It was par for the course in the life of a person who actively dated.

Maybe the difference was he'd really, *really* wanted a chance to kiss Mara. Wanted to feel her body pressed against his, feel her curves as he sank his lips into hers. He had a feeling that they would be very good at kissing each other.

But the moment had passed, and Mara Barretto was marked safe from Jay's Kiss Curse.

"—really don't think he's listening at all," Scott was saying, and Jay managed to bring himself back to the moment. Back to the ballroom, where the flowers looked even better under the lighting setup. To the food on the plate in front of him. They had apparently made it to dessert, which was a faux-Twix with sea salt and a caramel sauce that would follow Jay to his dreams that evening. To Scott, sitting beside him and telling a story about...oh god, he had no idea.

"So there we were, on the beach, and the dragon came down in front of us and asked if we were interested in checking out his hole."

"Don't you mean horde?"

"No, I mean hole, Mon. There was a hole in the cave, and there was treasure inside it." Scott's arms were spread out wide, mimicking... Jay was not completely sure what. What story was he trying to tell? "Right, Jay?"

"Right. What?"

"I think you finally got his attention," Mon pointed out. Not-so-subtly grinning from his side of the table. "Welcome back to the wedding, buddy."

"Ha-ha, very funny," he said sarcastically, rolling his eyes at the two, who seemed even more amused that he was acting all bitchy. He was bored, that was all! "I was distracted, that's all."

"By what?" Mon asked, at the same time Scott said, "By *who*?"

Then his phone started to ring in his pocket. Perfect timing, Universe, thank you. Jay had already planned to ignore them both anyway, but the ringing made it seem more out of necessity. Scott and Mon were great most times, but some days they came together and decided to share a single brain cell between them, and Jay was usually the subject of the organelle's attention.

There was also an email from his boss in Hong Kong, subject line URGENT: Return to Office. Jay ignored that for now.

"Ops, that's Ate. Gotta take this," he said, practically springing out of his seat to answer the call. He slipped out of the ballroom and to the hallway that connected this ballroom to the casita from earlier. Just in time, too. The hosts were just announcing that they were about to get the program going.

"Hey, did I buy the Nespresso machine, or did you?" Ate Irene sounded a little harried over the phone, and Jay pulled the phone away from his ear for a second to check the time. 9:00 p.m. was pretty early by most standards, but it usually meant that the baby had just gone to sleep and she was raring to do a whole list of things. "I can't remember."

Well, not a baby so much as a three-year-old, but, still.

"Capsule coffee? I would never." Jay scoffed, ignoring the little tug in the empty cavity that presumably housed his heart. Suddenly he knew exactly what his sister was doing, could practically picture her with a box in one hand and her phone tucked under her ear as she stared at the fire engine red Nespresso machine. "Isn't the coffee machine a more late-stage packing thing? You guys aren't moving until May."

"Well, I was panicking about it earlier," Ate Irene started. Jay leaned against the nearby pillar to listen, blowing a stray strand of hair out of his face. "And I called Nige, and he said I just needed to make a plan. So I made a Gantt chart."

"Of course." Jay wanted to laugh. Ate Irene liked charts—they helped her make big things seem smaller, actionable. They had several lying around the house, a memorable one in particular marked "Operation Baby Girl 2020" from when they realized that Ate Irene was going to have a pandemic baby in the middle of...well, the pandemic. A timeline of all the steps that needed to be taken to complete a project had been a lifesaver then. Makes sense she would make one now. "And the Gantt chart said 'pack the coffee machine'?"

"Something like that." He practically heard his Ate collapse into a chair with a deep sigh. Irene was three years older than him, but they had always considered themselves close. They knew how to speak to each other without actually saying what they meant. Like this conversation, for example.

"How's the wedding?" Ate Irene asked. Translation, *Will you be okay if we move away?*

"It's great. Hey, I apologized to Mara Barretto." *I'll be fine, Ate. You have to trust me, even if I don't totally believe it yet. I won't hold you back.* "I think she accepted it."

"You've always been hard to say no to, Jay." She made it sound like a bad thing. *We can stay if you want us to.*

"Hey, I made excellent points. I groveled well." *Don't stay for me.*

"Uh-huh. And Marina and David, they're happily married? No protests, objections from the crowd?"

"Documents were signed and notarized, and the wedding was drama free. They're together forever," he said. And if there was any bitterness in his voice, it wasn't because he was jealous, or sad. It was just… "Have you ever thought about how two people deciding to be together implies that someone had to be left behind in order for them to be together?"

There was a pause on the line. Jay could pretend it was because it took a while for a message to reach from the highlands of Tagaytay to an apartment in Pasig City, but he knew better.

"Are we still talking about the wedding?" Ate Irene asked. *Or are we talking about the fact that Luna and I are moving away from you?*

See, Jay and Irene Montinola were experts at saying things, without actually saying much. Jay didn't quite feel like facing it yet—that he'd reshaped and reframed his entire life around his family, only to find out that it wasn't going to be forever. But the Montinola siblings could hold off the emotional processing for another time. They should probably add it to the Gantt chart.

"Maybe." He sighed. "You know the bank is asking if I was going back to Hong Kong."

"Oh?" Ate Irene sounded like she was trying really hard to sound disinterested. "I thought you changed your status to freelancer so you never had to RTO?"

I did that when I thought you needed help raising Luna. "I did, but they can reinstate me to an analyst position if I want." It wasn't a terrible life out there. It was expensive, but Hong Kong had its delights and pleasures. Completely different from the ones in Manila, of course. But it wasn't wholly unfamiliar to him. "I'm negotiating a raise. Although I'm sure Hong Kong's only gotten more expensive since the pandemic."

"I bet," Ate Irene agreed. "Well…something for you to think about, I guess." *Are you really going to go?*

"Yeah. I'll be home tonight," he assured his sister. "Late nga lang. Is Luna down?"

"Only after some bribery and a promise that her 'Nong would be there in the morning." Ate Irene snorted, and Jay's voice caught in his throat suddenly, but he didn't want to think or talk about why. "I should let you get back to the wedding." *I love you.*

"Should I attempt to catch the garter?" Jay mused, tucking his hand in his pocket and fiddling with the buttons on his camera. It helped. *Love you, too, Ate.*

"Don't!" Irene laughed. "Between your powerful as fuck first kiss—"

"Ate you shouldn't swear when Luna is in the next room."

"—and the possibility of sukob, I don't think it's a good idea."

"I don't really see myself getting married this year." *Or ever.* "You should be safe."

"Yeah, but you don't want to mess with that wedding mojo, you know?" Ate Irene asked him. "Weddings are a hotbed of emotions. Things we hide feel like they must come to the surface, because two people were brave enough to say out loud that they were in love, that they were going to stay in love."

"Is that what love is? Bravery?"

"Love is closing your eyes and hoping for the best. But you have someone's hand to hold, so it's not so scary. So I guess yes, it's bravery. But weddings are love, bravery and alcohol. Bad combinations all around. You can't really trust that anyone's going to make a good emotional decision in that ball-room." *Especially someone who is deciding if he's moving away again.*

"That's reassuring, coming from someone who is getting married in, how many Gantt chart steps?" Jay teased, chuck-ling. He looked up and saw that the moon was full and bright tonight. Lighting up Luisa's parking lot and making the foun-tain in front of him look like fireworks. A good night to have a first kiss with someone.

"Hey, the bride and groom actually had time to make their emotional decisions," Irene pointed out. "Everyone else that follows is just swept up in a moment."

Ate Irene's words continued to linger in Jay's mind as he headed back to the ballroom. He was almost holding on to them a little too hard, tugging them to keep him grounded. He found himself still holding on to his silent phone, keep-ing his sister's words close.

Tonight wasn't the night to make bad decisions. Kissing Mara Barretto, who had love in her eyes, who wanted some-thing that lasted, would definitely be a bad one.

He walked into the ballroom, wondering why the sound quality of the music was suddenly so good.

The newly wedded couple was in the middle of their very first dance.

It looked like a scene from a fairy tale, if fairy tales ended in Tagaytay. A gentle fog made the dance floor look like it was a cloud. And floating on it, David and Marina held on to each other, all happy smiles as they swayed to the music. The music was played by a string quartet, and singing along with it was—holy shit?—the cast of *Hanggang Ulap*, the musical that Marina proclaimed to be her favorite.

Budget who? No wonder everything was wonderful and romantic. Freaking Erin Javier was singing, and, yep that was Ramon Figueroa with her, duetting the musical's Big Love Song. But as extravagant as it was, it somehow suited the newly wedded couple to be over-the-top. They both looked really happy. Flashed the kinds of smiles that you made when you forgot anyone was looking. Jay held up his camera and took a photo. It looked even more radiant in black and white.

"Here I was thinking you hated weddings," Scott said, moving to stand next to him, a tumbler of whiskey in his hand. The bar was apparently open.

"I don't hate weddings." Jay scoffed. "I just don't think they're for me. What David and Marina have. You and Ava, Mon and Olivia. Things that last? I can't have that."

He knew how to deal with things that weren't tangible. Other people's money, stock markets, boredom, feelings. Even his personal life held nothing permanent. The coffee machine he thought would bring him joy for years to come would end up in Irene's stash because he didn't actually like it. Conclusion? Things that were meant to last, well, not for him. He wouldn't even know the first thing about truly loving someone.

Thank you for being my last stop before the one, Selena had said in her post. Five years ago now, holy shit. *Your good luck kiss really worked.*

The last stop before the one. That was just the way his metaphorical cookie of a life crumbled.

"Hay nako." Scott sighed, taking a sip of his whiskey. "Here na me, you not yet."

"What?" Jay spluttered a laugh. That made absolutely no sense. Scott shot him a look of total seriousness, though. Even in the darker corners of the ballroom where they stood, it was a look that said, "Pay attention. I am about to drop Knowledge on you, dummy."

"Papunta ka pa lang, pabalik na ako," Scott said. That made way more sense. "You think you're the first person to think you don't deserve love? I went on a whole emotional, spiritual journey to Bali to finally decide that I was in love with Ava, and that I was worthy of her love. Mon went to New York thinking he was going to get a job, slept with Olivia and realized he was on the journey before he knew it."

"That sounds like Mon," Jay conceded. Although he was sure there was way more nuance to his friends' journeys than that.

"Even Teddy made the choice to stick to his guns when he asked Andi out to that date the first time." Scott looked entirely too smug at the mention of Mon's usually reclusive business partner. Teddy had been the one to ask Andi out first? Bravery, as Ate Irene said.

"My point being," Scott continued, unaware of the myriad of Jay's thoughts, "we make a choice to love someone, all of us. And choosing someone means you know you deserve love. Want it if you want it, push it away if you don't. But it's not because you don't deserve it. Everyone deserves love, Jay. And everyone who loves you is lucky, because we get to have you."

Yeah, those were tears that sprung in Jay's eyes. God, Scott was really, really good at this. Give the man his FAMAS Award already.

"What happened with Mara?" Scott asked. The woman in question got up from the family table and shuffled through the tables of wedding guests to stop and lean against a post, watching the couple. Jay could see her profile, and she almost looked…sad? Wistful? Her face was heartbreaking. What the hell had he done to make her upset earlier? What he really wanted to do was take her into his arms and tell her it would be okay. "Did you fix it?"

It would be okay, because he was going to do whatever he could to fix it.

"Not yet," Jay admitted, his hand loosening its grip on his phone. "But I will."

Six

"Defamation! Cyber libel! Emotional damages!" Mara listed, holding out a finger for each offense as her father listened carefully. Martin Barretto had the kind of listening face that was a mere tilt of his head, eyes gazing at his daughter above the frames of his reading glasses—he had been in the middle of doing his daily sudoku on his phone when Mara barged in and asked if she could sue someone. "What else?"

"Moral turpitude?"

"That can't be a real word," Mabel remarked from Mara's other side at the presidential table. They were just finishing up dinner when one of her dad's friends sent a DM inquiring about why Mara was expressing suffering on the internet via meme. With the way the internet worked, the photo had come from Instagram, then was meme-ified on X before it showed up on Facebook and Viber several weeks later. Which was why the boomers were only finding out about it now. It was difficult enough to explain that one of David's friends was trying to make fun of her, but more so when Martin asked his daughter if she was angry with him.

Was she? She was certainly feeling something. Something hot and fiery that made her want to growl and scream and sue him, apparently. But was that necessarily anger? She'd more or less forgiven him for all of that earlier.

"Also, Pops, we can't sue Jay," Mabel added, leaning forward a bit so she could speak to her father. "He's your future son-in-law."

"He is *not*," Mara snapped, shifting in her seat to glare at her sister.

"What about the curse, Ate?" Mabel asked. "You kiss him, and you end up marrying him!"

"That is a fundamental misunderstanding of how his kiss curse thing works."

"Sometimes I don't understand half the things you girls talk about." Martin sighed, resuming the sudoku puzzle he was trying to finish. Mara's father was a man who ate meals quick and didn't like dessert, which was why Mara and Mabel were currently sharing a second faux-Twix. He hadn't been quite present for the girls when they were babies and was only just getting to really know them now as full-grown adults. "It was easier reading laws in law school, and those you can interpret in many ways."

"Lucky for you, Popsi, it's vice versa when you and Mom are talking," Mara teased, making her dad raise a brow at her, as if to say, "Are you serious?" "Remember when she asked you about attending a webminar?"

"Or when you said we had to visit the deadly departed!"

Mabel said, sending the sisters into a fit of really stupid giggling, because that was *classic*. "Or, or when he got mad because he said we were half-hazardly parking the car!"

"Who's cursed?" their mother, Jasmine Barretto, suddenly asked, pulling away from conversation with Tita Claudine to glance at her daughters. Her faux lashes fluttered. In fairness to their mother, the faux lashes really suited her. "My son-in-law?"

"Not David," Martin said. Not even looking up from his phone. "Mara likes someone and she wants to sue them."

"Oh, you must really like them," Jasmine concluded. "You usually get angry at something before you finally decide that you love it."

Mara's giggle cut off quick as she gaped at her mother in horror. "Like…?"

"Oh! Like pizza with spicy honey!" Mabel said, which, traitor. Mara didn't like spicy things, but apparently adding chili flakes to honey was a revelation on pizza. Who knew?

"School," Martin added. Mara remembered lying on the floor as a seven-year-old and absolutely refusing to put on her uniform to go to "big school." Several academic awards later…

"Flowers!" their mother added. Ironic considering where they were now, and how far Mara had come. As a child she didn't like joining her grandmother in the garden, complaining that her hands itched when she touched soil. How wrong she had been about that, right?

"Hoy naman!" Mara said, taking a big part of her Twix. God, that caramel sauce was delicious.

Her family seemed oblivious to her distress, and the fact

that her cheeks were still hot after…whatever it was that happened between her and Jay earlier in this very room. "This is not the same thing. Jay, he…" *Looked at me like he wanted to kiss me.* "…made a meme out of me."

But she'd already forgiven him for that. She didn't care about that at all. But she needed to say something that made sense to them, because she couldn't quite make sense of this.

"Also, didn't the two of you say to me that you weren't ready for us to get married?" Mara asked her parents, indicating herself and twenty-five-year-old Mabel, who had a bit of cookie on her bottom lip.

Mara would never be able to really get it out of her head; the rare sentimentality in her dad's tone, the deep sigh he made as he and his mother sat next to Mara in the pews of the church. Jasmine had been crying, trying to make sure her makeup didn't run by pressing a point of the handkerchief where her tear ducts were.

"No more," her father had declared. "No more marrying you guys off. Not for a long while."

"Yes," Martin agreed now, several hours later. "I still want grandchildren, though."

Even Mara had to laugh at that. Yes, her parents were enigmas wrapped in mystery most days, but she loved them so much. Even when she wanted to put a GPS tracker on them at all times.

"Wait, who are we suing again?" Jasmine asked.

"The guy I saw Ate Mara almost ki—"

"I did not almost," Mara snapped. "There is no almost!"

"Anak." Her mother sighed, reaching over her father's body

to hold Mara's hand. While her temperament was closer to her father's, a lot of people liked to comment on how alike she and her mother looked. Mara never worried about what she would look like when she was older, because she was looking at it now—her mother's cheeks were still rounded. Softer now, but still. She had her wrinkles, mostly around her eyes and her mouth from smiling. Jasmine even had a few sun spots, which was why Mara had always been religious about sunscreen and moisturizer. A habit she was still trying to instill in her mother.

Point being, whatever happened, however she ended up, Mara knew she was going to be okay. Because her parents always made her feel okay. They worked hard and earned, and they bestowed it upon their children to make and do as they saw fit. Mara, Marina and Mabel all knew that the privilege of generational wealth was given rarely and to few, and they all sought to make something out of what their parents had built.

Yes, they were spoiled, and they were rich by most standards. But Martin and Jasmine taught their daughters that their work was their value, and that the measure of their lives was in how much they helped other people with their work. That was all they wanted for their girls. To live happy lives, in careers that they valued, giving jobs and futures to others.

Except sometimes, they also wanted grandchildren.

"You know when you were growing up, and all the movies said that a princess had to wait for their prince to come?" Jasmine asked her.

"Yes," said the girl raised on magic and happily ever after. Who still believed in it, to her core, after all this time.

"Well, sometimes, princes aren't the smartest. So you need to give them a little nudge to let you know that you would like them to pursue you." That was sweet of her mom to say, but also very not helpful at all. "Do you want cheese hopia? I have some in my purse."

See, this was the problem with Mara experiencing any sort of emotion in front of her family. Most of the time, whenever she felt something (anger, usually), she needed time to figure out why she was angry or upset. Feel first, analyze later. But it was hard to analyze when she was being relentlessly teased about it. Or when she was already being advised for a feeling she hadn't fully managed to break down yet.

This was why she kept her feelings close to her chest. Never told anyone about her delusions of David, especially not the people who understood her best. Maybe deep down she knew the answers and just didn't want to hear them out loud.

Jay had nearly fallen over when he caught her. Hadn't expected the weight of her body. But that hadn't embarrassed her or made her feel bad at all. What angered her (what *embarrassed* her, now that she was thinking about it) was that she thought that he was going to kiss her. Her lips pursed, her neck craned and her skin felt like it was on fire, so sure that Jay Montinola was going to kiss her.

But after David, and all her silly delusions, she had to shut it down. It did people no good to believe in things that had no basis in reality. Instead it was better to just make it happen yourself.

She was thirty-three, for fuck's sake. Enough of waiting for things to happen to her. Results would only happen if she did the legwork. Just like quitting her job, just like opening Wildflower. Who needed to wink-wink, nudge-nudge at the universe when you could just tell someone, "Hello, I would really like for you to kiss me."

So more a shove than a little nudge, but it would do.

"And now, for their first dance, David, Marina, can you please come up?"

Mara heard the whir of the fog machine as David helped Marina up from their seats in the center of the room. Music started to play, and the lights were on her sister and her new husband. He held her in his arms like she was the most precious thing his hands could ever touch and swept her across the room.

They had rehearsed this dance. Mara had already seen it in the practice room, in the family living room and at the rehearsal dinner just the night before. But tonight, with the lights, and the fog, and the fact that professional theater actors were singing their hearts out especially for the couple, it was…a lot. David tucked a flower in Marina's hair and ended up simply…holding her. They were smiling at each other with their eyes locked, hands clasped together, and *god*. God, it was so lovely.

"They're so beautiful together," Mabel whispered beside Mara. They were. And as happy as Mara was for them, a deep, dark pit inside her screamed of jealousy and desire. Called her selfish for wanting that for herself. Because, god, Mara wanted it for herself. She wanted to be loved and experience the relationship Marina and David had, where he could finish her sentences and she never had to explain to him what he meant, because he knew her, and understood her.

Could Jay "I Don't Do Relationships" Montinola do that?

She inhaled sharply and stood up, explaining to her mesmerized family that she needed to go to the bathroom. But what Mara needed was space. Distance, and space. Room to just breathe, and watch, and feel every rush of emotion that roiled inside her. She was so happy for them. So, so happy for them.

But she was sad, too, because the thing she could never admit to herself was the fear that maybe she couldn't have… this. That her walls were too high, she was too fat, too high maintenance, too shrill, too…everything. And while she knew all the reasons why marriage was "a rock that you constantly bang against your own head," deep down she still wanted it. And might never, ever be even a little bit close to having it.

"Mara?" a voice asked. Suddenly, Jay was beside her, his eyes brimming with concern as he gently touched her bare arm. "You're tearing up."

So she was. The tears in her eyes were hot, but they dared not to fall. Mara chuckled and pressed the back of her hand to her tear ducts, preserving her makeup, preserving her falsies! Oh god.

"Are you okay?"

Looking at Jay, Mara made a choice. It wasn't that she was desperate. It was just that, in the face of everything she would need to do to have what her sister had (lowering boundaries, meeting new people, being vulnerable, all the things that she didn't enjoy), it was easier to kiss a stranger. Easier still to kiss someone she had wanted to kiss a mere two hours ago.

Did she believe in the curse? That was like asking a Filipino how they could reconcile their Catholic faith, modern medicine and albularyo healing. She believed it like she believed in jumping when the clock struck midnight on New Year's. She believed it like the time she, Mabel and Marina giggled and stuffed twelve grapes into their mouth after jumping around because they wanted boyfriends.

Sure, why not. It never hurt to believe, and it didn't hurt to try. At the very least, Mara was determined to give it a try.

"Can I ride with you, back to Manila?" Mara asked. "If you're heading back, that is."

"Of course." Jay nodded. "I'm all yours."

Seven

Obviously, they didn't leave the reception right at that exact moment. There were programs to go through, and a couple trivia games to win. Mon scored a gift card to a Japanese restaurant because he happened to know that David was an Aries and Marina an Aquarius, amazing. The bride and groom also decided to forego the traditional garter and bouquet toss. Jay was a higher jumper than most and would have caught the garter without trying. Which meant he would maybe have to slide a garter up a stranger's leg, which was fine, but in public? Too weird. What *was* a garter anyway?

But the night continued, and like most Filipino celebrations, ended at a party. The DJ played "Y.M.C.A.," "Bongga Ka Day" and Sarah Geronimo's "Tala" in rapid succession, several representatives from every generation and friend group enthusiastically participating. There was always that one family member who ended up being the impromptu dance instructor for everyone. And that person happened to be David, who could take crowds through simple dance steps, with enthusiasm and gusto. He even pulled Jay in, the both of them more than game, because it was always easy to say yes to David.

"Great dancing, as always." David winked at Jay at some point.

"Once a street dance captain, always a street dance captain," Jay said, winking back at his cocaptain.

They hadn't even reopened the bar yet at that point, and already Jay had ended up swing dancing with Tita Claudine to "Wake Me Up Before You Go-Go" and "September." And he was going to remember that for a long time, because she'd winked at him and said something very complimentary about his "loose hips."

"Your friend," Mara said suddenly, appearing beside him at some point to hand him a bottle of cold craft beer. She was a little breathless—he had seen her dancing with her sisters and singing TLC's "No Scrubs" word-perfect a few songs ago. They looked across the ballroom, where Scott had somehow acquired a couple of glow sticks and was now dancing to Beyoncé's "Cuff It" along with all the titas doing the LA Walk. He was more than a little stiff, but you got the impression that he was doing it on purpose to be funny. To be fair, it really was. Jay took a video to send to Ava. "He's quite the dancer."

"Give him a whistle, he'll really go wild." Jay laughed, taking off his jacket and placing it across his lap. The cool weather and the open windows of the venue really made for perfect after-party dancing. He took a deep sip of his beer, which was also perfect. "Cheers?"

"Cheers." Mara smiled, clinking the top of her beer bottle with his before she took a sip. "God, my back is giving up. I am so going to need an Alaxan later. I just turned thirty-three last week!"

"I was due to drink maintenance meds an hour ago," he said, holding up his smartwatch for her to check the alert. "Welcome to your midthirties."

"Oh no." She laughed, shaking her head, because Jay's alarm was pretty peeved that he hadn't listened. It was fine, he could drink before bed. "Are you—"

"Mara!" someone called behind them. "Tito Pedring and I are leaving na, can we bring home these flowers?"

"Isn't that bad luck?" Jay asked, raising a brow.

"That's funerals, dummy." Mara chuckled, using his shoulder as an anchor to help her stand before she turned to the wedding guest. She was clearly getting tired. But that didn't stop her from smiling at the guests. "Yes, tita! I'll walk you to the exit. But not the vase po, we still need those—"

"Ha? But they're the best part!"

Jay grinned as she walked away, clandestinely keeping her beer bottle at his side as she smiled and nodded to the unfamiliar couple. This happened a couple of times that evening, even as the taco bar finally opened and more ice cream was served to guests taking a break from the partying. The line to the tacos was so long that most of the guests had gone home by the time Jay managed to get a hold of a plate.

Hello, my love. We reunite.

"Taco?" Jay asked as Mara waved goodbye to a younger family heading back to the parking lot. In particular the ring bearer, sleepily waving at them from his father's shoulder as they walked away.

"Jay!" Mara said. The surprise that registered on her face would have stung, but Jay had a little beer in him, which probably dulled the sting a bit. "You're still here."

"I agreed to drive you home, remember?" he asked, and if she'd forgotten *that*, he definitely would have been hurt. It was absolutely no burden for him to drive her back wherever. Not like anyone was waiting up for him to get back, and it was a Friday. "Where else would I be?"

"Your friends…?"

"Scott's driving Mon to Starbucks Reserve. They're meeting Ava and her cousin there," Jay explained. It was nice of her to think of his friends like that. "Like I said earlier, I'm—"

"All yours. I remember." Mara nodded, and it seemed like she came to some sort of conclusion in her head. "I'm sorry I'm making you wait. There's a lot of stuff for egress. I just want to make sure it's done well."

"It's no problem," he said, squeezing her arm with his free hand. "I'm having fun. I met your mom! She's hilarious. She was trying to guess whose friend I was, because she was convinced she'd met me before."

"Oh my god," Mara groaned. "That's her thing, and she's really bad at it. I'll try to hurry it up. Sorry, Jay."

"Mara," he said, placing the tacos in her hand. "Eat tacos. I'll be here whenever you're ready, okay?"

He smiled to reassure her that everything was fine. And he really didn't mind waiting around a little longer. But he couldn't quite read the emotion brimming in Mara's face as she took the tacos from him. He didn't miss that her eyes were a little more shiny, her lips moving as if there were more things she should probably say. Instead she took the plate, picked up a taco and took a bite.

"Mmm," she moaned. The sound made Jay's throat feel a little thick suddenly. Was he coming down with something? "That's really good."

"I know," he said, clearing his throat because it definitely was not his throat. Because he could very easily picture Mara wrapping her lips around something else entirely. "Go, go."

"Thanks, Jay!" Mara said, ducking back into the ballroom. Jay was about to head back himself when he heard a low chuckle from the benches nearby.

"So you're the famous Jay." He couldn't quite make out his features, but the impressive fit and embroidery on the piña cloth was unmistakable. The face slightly glowing from the screen of a sudoku puzzle was that of Martin Barretto, Mara's dad, and the father of the bride.

Marina looked a lot like her father, now that he was looking closer. Except where Marina was smiley and approachable, her father radiated an intimidating aura, one that told everyone in his vicinity that he was the one in charge. Funny enough, Mara was more like her father in that way.

"My daughter wants to sue you."

"Which daughter?" Martin narrowed his eyes at him. They both knew which daughter.

"For stealing her heart?" Jay squeaked, feeling his heart lodge in his throat. He'd just been thinking of this man's eldest daughter eating not-a-taco. If Martin (*Tito* Martin?) was going to murder him then and there, he would not be entirely unjustified.

The older man laughed, and Jay could not tell if it was because he thought Jay was funny, or because he was about to make Jay's life a miserable hell. It was very unclear which one it was.

"Which daughter talaga. How very brave," was his conclusion, spoken as he peered at Jay over his reading glasses. "I'll have to keep an eye on you."

Earlier that evening, Martin delivered a speech about raising his daughters to work hard and how he expected David to be of the same standard. He also inadvertently quoted Lil Wayne in saying that "real Gs move in silence like lasagna," as he claimed most husbands will have to. It was a good speech. Jay thought it was funny, and touching, and quite right for the man that raised the hellions that were Mara, Mabel and Marina Barretto.

"You're exactly her type pa naman."

"Pops!" Mara exclaimed, stepping back out from the ballroom, sans tacos. "I thought you were going to find Mom and head back to the hotel?"

"Well, your sister forgot to book transpo to take her and her lovely groom back, so we're all carpooling."

Mara did not seem the least surprised that this was the conclusion. She sighed and held out a hand to her dad. "Let's herd the family, then. The Luisa's people are waiting for us to leave."

She glanced at Jay, and he hoped she couldn't tell that he was still feeling a little shaky in his leather shoes. But they left him quickly, and Jay headed back to the ballroom himself. He might as well help encourage people to go home to make the job easier.

After grabbing another cone of ice cream (honey and milk, yum-yum) and telling a few guests that the venue was closing, Jay found himself back near the dance floor, staring at the last remnants of the Barretto-Gonzales wedding. Most of the flowers were gone—the guests had clearly helped themselves. But the red-tinted vases were lined up perfectly on top of the presidential tables, one of the staff wrapping them up in newspaper to pack away. There was confetti on the dance floor from when the party first started, and Bruno Mars was singing mournfully from the speakers like the last tito left at karaoke. The remaining guests waved at each other, in varying shades of disarray and a little too much partying.

He heard a laugh from a corner and saw Marina and David emerging from the photo booth. The booth had a backdrop that was especially created for tonight—tall velvet arches holding cascading flowers and a large version of Marina and David's initials monogrammed together. There were flowers tucked behind their ears, and they were unable to keep their hands off of each other.

They tumbled out of the photo booth together, laughing at the faces they made as they looked at the photo strip. They looked deliriously happy, like absolutely nothing could ruin it, especially not tonight. And in this moment, he felt that rare moment of being happy that he had the smallest hand in getting them together. Curse or not, they were both good people, with dreams that they found fulfilled in each other.

Jay turned on his camera and snapped a photo. He felt strange, preserving this version of his friends. Would they stay this much in love? What if they fought? What if their dreams changed—would they stay together? If they had kids, would they bury their resentments so deep they only came out after being married for thirty years? He sincerely hoped not. For now, at least they were together, and happy. Sometimes that was more than what one could ask for.

"Shall we go?" Mara asked, coming up beside him. Her cheeks were flushed red, her breaths short, and she was sweating just a little.

"You're all flushed," Jay said, brushing away a strand of hair that had come undone from its hold. The action was instinctive, and made Mara's eyes go wide in surprise. He quickly dropped his hand. "Let's go home."

They made it to his car soon enough. Jay was already sitting in the driver's seat when Mara opened the door. He hadn't remembered that he left his Snoopy plushie on the passenger's seat, and the poor guy's head tilted toward his guest.

"Sorry!" he said as Mara quickly caught the plushie in her hands. "He gets excited."

"Whoa, down, boy." Mara giggled, clearly in a good mood. Or maybe she was a little nervous? She tucked the doll under her arm and sat in his passenger seat, juggling the plushie, her purse and her skirts with the expertise of someone who did this sort of thing her whole life.

"Bad dog." Jay fake scolded the plushie and put him in the back seat, relegated next to an odd-looking heart character with tentacles and a pouty lip. He had to remember to bring that up for Luna.

"Oh. Snoopy has a friend?" Mara asked curiously.

"That's my niece's," Jay explained. "She keeps telling me Snoopy is lonely."

"That's sweet," Mara noted, grabbing the seat belt. When she struggled to find the place to put the buckle, Jay helped her, tingles shooting up his arm when their fingers touched. "Thanks."

"Sure," Jay said. They were both quiet for a moment, letting the fact that they were about to do this sink in. It was no easy feat, committing to spend two hours (or longer) in a car with someone you, for all intents and purposes, just met. "Um. Just let me know if you need to make a stop on the way or whatever."

"Okay," Mara said, her eyes fixed on the figurine on the dashboard. The little squirrel bobblehead happily offered them an acorn as Jay started the engine. "Yours, or your niece's?"

"Mine. My front teeth grew in before the rest, and I was a squirmer when I was a kid, so my family called me a squirrel." He sighed fondly, shaking his head as the car hit the highway. "Imported rat, as my sister joked."

Mara laughed, and Jay thanked his younger self. The poor kid didn't know that more than twenty years later, his little origin story would make a beautiful woman smile. But first things first. One thing that Jay had not considered when he offered to drive Mara home was *where* home was for her, exactly. Marina had a car for the short period of time that they dated, and the subject of where she lived on the weekends didn't exactly come up.

"Our house is in Timog, near ABS and GMA," Mara explained. Driving through Metro Manila was all vibes and GPS locations, but Jay got the picture. The GPS estimated a one-and-a-half-hour drive ahead, which was excellent time, considering it took them about the same time to get from the church to Luisa's just that afternoon. "There's probably a McDo or Jollibee wherever you exit the Skyway, so you can just drop me off, and I'll get a Grab."

"It's a Friday night," Jay pointed out. When Mara stared at him in confusion, he continued. "Friday night in Manila means traffic. Traffic means less Grabs and price surges. You're still in a dress—you can't just walk into a McDo in a dress. I'll drop you off at your house if you direct me."

"But—"

"—stuff," he said, laughing because he was fourteen years old. He didn't even have to look at Mara to know that she was rolling her eyes.

"Where do *you* live?" she asked when he settled down.

"That's for me to know, and you to find out at a later date. Maybe."

The car was quiet after that, as if an awkward silence had been laid between them on a blanket. And now a metaphorical cat was rolling around the blankets and enjoying the awkwardness. Jay's palms were sweating. He wasn't sure why. He was just doing a friend a favor, that was all. He was the kind of guy who liked doing things for other people. This was not supposed to make him nervous.

He connected his phone to the car's speaker system. Jay was a firm believer that the right playlist set the right mood and chose one. Unfortunately, his finger slipped, and he ended up playing "Don't Go Home" by GD & TOP. Wow. Hello, 2012.

"Ah, fuck," he said. Thank god she couldn't tell how embarrassed he was since it was dark. He held his phone up to her, the screen showing the music controls. "Here, you can change the playlist. Just, no podcasts or audiobooks, please. I will fall asleep."

He heard her chuckle as she took the phone from his hand, and there was silence while she browsed. Jay undid one of the buttons of his shirt, feeling the skin under his collar heat up. What was it about sharing your playlist with someone that made you so vulnerable?

"This is…a lot of K-pop," Mara said. "Second-gen K-pop to be exact."

"My era." Jay sighed dramatically. "I was deep in the Hallyu wave until 2013, I think. EXO had just released 'Growl' when I quit the game."

"Interesting," she said, and it was killing Jay that he couldn't see the expression on her face. It wasn't cool to like K-pop when he was in college, but at the time he enjoyed it too much to care. When he was in his twenties, he changed music tastes, moved to Top 40 songs and a sentimental love of early 2000s R and B. But now in his thirties, he kept looking for those familiar K-pop sounds and found himself discovering the new, younger acts, too. Mamamoo was his favorite. The screen on his dashboard showed that his phone was playing "Gee," by Girls' Generation, because of course it did.

The familiar intro started, and Jay spoke along. "Uh-huh. Listen boy."

"My first love story," Mara said back, much to his surprise and delight.

"Oh my god." He started singing the vocal harmonies. She knew them just as well as he did. Mara clapped along to the beat, and they continued in tandem just before the verses started. Jay tried his best to fake his Korean, as he had ever since he first heard this song in 2009. He knew...some of the words. He definitely knew, "Gee gee gee gee."

He was sure Mara knew the words, too. Knew them better than he did, actually, because he stole a glance at her and she was mouthing them perfectly, not missing a single beat. And just when he thought she was lip syncing, he heard the softest little voice singing the chorus sweetly. The music wasn't that loud, and there were only the two of them in the car, so he could catch words that were *definitely* Korean.

"Mara, if you know the words, you should sing them out loud."

"But—"

He didn't wait for her to make any excuses. "It's just me." Wasn't that enough inducement? He could feel in his bones that Mara wanted to sing out loud. Loving K-pop was 99 percent feeling and 1 percent knowing the words. It wouldn't do for her not to do the 99 percent. "Sing your heart out."

And she did. She hit the high notes perfectly, like the girl group's unseen tenth member. Jay would never know or understand the feeling of a young girl's first fluttering of love the way the song described, but the way Mara sang the song, smiling and shimmying in his peripheral view (she knew the dance, of course she did)…man, he wished he could dance along.

They cycled through a few more songs at her choice, which contained her favorites from 2NE1, SHINee, and KST, a newer boy group. It made the drive feel faster, and Jay liked that she was letting loose in front of him.

"You know more words than I do," Jay teased her.

"Well, I took basic Korean as one of my electives." Mara snickered, like the idea was hilarious to her now. "My course let me take two electives my entire college life. Because I was fully convinced that I was going to shed all of my interests after college because of work, I chose musical theater—"

"Oh my god, you're an ex theater kid." Jay shook his head. "No wonder you can sing."

"And basic Korean," Mara finished. Laughed like it was the silliest thing in the world. "For my final, my teacher let me act out a scene from *Dream High* where IU is singing a phone ad? Peak of my acting career."

"That's daebak." He stole a quick glance at Mara just in time to catch her rolling her eyes. She was smiling, though, which was likely a good thing. "And are you still into Korean things?"

"Oh yeah," Mara said like it was a given. "The music, the food. My usual weekday post-work vibe is watching a drama while crocheting."

"Crochet?" he echoed, immediately picturing her sitting in one of those wooden rocking chairs with the long arms, her brows furrowed as she glared intensely at her yarn and her TV screen. "Like…potholders?"

"Like blankets? Cardigans? I've made bags, bucket hats, holders for things. I made Mabel a top with these puff flowers." She grumbled a little and held up her screen to quickly show him. What he saw was Mabel, posing in a foreign country (Japan, maybe?), wearing a sweater made of cute, puffy flowers.

"Whoa. You made that?"

"Yuh. It gets weirdly cold in the studio so I decided to pick it up. Crocheting helps me not think so much, after work. And I get to do something with my hands, which I really like."

"You should make me something sometime." He grinned, and yes, he was being flirty, and he was teasing her a little bit. But crocheting your days away was unexpected. "I would love to see your yarn stash."

"Oh my god." Mara laughed, shaking her head at his little innuendo. "That's where you live, on the corner of maginoo and bastos." She sighed like it was a damn shame. "What do I do with you, Jay."

What indeed.

"So…" he started when Mara put on a different song, this time "Jeepney" from Sponge Cola, which was such a throwback that Jay actually felt his thirty-five-year-old back spasm. "You're the only one heading home tonight?"

"Marina and David have a second reception tomorrow at Seda in BGC." Mara sighed, sinking back into her seat like her little K-pop high was wearing off. "I want to get to the studio as early as possible tomorrow to help with setting up."

"Ugh." The sound came out of Jay's mouth before he could stop himself, and even then it was too late because he'd already rolled his eyes to the back of his head. Beside him, Mara laughed.

"You want to say that to my face, Jay?"

"No, it's just…" He tried to formulate nice words, he really did. But the annoyance was real, and this was really annoying. "Seriously? They're having a fake wedding for the people they didn't think were important enough to invite to their *real* wedding?"

"Well," Mara said. He wished he could look at her, steal a glance, glean what she was thinking. But did he detect a bit of…amusement in her tone? "Some of our cousins couldn't make it, and David has a few people he didn't invite to Tagaytay, so—"

"So they're spending, what, another five hundred thousand—"

"Closer to seven hundred, actually."

"Seven hundred?" Jay repeated, flabbergasted. That was an *insane* amount, considering tonight's festivities would have cost them a million at least. "Oh my god. Weddings are so *stupid*."

"Are they?" Mara asked. He could tell that she was trying very hard to hold back her laughter.

"With 1.7 million you could make a down payment on a house!" Jay said, his hands loosening their tight grip on the steering wheel. "Okay, maybe not a house. A nice two-bedroom condo in QC or Pasig, maybe. Pre-selling. Rockwell, or some other A to B class developer."

"Are you sure you're not a real estate agent?"

"You could also invest that same amount and earn 5 percent on a time deposit, and that's if you stayed conservative." He'd seen people make more. Way more, and sometimes at his advice. He'd made millions on paper in the span of a minute. His work was terrifying that way, but when he managed to do well, the thrill that it sent him was incomparable.

Nowadays Jay's clients—people with way more money than him—preferred stability. They were either keeping the funds for a rainy day, or transferring the earnings to their children and asking Jay to give them a crash course on money management. It was surprising how much one's goals changed when you changed clientele, which was probably why Jay wasn't inclined to go back to Hong Kong anytime soon. Maybe.

"Different people have different priorities," Mara reminded him. "Marina and David don't mind, and everyone's happy."

"Even you?" he asked, the question out of his lips before he considered the words. "You're sitting in a car with a stranger, and you were planning to take a Grab from wherever to get ready for a reception that already happened."

His question was met with silence. Jay didn't know if it was because he'd said something dumb, or if she was really thinking about it. Either way it took some time before Mara gave him an answer.

"That's not a fair comparison," she finally decided, her voice sounding blithe and dismissive. "You can't ask someone if they're happy while they're doing something inconvenient. Of course they will say they aren't. But happiness is happiness because it happens in between inconvenient things. Hard things."

Jay said nothing, getting a sense that she wanted to say more. But really, half of his being silent was because, goddamn it, he'd upset her again. How the hell did he keep managing to do this? Was this all part of Scott's Journey to Love or whatever?

"Take this wedding, for example," Mara said, pulling Jay's focus back to the road, and to her. "I've been up since 5:00 a.m., wearing a dress that isn't exactly comfortable. My hair is flammable, my eyelids are itchy, and I'm going home in a car with a guy I met once a year ago, and loathed for just as long."

"Loathed makes it sound like you wanted to eat me like a piece of bread," he said, the words spilling out of his mouth before he thought about it. He didn't need to see Mara glaring at him, because he could feel it on his skin, like goose bumps but worse. "Sorry. Go on."

"All of that? Inconvenient. Some would even say shitty. But, my sister got married to the man she loves today." He didn't miss the way her voice caught at the end of that sentence. But it was a fond voice, a loving one that wrapped around him like a gentle caress. "She will spend her entire life, if she wants, with someone who will always be in her corner. Someone who can reach high shelves and open guava jam jars so she can spread it on kesong puti and crackers."

"And that's your happiness? Seeing your sister being roommates with someone else?"

"Is marriage just being someone's roommate?" There was that dismissive tone again. "Come on, Jay. You can't be that cynical."

"Come on, Mara. You can't be that idealistic," Jay argued,

because she was Mara Barretto. An eldest Asian daughter practically made of high boundaries and cynicism, because she needed to be on her toes for everyone else. "You have to know. Relationships aren't just jam jars and high shelves. It's absorbing all of another person's bullshit, and hoping to god they can do the same for you. But because it's life, and life is never fair, it's never exactly equal, and you spend the rest of your relationship—the rest of your *life* in this country because we *still* haven't passed the divorce bill—a little disappointed, or worse, fucking trapped."

Jay's grip on the steering wheel tightened, and he felt his face heat up. He was pretty sure he'd never said any of this to anyone, but he didn't want Mara to have any illusions of what life was going to be like for her sister. Was she really going to hitch her horse to that?

"People disappoint each other all the time," he pointed out. Could give her a long list of people he'd disappointed just by being himself. "And I wish it doesn't happen to Marina and David, but... I don't know. I think it's a waste of time and money."

"Argh, can you cut the condescending bullshit?" Mara snapped. Jay froze, taken aback at how angry she was. He was trying to be conciliatory here! "*You have to know.* Tang ina. Of course I don't know. I've never been in a relationship! How very ilusyonada of me, to want my sister's husband to love her."

"I didn't say that," Jay groaned, running a hand through his hair. He'd seen *Pride and Prejudice* enough times to know when he was being a Bingley, in his words, an "unmitigated ass," and he seemed spectacular at doing that with Mara.

She'd never been in a relationship. Marina had told him, and David had worried about it once. It wasn't exactly a secret. Yet here he was, projecting his insecurities at her. Amazing. "I'm sorry, Mara. I've been in a lot of relationships. I feel like I've seen it all, you know? I've disappointed people in spectacular ways, you included. I just... I don't want you to regret anything, if you do decide to want the same thing."

And he could have been better for those other people. Could have fought for those relationships, stood outside their door with a boom box, met them on top of the Empire State Building, run after them through the airport. But it was easier for everyone involved if he just moved on, tried again. Clearly, ten out of ten times, it had been the right thing to do. He was happy with his life, satisfied that he could provide a home for people he loved.

Except those people were moving somewhere else. So was he really happy, when he was in the middle of it all?

"Teach me, then."

"What?"

"Teach me," Mara repeated. Her voice lost all vitriol and anger, and all that was left was...hesitation. She was nervous, and he wondered if this was the first time she'd entertained the idea of someone telling her how to do this.

"Teach you what exactly?"

"Your vast wealth of knowledge in the trifecta. Love. Relationships. Sex."

She listed them like they were things you could pick up

in a single afternoon workshop. As someone who had been dragged to calligraphy, watercolor, ceramics, floral arranging, journaling and gratitude workshops (Ate Irene liked a workshop, okay), he knew that definitely wasn't the case.

"I want to experience one of each at least once in my life. I've liked people before, and I just... I can never get their attention. They can't see me, or they can't see me as someone they find attractive. Hell, I signed up for those dating apps and I didn't match with anyone. And since you feel very strongly that there are things I *have* to know, and other people feel very strongly about deficiencies in my physical appearance that keep me single—"

"Mara," he chided her weakly. She ignored him.

"—I might as well ask someone to just teach me and get it over with. Make someone fall in love with me. Have sex. Discover all the ways we can disappoint each other, and I can be satisfied and tell myself it's not for me. I want to stop wanting it, Jay. And if you think that you're so good at this that you know why I shouldn't want it, then teach me."

She was saying these things like she was talking about trying a food she didn't enjoy. And the thing was—and Jay *knew* this—he could do it. Knew it like he knew where the exit ramp to the Skyway was, and that he could easily navigate the car up the ramp.

He could tell Mara what to wear, where to go, what to say when someone came up to her (because people would come up to her, for sure). Show her the little things about dating that he enjoyed, how people played a song and dance of wheedling the red flags out of the other before they committed to anything serious. Show her how he liked to be touched, what turned him on. Encourage her own sexual explorations, whatever her experience. He would be lying if he said that the thought of *that* didn't turn him on. Not at all.

But he also knew that it was a bad idea. Because agreeing to do it would mean Mara admitting that there was something—what word did she use?—*deficient* about her. That there was something she wasn't doing right. And he didn't want to validate that, no way.

They cruised through the Skyway in wretched, sixty-kilometer-per-hour silence, nothing but the agonized tones of Yeoeun's "Let's Forget It" to accompany them. All that time Jay agonized over what he was going to say, and he could feel Mara's anxiety grow and grow beside him.

They finally made it to the Quezon Avenue exit. Only a few short streets away from her place, ten minutes if the traffic wasn't bad. There was a second where they needed to stop at the exit booth, and Jay glanced at Mara. Her eyes were focused on the road, her face blank and placid, like she hadn't said anything that changed their whole dynamic.

But he noticed her flicking her thumb against her nails, peeling off her nail polish. He reached out and placed his hand over hers, making her stop. He sighed deeply, suddenly feeling bone tired.

"Stop ruining your nails." He kept his eyes on the road, driving with one hand. "Sayang the manicure."

"I'll live, thanks." Mara gently pulled her hands away.

Silence again, except for when Mara told him to turn from Quezon Avenue, on to Timog, around the rotunda and through a few more side streets. Jay kept his laser focus on the road, further hammering in how easy it was for him to disappoint someone, Mara now included. After everything he said, and everything they had said, ultimately he was too selfless to take her up on her offer, and too selfish to do it so that she could just find someone else.

How very fucked up of him.

"This is me," Mara announced on a seemingly random street. Jay pulled up in front of a small brick house, tucked away from the street by a black iron gate. The property was definitely worth more than the house—nobody lived in residences in this area without being of some generational wealth anymore. These lands went for hundreds and thousands per square meter. But there was a fond look in Mara's eyes as she looked at the house, an ease in her posture that told him that the family probably wasn't going to sell anytime soon.

"It's lovely," Jay said, and he meant it. The gumamela planted in front of the house were in full bloom. From the street, he could see a warm, yellow light from the inside turn on. Someone had probably seen them pull up and left the light on for Mara. It was a different kind of comfort, someone turning a light on for you that you could see from the street. It was a totally different world from his Pasig condominium here, and they lived (for all intents and purposes) in the same group of cities.

Mara shifted to unbuckle her seat belt, but Jay did it before she could find the buckle, slowly easing the belt back without smacking her in the face. He heard her breath hitch. Which was fine because he wasn't breathing at all as he leaned in.

"Jay," she said. He turned to her, trying (probably failing) to act like everything was fine. They were parked near a street lamp, and he could clearly see the confusion in Mara's face, her eyes bright as she nibbled at her bottom lip. "Let's not talk about this ever again."

His heart sank. Why did his heart *sink*? (Because she was upset, and it was his fault, again.)

"I had a long day, and I'm delirious," she added. Seemed to sink into her seat, all bluster and bravado and anger gone now that they were so close. The world was still quiet around them, consisting of nothing but the space between them, inside this little mirage.

She'd opened up to him. Said things that he needed to keep safe, that he cared about. Her feelings were so precious and delicate in his hands that he didn't want them tucked away without proper acknowledgment. She deserved that, at least.

"Mara." He sighed, without pulling back. He wanted her to know that even if they didn't want the same things, he understood her not wanting to desire love. To yearn for it, and feel foolish yearning for it. "I can't let this end like that."

He wanted her to know that she had nothing to worry about. Because if he could want her so much after one night, someone else—someone else who truly deserved her—would, too.

All she wanted was for someone to look at her the way she hoped for. And Jay knew what he could do to make her feel like it was going to happen.

"So what do you want to do about it?" she asked him.

"I'm going to assume your sister told you about my…thing."

He'd never put any stock in his kiss curse until tonight. But if ten times wasn't a big enough indicator… Jay worked in finance, and numbers. He knew what they meant, even if he didn't love it. He'd put his faith in a lot less. "With the kissing and the marrying other people."

"That's one way to put it." Mara smiled. If the change in subject confused her, she didn't let it show. "But she did."

Of course she did. Because Marina needed to hear that she was still a good person when she first told Jay she wasn't interested in him, and Jay told her about the kiss curse to make her feel better.

Most of the time, it helped. He didn't feel bitter or rueful about it, especially not right now. Right now, he just needed it to be true.

"May I kiss you?" he asked, and her eyes widened in surprise. But she knew what he was really asking her. *May I kiss you, so you can find someone else?*

"Okay," she finally said. She sounded nervous. Why nervous? Unless she… Oh fuck.

"You've never kissed anyone, have you?"

"Well. Not like this," she admitted. His face blocked her light just enough so he could tell she was blushing. "Once. High school in an exclusive girls' school can get confusing. She was very good at it."

It was enough to ease the tension between them, just enough that Jay could reach for her with the hand that wasn't anchored on the middle console. Touching her arm, fingers creeping up until he made it to her cheek. His hand cupped her soft, supple skin, and he didn't know what was louder—

his thumping heart or her short breaths. His thumb brushed against her lips in a gentle caress, teasing them slightly open.

Then he kissed her. He hadn't intended to do more than to press his lips on hers, to infuse…whatever it was about him that made others find love in a single kiss.

But Mara parted her lips more, invited him in. And Jay was lost to the kiss, taking her parted lips as his invitation to take away her longing, to kiss her like there would be no other kiss after him. And he let her take everything she wanted from him, everything she wanted to experience. Her hand gripped the front of his shirt, fingers slipping through the buttons and on to his heated skin. Jay's lungs constricted, and his heart wrenched. She was very, very good at this.

But as he thought about what else he wanted to do, how he could push this further, he was struck with a mental picture of her with someone else. Someone tall and handsome, with a soft, cheeky smile, who could open any guava jam jar she wanted and stick around for the next morning to have SkyFlakes and kesong puti with said guava jam.

He was kind of picturing Tuxedo Mask from *Sailor Moon* filling that role. It definitely wasn't him, and it made him pull away suddenly, abruptly.

He instinctively raised his hands to stop Mara from losing her balance, and he felt his chest ache when she looked at him in pale-faced shock. After a blink, she cooled and wriggled herself free from his grasp, collecting her bag and exiting the car. With the door still open, she paused and turned to him, bending forward, one hand on the door and another over her cleavage.

Jay tried very hard not to look at the hand covering her cleavage.

"Do you live in Quezon City?" she asked.

"Pasig," he admitted, and she nodded like he had absolutely confirmed something for her that he wasn't prepared to admit. He knew what it meant, driving someone to a different city. It was a commitment, in this country with a broken transport system, to drive someone home. It was expensive to take the Skyway, the gas wasn't cheap. The roads were nuts. But it didn't matter. *You're home, and you're safe. That's what I said I would do.*

"You still have a long drive, then. I'll let you go," she said, nodding then slamming the door. Jay rolled the window down, because this wasn't how this was going to end, was it? All his instincts told him to get out of the damn car, follow her to her gate, tell her not to go, tell her that he could be everything she wanted and more. "Night, Jay."

"Good night, Mara."

Jay took all of those instincts, balled them into his fists and kept them clamped down. He watched Mara slip her hand through the bars of the gate, wriggle the lock open and walk through and up to the warm light of the home that waited for her. She didn't turn around. Didn't give him one last look.

All chances gone.

Just as well. She was about to fall in love with someone else. And Jay would have a squirrel, a bunny and a beagle to keep him company all the way to Pasig.

Alex and Tori are getting married!
See you at the beach.
Shorewinds Hotel, Station 1, Boracay

Eight

It took three months, some logistical finagling and careful consideration for Mara to decide to spend her wedding money on a summer trip to the beach. It took a week for Mabel to say she was joining her, and another week for her to then back out. Marina and David considered coming for about two days—until they decided against it, and Mara was alone.

So one warm March day, Mara sat her parents down and told them she was going to the beach for a week. And her parents, knowing fully that there was nothing they could do when their daughters made a decision, could only ask, "Which one?"

Which beach was a question as essential and philosophical as asking someone their star sign. In a country where moving in any direction will eventually lead to a beach, which *kind* of beach was an important distinction. Beaches to the north—La Union, Zambales, Bataan—were all black sand and warm waters. They were made mostly for serious surfers, getting tanned in the sun while dining on niche food concepts among Manila folk who were looking for a hip, young surf town vibe. Mara never enjoyed a beach she couldn't swim in, and she was never a party girl, so pass.

Slightly to the south of Manila was Anilao, a diver's paradise that had since evolved to have gorgeous resorts with even better pools. But it was a two-hour drive with no commute options, and it made no sense to rent a van for just one person. Venturing farther to the west via plane landed you in Palawan, God's gift to the Philippines in the form of gorgeous rock formations, open sea, hidden lagoons and lakes to discover for the more adventurous tourist. These were the tourists willing to sit for an hour or longer on a little boat to experience the islands' otherworldly beauty.

But Mara wasn't looking for adventure. What she was looking for was a Lazy Girl's Fancy Beach Vacation, one that didn't require a car, much thought or consideration, and with enough convenience and people for her to still be relatively safe on her own.

And so, Boracay.

Mara loved Boracay. She loved it as a child, willing to sit through a nine-hour ferry ride and another thirty-minute small boat ride just to get to the island's crowded, noisy Station 3. She loved it as a younger adult, blowing her parents' money to party with her college friends in May for Laboracay in Station 2. But she loved it the most as an adult, spending her own money on a proper flight, an even shorter fast craft ride and a nicely appointed hotel in Station 1. It was quieter on that part of the island, with more space to enjoy the perfect white sand, crystal blue waters and her favorite sunsets. The fact that the restaurants along the beach rivaled those in Manila, and the café there was slightly better, was also a big plus in the island's favor.

Mara wasn't even there yet, and already she didn't want to leave. But before she could get there, it did mean having to ride a fast craft from Caticlan Jetty Port to Boracay.

"Ate, it's a chill ten-minute ride at most," Mabel tried to reassure her over the phone as Mara huddled into the corner of her bench seat. "You'll live."

"Say that at my funeral, thanks." Mara sighed dramatically. She leaned her forehead against the open window beside her. Her face desperately turned toward the sea, letting the weak breeze allay the dizziness that was threatening to overwhelm her with each rock of the boat. Inside, the fast craft was full of activity. Crew making sure the passengers were seated in the right places, porters who didn't really have to be there getting PHP 50 per piece of luggage from the passengers who hired them, *more* porters, and staff and passengers arguing about how the bags should be stacked up front, in a way that they were in the passengers' view at all times.

Chaos, chaos.

"Anyway," Mara continued, keeping her eyes on the calmer seas. "Are you still hiding from Mom and Dad?"

"You bet!" came Mabel's overly cheery, sarcastic reply. "It's all yelling and no communicating, and I thank god every day that I learned to drive in these insane streets so I can escape Mom and Dad creating more marriage counseling fodder."

Mara laughed, mostly because Martin and Jasmine would

never go to marriage counseling, even with their daughters' urging. Another side effect of the three girls entering their thirties (or in various precipices of), was that very suddenly they were old enough to read between the lines of their parents' arguments.

They could boil it down to this: waking up one day and realizing that the person you had been sleeping next to for the last thirty-something years wasn't the same person you married. That you didn't fully know or understand this new person, because you expected them to stay exactly the same. This resulted in a lot of yelling, lines being drawn, and three daughters playing unlicensed marriage counselor once a week. Mara was their particular favorite for this, the only daughter who didn't snap at them for being unreasonable.

But as she was in a completely different group of islands at the moment (shout out to you, Visayas!), this left Mabel to be the one to say things like, "Why didn't you tell her," or "Maybe you could tell him," or the classic, "Yes, that's what we call communication."

"I ran away to the mall because Mom had that *'I need to talk to you'* look on her face," Mabel explained. It wasn't hard to hear the guilt laced in her tone. But by tacit agreement between the sisters, they made the decision to be firm with their boundaries, and that meant walking away from their parents sometimes. "And they wonder why we're in no rush to get married!"

"Ikaw naman," Mara chided her little sister. "Fighting is normal in a relationship, we know this."

"In *their* relationship," Mabel corrected her. "We're not supposed to be involved!"

Mara sighed. She'd had these conversations with her sisters about as many times as her parents blew up at each other. So there wasn't really much she could say except, "Fair."

"And yet we're the ones who have to hear them yell at each other, commiserate when they complain about each other, and not be there at all when they make up!"

"Do you *want* to be there when they make up?" Mara joked, and Mabel made a gagging noise in response.

But really, there was no need for her to explain any more, or for Mabel to rant any more, because they were sisters. And the great thing about having siblings with a group chat was that there was nobody else in the world who understood the phrase, "My parents are driving me up the wall," more than them. They had the context, the language, the phrasing, the reassurances. Emotions waxed and waned like the tide. And Mara enjoyed that predictability of their relationships, as complex as it all was.

"You could always move out, Mabel," Mara pointed out. "You don't have to live at home."

"Oh please." Mabel snorted. "In *this* economy? We're so fucked that I'm losing 40 percent of my income to a government who uses our money as a fun expense account. The salary I am paid is not equal to the amount of work that I put in to a company that doesn't care about me, and I am expected to be able to afford my middle-class life on that? No."

Facts. And it didn't at all help that the supposed head of the government owed billions in taxes himself. It was a mess on all counts that, surprise, surprise, affected everyone. Both Mara and Mabel sighed. It was not a fun conversation for ten in the morning.

"It is what it is," Mara told her sister. The best platitude she could give her at the moment. They knew there were worse things. But that didn't change what it was—still pretty shitty.

"Isn't it always. I'll have brunch here at the mall and then do some errands before I go home. I'll send updates on the group chat so Ate Marina knows, too."

"Okay," Mara said, the two of them promising to report their whereabouts later on in the chat.

"Rosplenda, Rosario and Rosemary" was a safe place online where the Barretto siblings could keep tabs on each other, talk about what restaurants were cool, share reels and discuss their dislike of Taylor Swift. There had been a recent debate on if David should be brought into the fold, but he stayed in a separate chat, now called, "Lady Whistledown's Chika Room."

She hung up just as the fast craft pulled away from the docks and the engines roared to life. Everything that rocked also started to vibrate, only magnifying Mara's dizziness.

Ten minutes, she reminded herself, closing her eyes. *It's only going to take ten minutes.*

She was pulled out of her own misery by the feeling of someone tugging her free hand. Someone small. She cracked an eye open and found herself holding hands with a small child. The child sat beside her on the bench seat, head facing forward, face mostly obscured by the cutest little checkered bucket hat crocheted with red and pink squares. Clutched in the child's other hand was a very familiar-looking heart-shaped alien with tentacles. Why was it familiar?

The child turned their face toward Mara. Then the child smiled, and their entire face lit up, cheeks pressing up to the corners of their eyes. Mara's heart felt like it was producing heart emojis out of cuteness. It was the kind of smile that could make any Grinch believe in Christmas.

"I'm being a good girl," she announced.

"Uh, I guess you are," said Mara, nodding. Although this child could tell her the sky was green and she would agree. She might be confused, but she did feel the strong urge to put this little girl in her pocket, she was so damn cute. "Hi."

"Hi!" she said back, her little legs kicking under her. "Mama says you should hold hands on a boat."

"That's good advice." Mara wondered how she could subtly ask this child if she was supervised. Because if she was not, then there was a high possibility that Mara was having heat stroke and imagining a ghost baby. "Um, your mama is…" *Please don't say a ghost.*

"Luna!" an unfamiliar voice exclaimed, a whirl of flowy fabric swooping in to wrap itself around the little girl. "Thanks for finding our seats, baby."

"Mama!" The little girl squealed as her mother attacked her with kisses. Luna's hold on Mara's hand broke as she hugged her mother back, giggling wildly. The woman pulled the hat off of her child's head, revealing a slightly sweaty anit. She pulled out a previously unseen hand towel and swiped the sweat off the little girl's head, quickly replaced it with spray-on sunscreen and put a couple of spritzes on top before she leaned in and took a deep sniff.

"Mmm. Bantot!" She laughed and put away the spray bottle. Then she gave her daughter a portable electric fan in a bid to stave off the heat.

"I was holding hands," Luna explained, and her mother turned to Mara with an appraising eye. It was a little scary, mostly because Mara knew Luna's mother was trying to ascertain her intentions. Mara blushed, suddenly feeling like an intruder in what was clearly a very sweet mother-daughter moment.

"I see," Luna's mother said, smiling. "Say thank you to your friend, Luns."

"Thank you po." Luna's voice was uncharacteristically small and shy as she leaned against her mother. "Tita."

Aray naman. Shot through the heart right there. Mara smiled, though, and told Luna that it was her pleasure. All the while, she endured Luna's mother's assessing glance, like she was trying to categorize the purpose of a single woman riding a boat to Boracay on a weekday.

"Luns, why aren't you wearing your life vest?" a new voice asked. Well, not new. But a voice she didn't think she was going to hear again anytime soon. "Do you need candy? I have some right here."

Motherfucker.

Just when Mara thought she'd run away far enough, Jay Montinola stood in the middle of a fast craft to Boracay. Mara choked on air, like a spirit had possessed her and tried to deliver her from this moment via a swift death. *Not today, Satan.*

"Arms out," Jay said to his niece. Apparently not seeing Mara. She put her sunglasses over her eyes and sank into her seat in a bid to make her 5XL frame feel just a little bit smaller. He looked very much like a harried tito, wearing a rattan fedora, a sleeveless sando (complete with puka shell necklace, *why?*), Islander flip flops and blue tinted shades.

(But how did he manage to still look so cool—that was Mara's question. He literally had a little cross body pouch?)

There was a stripe of still wet sunscreen on his chin. He was also inexplicably carrying a deflated duck floatie, a child-sized bright orange life vest and two more bags. Not including the previously clocked little Snoopy pouch, from which he procured a mint candy for Luna.

"Jay, she's already sweating from your bucket hat!" The woman Mara now assumed was his older sister swatted her hand in his direction, like he was a fly that needed to buzz off. "And she doesn't need the life vest. Save it for the ocean."

"Huh! Ate, this *is* the ocean," Jay pointed out. "What if—"

"Nong, you're not holding hands!" Luna said it with the same vigor as her mother, like it was of equal importance that her ninong was holding someone's hand. Luna splayed out her little hand toward Mara as if asking for a screwdriver. "Tita."

Mother*fucccckkker.*

"Er, Luna?" Mara quickly straightened herself in her seat and smiled innocently at the girl.

"Mara?" It was comically hilarious how Jay nearly dropped everything he was carrying when he realized who was sitting next to his family. If this was an anime, a large drop of sweat would be right over his head.

"Oh, Mara," his Ate exclaimed, fully whirling in her seat to face Mara. Her eyes were brimming with perky interest and excitement. Mara was only a little bit scared. "You're Mara!"

"One of many?" Mara asked hesitantly.

"The one and only," Jay corrected. He looked like he didn't know if he was going to jump out the window and swim to Boracay or make his sister move so he could sit next to her. If she were being fully honest with herself, Mara was thinking the same thing. He moved to sit in the empty seat across the aisle.

"Oh no, don't sit *away* from her, anuba!" Jay's Ate said. A quick glance at his older sister told Mara that neither she nor Jay were in control of what was going to happen next, because Ate was already putting the hat back on her daughter's head and standing up, seemingly unconcerned at the rocking of the boat. "Luna and I can take your seat, Jay. Hi, nice to meet you, Mara. I'm Irene. Go lang. Bond. Reunite. Recreate."

"Ate—" The engine of the boat roared to life, and Jay stumbled.

"M'amsir, please stay seated," one of the staff yelled over the sound, and all of a sudden (intentional), Mara was right back where she was three months ago, inside a moving vehicle with Jay. The circumstances were completely different this time around, but still it was him, and her, and all the words they had said to each other.

A couple of bags were passed between Jay and his sister, the deflated duck and the life vest staying firmly on his lap. Mara noticed Jay's knee was shaking. They exchanged nervous smiles, as if their lips had never touched before. Mara felt a tug in her chest that she was wholly unfamiliar with. A yearning she hadn't expected to feel around him. She pushed it down into that deep place where she'd placed all the other swirling emotions of the last three months, left there to be unexamined until she needed them.

What was it Jane Austen said about exes? Strangers that would never become acquainted. Sitting there now made her feel it, that ache of sadness about the things that weren't going to happen between them. That he decided were not going to happen.

Not that Jay was her ex or anything. He wasn't actually *anything*, really, but still his knee shook, and Mara was… She was mad at him. She knew this because it was the predominant feeling she'd been carrying for Jay Montinola since she met him. But while she was angry, she could be polite. Ten minutes' worth of polite.

"So," Mara started, because she was the bigger person, and she didn't plan on letting him know that she was angry with him, "your Ate and niece?"

Her voice was almost snatched out of the air by the roaring engine and the wind that whipped through the boat.

"What?" Jay asked. Because it was the polite thing to do, even if there was no use to start polite conversation on a moving boat. Mara had forgotten how *loud* it could get.

"Your family?" Mara screamed, gripping the bench in front of her to keep herself steady. She used her lips to point to Ate Irene and Luna. He still looked confused. "Oh my god. YOUR FAMILY?"

"YES," Jay yelled back. Both of them were making a valiant

effort to pretend that Ate Irene wasn't doing a terrible job of trying to eavesdrop. "Wedding! We're attending a wedding!"

"OH NICE," Mara said, smiling a little too sweetly while she imagined kissing his face off. See how *he* liked it. "Are you—"

"Best man!"

"Great! Have you seen Marina since—" *Since we deeply kissed in front of my house and never spoke to each other again?*

Because it could only have been a deep kiss, what they did that night. Mara didn't have a wealth of experience on the matter, but it felt deep, like he wanted it to last longer, like he wanted to hold on a little tighter. Or maybe she was projecting, and all kisses, deep or not, felt like that.

The boat jerked suddenly, in a way that made Mara and Jay jump, lose whatever grip they had on their seats and slide into each other. Mara gasped, and Jay shouted in surprise. His hand flew out and reached for her shoulder, keeping her steady as she found herself looking into his kind eyes. At the little wrinkles in the corners that were beginning to form as a result of what she assumed was excessive smiling. The boat carried on like nothing was amiss, and yet everything seemed to have changed.

Mara looked up at his face, and, to her horror, angry tears sprung into her eyes. Oh *god*. Thank god she was still wearing her sunglasses. As angry as she was, as annoyed and embarrassed, she didn't want him to let go. And wasn't that just the most fucking fantastic thing.

"Jay."

The boat steadied, but his hand stayed. Was that the engine still roaring in her ears or the beat of her heart? Mara couldn't tell. She could barely hear as it was, but she was already picturing this moment with a soundtrack, like Stevie Nicks, or Armi Millare.

"Mara."

The smile on his face was like a hand that squeezed fondly over her heart. The tension eased between them, like they'd never left his car. "How are you?"

"I'm good," she said, because it was true. "Busy."

"With someone new?"

Anger made Mara move to slide back to her seat, thanking god again that she had her sunglasses on. She was not going to let Jay Montinola see her break. She shook her head. What an asshole. He had *no* idea. "You might need to revise the statistics on your little kiss curse. Didn't quite work."

"What?" he asked, and Mara shook her head.

"It's okay," she told him. Which was a total lie. Of course it wasn't okay that he resorted to kissing her to reject her, that he'd embarrassed her and made her feel even more unwanted than before, and—no. She had to stop dwelling on that. She was on vacation. She was going to enjoy herself and move the fuck on.

"Mara…"

"What?" she snapped, turning to him. His hand was reaching out to her cheek, but she pulled back and touched the spot he was about to. It came away wet. "I had something in my eye."

"Oh. Um. Where are—"

"Um, guys?" Ate Irene asked. Mara looked up just in time

to see Irene holding her daughter's hand while standing in the crowded aisle, facing them. "The boat's docked."

And sure enough, it was. The engine had been turned off, and the boat was now floating idly by the dock. It was amazing how quiet the world suddenly seemed after loud noise. The sound of waves lapping lazily against the shore was perfect and tranquil. The crew was busy dropping anchor, tying the boat in various places. As Pinoys were wont to do in every travel situation, people were crowding the aisle, each person seeking to get out of the boat before anyone else, wanting to be the first out for no discernible reason.

"Fastest ten minutes ever," Jay said, and Mara had to agree. He stood up and squeezed into the line of people, shuffling backward to give her room. She ignored him.

"We're staying at the Shorewinds Hotel in Station 1," Ate Irene informed her, turning to face Mara, Luna holding on to her skirts. "Just FYI."

"I'm right next door," Mara realized out loud. "Seasprite Stays." Thank god. She'd almost booked at Shorewinds.

"What an *amazing* coincidence," Ate Irene cheered, enough that even Luna looked excited. "Isn't that also where they sell that coconut dessert—"

"Cocomo? Yeah. I might have…chosen Seasprite because of Cocomo," Mara admitted, ignoring the chuckle from Jay.

There was a well-known trifecta of restaurants within ten steps of Mara's hotel. Cocomo the dessert stand, Sunnydale the café and Amano Po the Italian restaurant. A ten-minute walk away was a restaurant that served world-famous oyster sisig and four-cheese pizza. Another ten-minute walk in the opposite direction was a place that served fruit shakes. Mara's vacation plans consisted of never straying far from any of those places. And with the beach right in front of all of these establishments? It was a lazy girl's dream come true.

"Cocomo?" Luna repeated curiously. "Is that good, Tita?"

"Yeah, it's ice cream made with coconut milk and other yummy things." Mara smiled. God, Luna was cute. She was still that age where she had perfectly round baby cheeks, even if she was quickly growing taller. "You should join me. I think I get a discount because I'm staying at the hotel."

"We will take you up on that offer. Right, Jay?" Irene asked her little brother pointedly. Her smile was both diabolical and amused. Mara had intentionally not included Jay in her thoughts of inviting the Montinolas to dessert. "Luna, you want to put on your hat?"

"Yes please," Luna said, reaching for the hat. Upon closer inspection there were still a couple of loose threads inside. It was clearly handmade. Luna saw her looking and held it up for Mara's inspection. "Tita, did you know Nong made this for me?"

"Really?" Mara blinked in surprise. "Nong?" she echoed, turning to face Jay, who looked sheepish. "You crochet?"

"I wanted to try it after what you said. You're right, it is soothing."

Curses, he was cute. Mara rolled her eyes at her own fickle emotions. It was really, really hard to hold on to a grudge when Jay was making his niece cute bucket hats. Hats were hard to make, and she should know! You needed to stitch in a round, with a magic circle base, and...wow. He really tried crochet. Because of her. Mara inhaled deeply to store her kilig.

The line started to shuffle forward, and Jay squeezed past his sister to grab his family's luggage before someone ported it out. Mara sighed and took her place in line. It was almost over.

"I feel like I should ask," Ate Irene said over her shoulder to Mara.

"Don't ask," Jay yelled a few places ahead of them. But clearly Ate Irene had chosen to ignore her brother's sage advice. Jay was quickly lost to the dearth of porters and passengers grabbing luggage left and right. It was actually kind of scary.

"What did he do?" Ate Irene asked, as Mara lifted her sunglasses to the top of her head. "Is it the meme thing?"

Mara shook her head. "He already apologized for the meme thing."

"So he did something else," Ate Irene mused. God help all the younger siblings who had to endure the scrutiny of their Ates. Mara pulled a half-empty water bottle from her purse and started to take a sip. "Is that why you guys aren't dating?"

Mara choked on the water, making Luna laugh as some of it sprayed on her hat. Mara apologetically patted the little girl's head. So cute.

"Why would we be together?" She laughed like it was the most ridiculous idea she'd ever heard, even as her heart ached in such a familiar way. Like she knew exactly how long it would take, how much it would hurt, when it would go away.

"Because he said that he kissed you," Ate Irene pointed out.

"I asked him for a...different favor." Mara huffed, but she

looked down at Luna to indicate to Irene why she wasn't going to elaborate more. "A more hands-on one. He declined and thought his magical, not-real kiss thing would be better."

"Hay Jay." Irene rolled her eyes. Again, a familiar reaction to a sibling being particularly obstinate. "I swear, his Leo placements get the better of him most of the time. He's just had a rough time with love. Our parents, Selena…" Mara did not remember right away that Ate Irene meant Selena Guerro. "Plus, I haven't exactly been a stellar role model for him when it comes to long-lasting love."

"Yes, but *he's* making these choices. He's an adult, making them."

"Oh, I like you." Ate Irene gasped like she just realized how awesome Mara was. "I can see why he was mopey these last three months."

"Mopey?"

"Like Snoopy but sad," Luna supplied, which was only kind of accurate. Mara laughed, even as every part of her itched to ask Ate Irene just *how* mopey Jay had been. If it was anywhere near as mopey as her…

"And there's nothing going on between you. Your interest in him was—"

"Academic."

"Sure. And he was being—"

"Philanthropic, he thinks."

"Uh-huh. Is that what we younger millennials are calling it these days?" Mara had the distinct impression that Jay's older sister was trying not to laugh. "You know, I think I will take you up on that Cocomo date. We have so many things to discuss."

Ahead of them, she spotted Jay already holding two pieces of luggage on top of everything else. He was scanning the pile for a third. What else could the family possibly need? His eyes brightened, and he reached over to Mara's luggage and pulled it from a pile. Of course he knew it was hers. Mara could read her own last name from the gigantic luggage tags her mother had gotten them for Christmas, hanging from the side of her carrying case.

"Jay!" Mara said. "What are you doing?"

"Helping you," he replied as she, Luna and Ate Irene made it to the front of the boat, people passing them to go ahead. "That plank to the dock is rail thin and rickety. It's really hard to do it without bags."

"And yet somehow I managed to get on the boat by myself, like a big girl. Give me the bag."

"It's fine, I got it," Jay insisted. He was holding both handles of his family's strollers in one hand, carry-on bags on his other shoulder and the deflated duck looped around his neck as he held on to the handle of Mara's case in his other hand. He looked extra ridiculous, and Mara could feel a familiar heat of anger rise from her belly.

"Jay, let go of my bag," she repeated.

"Why won't you let me help you?" He sounded annoyed and exasperated. "If I was your boyfriend, you would have expected me to help you."

"I already asked you to help me, remember? And you said

no. Now, aren't you glad you aren't my boyfriend, pretend or otherwise?"

She turned away from his flabbergasted face and called a porter over. She could have sworn she heard Ate Irene choke back a laugh. The man was eager to help and quite surprised when Mara made him grab Jay's carry-on bags and the two strollers. Before Jay could protest, Mara snatched her case from his hand, urging the porter to go ahead of her.

When she managed to make it up on the ramp, fueled by spite and zero self-preservation, she handed the porter two hundred pesos and thanked him. Then she turned to face the Montinolas, who were still standing on the fore of the boat and watching her in varying expressions of confusion (Luna), amusement (Irene) and what-the-fuck-just-happened (Jay).

She grinned at him and used both hands to put her sunglasses on, Horatio Caine style. *Yeeeaaaaaahhhhhhhh!*

Jay rolled his eyes in response. His sass was massive, but Mara's spite was only just bigger. Because if she was completely honest herself, what she had refused to tell Ate Irene, to tell Jay or anyone else, was the real reason why she booked this trip. Why she thought it was time to use her good luck wedding money.

It wasn't her sister getting married, wasn't the first or the second reception. It wasn't even that it was the busiest time of the year for the studio, or that her parents' relationship was a daily tightrope walk of other people's problems.

It was that he'd tried to soothe her with a kiss. A kiss that he knew had to ultimately mean absolutely nothing, but still made Mara feel good. Made her think that it actually agonized him, saying no to her. Made her think sometimes that today, *today* it was going to work. Only to realize that she wasn't a little girl, and she didn't believe in fairy tales that way anymore.

She had gotten so used to waiting, waiting and hoping. The prince would approach her, everyone said!

But no. Jay had kissed her because he pitied her and thought it would be enough. And the humiliation was, quite possibly, even worse than when he'd made her social media's favorite joke. So Mara was going to hold on to her triumphant pettiness for a long, long time.

"We're just waiting on the other group to join us," the driver of the transport told her when she loaded her belongings into the van. There was a fifteen-minute van ride to get to Station 1, and most hotels booked proprietary third-party services to handle that transportation.

So Mara ended up holding on to her triumphant pettiness for about, oh, ten minutes. Because the doors to the L300 opened to the sight of three very familiar people.

"Tita!" At least Luna was genuinely delighted, waving happily from the open door. Ate Irene was busy speaking to the driver, checking their belongings, and Jay was on the phone with someone, even if his eyes had zeroed in on Mara. The gaze was heated, but she couldn't tell if it was a good or bad thing.

"—yeah, we're here. What do you mean a disaster?" Jay said to the phone. "No, it's not a disaster. Hold on—want Nong to carry you, Luns?"

The little girl nodded and held her arms up without turning

to face him. What followed was a funny scene of Jay hoisting Luna up to the single step up to the back of the van, the girl keeping her arms perfectly straight at her sides like he was about to toss her in the air. Luna giggled and moved to sit next to Mara while Jay kept talking, tucking the phone between his chin and shoulder as he helped Ate Irene load their many, many belongings. "I'm sure it will be okay. It's Boracay! I'm sure there are suppliers somewhere out there."

He sat in the spot closest to the door as he helped pull his sister up. Ate Irene's eyes widened at the sight of Mara and Luna, but they softened at her daughter's smile, and she sat across from them.

"What a coincidence," Ate Irene said, "I mean it, though, Mara. I really like you. That—" she jerked her thumb at her brother "—notwithstanding. And not to defend him or anything—"

"Oh, Ate, you don't have to—"

"—but he really does think that kiss of his is a curse. It's the first time he's done it intentionally to spare someone, and I think he wouldn't have done it if he didn't think you would be better off. He can be a real dummy that way."

Ugh. Her conscience had no voice, but it did feel a lot like a rock weighing her down. She should trust him more, but trust would mean letting go of her feelings, of packing them up and putting them away neatly, never to be felt again. Would he have listened, if she told him, about how he'd made her feel that night?

"Alex. Breathe," Jay said into the phone, unaware of the conversation about him happening from the same car. "Ate

and I will be there in about fifteen minutes, then we can figure it out, okay? Now, who's the best man? That's right. You
can use me as a stress ball as soon as we get there."

He hung up and put away his phone.

"Everything okay?" Irene asked.

"Nothing a best man can't handle." He smiled at them, but
it was a polite, strained smile.

The ride continued on in silence, filled only by Luna asking
her mother questions, or Irene fielding questions from Luna
that were supposed to be meant for Jay. Mara could almost
feel his aura radiating...something from his side of the van.

Thankfully, her hotel was first.

The van pulled to a stop, and the driver grabbed Mara's
bag from where he'd placed it in the passenger seat. Mara
made sure he had it by the door of the hotel before smiling
at Ate Irene and Luna, waving as she awkwardly shuffled to
the end of the van.

It wasn't going to be easy to alight from the van, she realized.

She sat in the seat at the very end, closest to the door, before
she remembered that someone was supposedly sitting here.
Only for her to look at the door to find Jay holding his hand
up to her, his smile kind. And she knew what his apologetic
face looked like, because she'd seen it so many times already.

"I'm sorry," he said to her.

"Do you even know what you're apologizing for anymore?"
Mara asked. She was tired of this, of not understanding how
he felt, and not being able to ask (because why, again?). She

was tired of picturing him walking through the door, of still being lonely.

"You're angry."

"I'm a lot of things. But yes, I am angry," she admitted, and a weight lifted from her, just by admitting that out loud. "Frustrated, annoyed, really, really pissed…"

Jay winced, and all the fight left Mara, her shoulders dropping.

"But I'm really happy I ran into you. All things that are true."

He seemed relieved.

"Let me help you down." He held a hand out for her. She took it and let him guide her down from the van, the two of them standing in the street together. Electric tricycles, other vans and cars passed by them, but it was really hard to notice when Jay was looking at her like…like he understood her. Like he could see her for all she was, and how she felt. He was sweating. And that stripe of sunscreen was still on his chin. Mara wiped it off, and she didn't miss the way he closed his eyes at her touch. The way it made her heart skip a beat.

So maybe he hadn't rejected her because he didn't want her. He did. And the way she was reacting to him, the way she wanted him? The feeling was mutual.

"I think we need to talk," he concluded. She nodded.

"You know where to find me. I'll see you later."

As it happened, later was in about thirty minutes. After a very painless check-in and a quick change, the vacation was officially on.

Mara was at the beach, fully protected by sunscreen, nursing a glass of complimentary ripe mango shake and holding her phone. She'd taken a quick dip in the ocean. Not long enough that her fingers got pruny, but just enough to cool her down. Her view was obscured by bamboo scaffolding that kept patrons from view of the public, but it was perfect enough for her purposes. The beach and the lounge were almost completely empty at noonish, which was understandable.

Mara wouldn't be caught outside in the blazing heat of the too bright, too hot sun, either, but she found a lounger situated under a strategically placed palm tree, had re-slathered herself in sunscreen and kept her legs under her sarong. The key to enjoying the beach was getting *just* enough sun.

Her phone was currently playing catch-up with messages and texts—mostly questions from the team regarding the Impressionist Cosmetics tinted lip gloss launch next week. Would they be able to accommodate more students for the flower workshop? She had three hours left in her workday, and that was fine.

Over on the "Rosplenda, Rosario and Rosemary" group chat, Mabel sent a photo of a cake. It was a gorgeous cake from Caramello's, with a creamy yellow caramel layer and roses piped expertly in buttercream.

There was no dedication, no note. Only a caption from Mabel. *He bought a cake, guys. I think they're fine na.*

Nothing spelled, "Can we sweep our issues under the rug now?" better than a cake from Caramello's. Mara sighed and laughed ruefully, shaking her head. Some days, she didn't regret her current single situation, when it meant not having to deal with this kind of thing.

Locking her phone and leaving it on Do Not Disturb, Mara just settled in for her first round of sunbathing when something wearing a sando, a Snoopy pouch and a puka shell necklace blocked her view. Her eyes un-squinted and she looked up at the space invader.

"I have questions about the pouch," Mara said without moving.

"It contains essentials." Jay shrugged like it was all the explanation he needed to give. "You want a candy?"

"You know when I said I would see you later, I meant I would come to you, not the other way around."

"You did tell my sister exactly where to find you," he teased, and his grin turned into a soft smile. Mara's eyes lazily drifted to his exposed collarbones, the way the sleeveless shirt hugged his trim waist. She felt a sparky, electric heat shoot up from between her legs, to her chest and back between her legs. Jay was openly staring at her lying in front of him, bikini on, her thighs and cleavage on full display. Her toes curled under her sarong to contain what her high school religion teacher called "urges of an impure nature."

"I really can't decide if I like the necklace." She suddenly had to change the subject, sitting up on the recliner. "I'm getting boyband flashbacks."

"It's vintage 2000s, baby," Jay chided her. Upon closer inspection, Mara clocked that he was nervous and sweaty. Sweaty she understood, but nervous, not so much. Not for Jay. "Okay, I know we need to talk. We need to talk a lot."

"Do we?" Mara sighed. "I kind of thought we already didn't say everything we needed to not say."

Jay blinked, absolutely confused by the double negative. Mara couldn't repeat that if she tried. But she was the child of two people who perpetually didn't communicate. She learned things.

His eyes darkened. "I'm not here to talk."

There it was again—that warm, shivery little *zing* that shot through her body. Maybe it was her thirties. Maybe it's Maybelline.

"I actually need your help," he said.

And let's be honest. To the part of the population that was at the intersection of being an eldest daughter, Asian and an earth sign…was there anything sexier than someone asking your help?

Today, Mara learned, that the answer was no.

"It's the wedding. There's a floral emergency."

"Brief me while we walk," Mara said, throwing her tapis on. "What's the emergency?"

Nine

What isn't *the emergency?* Jay almost snorted as he led Mara through the beach, past the property line of her hotel and the approximate fifteen steps to his. As it turned out, the best man could not have come at a better time.

The wedding was tomorrow, and Mon, their unofficial officiant, and his plus-one, Olivia, weren't arriving until two hours before. A last-minute preproduction meeting for Olivia's latest project meant the soonest they could leave Manila was tomorrow. Luna had seen Alex try on her wedding outfit and cried in a shocking bout of hysterics because she couldn't conceive anyone being "prettier than her." Red tide hit Aklan so half the seafood was no longer available, and neither Alex nor Tori had finished writing their vows.

All these things he could handle. Jay was a finance guy; he knew how to handle disastrous situations when someone was yelling at him from halfway across the world on two different phones. The key to managing a situation was to, one, decide if the problem was something you could fix, and two, if you couldn't fix it, find someone to do it.

So far he'd been doing well—Mon was in charge of figuring out timings and keeping them updated if there were any changes. Ate Irene was with Luna, distracting her with a treat from Jonah's Fruit Shake while trying to explain to her daughter that more than one person could hold the crown of "pretty." He'd spoken to the chef and recalibrated the menu for taste testing tonight, and tasked the maid of honor, Ava, and Scott on locking their friends in their rooms until vows were written.

Things were fine. Things were under control.

But everything changed when the flowers attacked. Sorry. *Arrived*.

Jay instantly knew that there was only one person on this island that he could trust to help. Lucky for him, she was right there wearing a red bikini while lounging on the beach.

Logically, Jay knew that the possibility of seeing Mara Barretto in a bathing suit was pretty high considering they were on an island made for bathing. But thinking something logical was completely different from something being actually true, and Jay found that out the, uh, slightly *hard* way when he saw Mara on that lounger. Slow down, boy.

It did things to him, seeing her body facing the sun, the lazy way she stretched. The suit clung to the softness of her, and he wanted to hold her, revere her curves. He wanted to wrap his body around hers, kiss the skin on her generous cleavage. Mara had looked so content lying on that lounger. He almost curled up next to her to take a nap.

Almost. Because he was a good best man. And the best of men risked the ire of women they wanted to sleep with to help brides out of a tight spot.

"I'm sorry I'm pulling you out of your vacation," he said. At least he knew what he was doing wrong this time.

"I know you wouldn't have done it unless it was really important," Mara said dismissively, tightening the knot of her sarong on her waist. Jay already missed the skin her bikini had exposed, that space under her breasts, and the top of her waist, lined with stretch marks and itching for his touch. "What happened?"

"Well—" he cleared his throat "—that."

They crossed a low line of strategically planted beach fauna to enter Shorewinds's open air space, one that doubled as their restaurant. They were immediately greeted by the chaos of the flower company staff moving its blooms in to the venue, restaurant staff telling them they couldn't and diners eyeing the scene unfold with the interest of old men watching construction sites in their spare time. Tension was getting thick as the oppressive beach heat only made everyone more irritable.

"Apparently the supplier got the dates confused and delivered the flowers today." Jay spoke quickly as they rushed in to diffuse the tension. "I couldn't get them to take it back because apparently the owner has a job in Cebu and is currently on a plane. So I—"

"Haven't told the couple, have you," Mara guessed, assessing the situation.

"Neither of them have finished writing their vows! And it's not a *huge* emergency yet."

"This is pretty huge, Jay." Mara held her hands out at the unfolding situation.

"That's why I called the best florist I know." He winked.

"It's floral designer," Mara corrected him, rolling her eyes. But it lacked any kind of heat and so he took it as affectionate. She sighed and surveyed the situation again. "But you're right. You are so lucky I came."

"I know I am." He grinned at her, because what was a better inducement than charm and total honesty? It was all he had, really.

"Boss," one of the flower guys called, apparently recognizing Jay. His eyes widened at the sight of a whole fucking arch being unloaded from the back of a small truck. "The waiters said we can't set up."

"Sabi ko sayo, sir, this is a *dining area*," the waiter said, sounding exasperated.

The flower guy responded with a roll of his eyes, muttering something about "eto pala si Optimum Pride eh," which was both funny and a sure sign that patience was wearing thin on both sides. Jay really needed to come up with something before his charm stopped working on either party.

"Should I call the manager?"

"Huy, mga lodi, let's chill!" Jay held his hands out to calm the situation, giving both sides an amiable smile. He turned to the flower guys. "I really need these flowers, but I don't need them until tomorrow. Can't you come back tomorrow to set up? As you were scheduled to do?"

The flower delivery guy shook his head. "No can do, boss.

We have a wedding at Shang tomorrow. We deliver these today or your event doesn't have flowers."

"Where's your room?" Mara asked suddenly, looking around the place. Was she giving up already? "Shorewinds only has villas, right? We can move the flowers there and figure it out tomorrow."

Genius. Mara Barretto was a genius, and Jay wanted to kiss her.

"You think all this will fit?" Jay asked doubtfully, waving his hand at the nosegay (nosegay?) of flowers that was building up literally at their feet.

"We're going to have to make them fit." Mara's lips pursed cutely, hands on her hips. Jay grinned. The fortunate upside of this was that he was going to get to see Mara in her element, and he was surprised at how much even he was looking forward to it. "Is there some kind of layout or a plan for the event?"

Yes, there was. They also had a copy of the signed contract, which Mara quickly flipped through, her eyes squinting at the print. It was almost comical, seeing her with her sunglasses perched on her head, bikini and all as she examined the very serious documents.

"I also need to know when your boss's flight lands in Cebu." Mara frowned at the paper in her hands. "If the couple is hiring a new team by tomorrow, we need to enact a couple of these refund options. The contract says the install for the flowers is tomorrow, not today."

Everyone within hearing distance winced. What Jay had told himself was a small problem was suddenly a huge one.

"I have a friend who has a floral design business here in Boracay. I can call to see if he's available for the setup tomorrow. But for today, I can start on the wedding party bouquets."

"Jay, what the fuck!" Alex lightly swatted his chest with her hand as the rest of the currently present wedding party watched the march of the flowers currently occurring in his villa. Jay gave a loud yelp, jumping back in shock at Alex's sudden yell.

"What the hell, Alex! You can't sneak up on me like that!"

"I have so many questions."

"And so many flowers," Scott commented dryly, moving out of the way of a staff member who couldn't see much because the roses were blocking his view. Jay shrugged, although the effect was quite lost, as his shoulders were obscured by the massive buckets of bloodred anthuriums and pastel purple ranunculus that he was carrying.

"And zero florists," Ava, the maid of honor, added, glancing nervously at the growing forest of florals. There was a holdup at the door. Inside, Jay heard Mara loud and clear, directing the people to keep things by event and by color, and—if it was for the wedding arch—placing them by the bathroom. Jay had been effectively unhoused in favor of party decorations.

"Floral designers," Jay corrected her. Tori, the other bride, shook her head in disbelief at what was unfolding before them. Alex smacked his arm, telling him to focus, and he recoiled in surprise. "Aray! Hey, I got you guys a refund on the design fee!"

"Thank you for the money, but what about the flowers?" Tori said.

"Oh no, you don't get the money. We're repurposing the funds for a new investment."

"A new what!"

"O-kay. I can sense this should be a conversation, not an announcement," Ava announced, looping an arm around her cousin's, the other around her boyfriend's and dragging them toward the restaurant. "We should go see if the restaurant is ready with the new menu. Come on, Tori, I know writing makes you hungry."

Scott was protesting that can they please not leave "because the drama is *here*!" but Ava probably was trying to give Jay the room to explain himself to the soon-to-be-wedded couple. "Best of luck," she said.

"I'm the best man, I don't need luck." Jay chortled.

"I was talking to Alex," Ava called over her shoulder as she, Tori and Scott left the vicinity of the area. Leaving him with one very confused, very angry, but still very cute bride.

"Jay. Sweet red bean. Idiot of my heart."

"Oh god." Jay winced. "Red bean?"

"You just made me one shot my vows. I am way too emotionally vulnerable to be calm," Alex said, rubbing her temples and closing her eyes. She was stressing. He was doomed. "We have no flowers. No officiant. No oysters. Tori and I might as well just spend tomorrow swimming in the ocean! What the hell are we even doing here?"

Contrary to what Alex was saying, Jay knew that *she* knew that he was not an idiot. He also knew that his friend could be testy (and that was an understatement) when she was stressed, and this definitely counted as a stressful situation.

Jay and Alex met a few years back after being matched on a dating app. They gave it a good try, dating a few times, but called it quits and remained really good friends instead. Alex had gone to Bali for a production job and came back to Manila dating Tori, who was cousins with Ava and also in a barkada with Jay's high school friends Scott and Mon.

Which was purely proof that the world of middle-class Manila was really not that big.

Alex and Jay were low-maintenance friends, the kind that sent each other memes and talked about shit every day, but never saw each other more than a few times a year.

Being Alex's best man wasn't surprising to Jay. Mostly because Jay was Alex's last straight boy kiss before she decided to date women exclusively and met Tori on a work trip to Bali.

Yeah. Meet Alex Suarez, kiss curse victim number eight. Jay should *really* stop kissing on the first date.

So Mara really didn't have to worry about the kiss not working out for her. He didn't have metrics, obviously, but the successes happened eventually. Patience was a virtue, although he was pretty sure his teachers weren't specifically thinking of this context in particular. There was nothing Jay could do about that for now.

Right now, Alex was on the verge of panic, and Jay needed to talk her down a bit.

"Hey, hey. You're declaring to everyone you know that you want to wake up next to Tori for the rest of your life. Isn't that beautiful?" Jay said, putting his buckets down to usher his friend next to him on the elevated ledge of the villa, facing the beach. Alex's face stayed in a frown as she glared at the ocean, as if willing a tsunami to wash him away. Well, tough luck. "Well, it is, Al. You're in love, and you want people to know, diba?"

"I do."

"See, you know the words already! It'll be easy for you," Jay assured her, patting her on the back. "And don't worry about anything when it comes to this wedding. Between me and Ava, we have it covered. You and Tori picked good people."

"The best people," Alex conceded with a little sigh. Almost like she didn't really want to admit it. She shot Jay a long, assessing look. "You know I almost didn't choose you."

"Me? Why?" He pouted.

"You don't believe in this stuff, Jay. You never have." Alex chuckled. "And don't lie. I have the receipts. All the lengthy conversations we've had about why you don't believe in love. Literal nightmares you've had about it. Do you still get the one where you're a hoarder?"

"I don't think *I* was the hoarder in the dream," Jay corrected, but just the mention of the nightmare made him shudder. "Families collect a lot of junk."

The nightmare always started in the same place. Him kicking ass at a billiard table, which was already weird because he never played billiards. Then a woman would show up—he would never remember who it was—and demand that he go home with her. Only for them to pass through a door and into a room cluttered with, just, stuff. Rattan furniture that was frayed with even-more-frayed cushions. Pirated DVDs.

Books, stuffed toys, cassette tapes. Cables. So many cables. Empty fish tanks. There was barely room to breathe.

And then the kids entered. Cute kids who needed food, needed him to play with them, needed his help with homework. Bills would slip through the bottom of the door behind him, all demanding to be paid. Then his phone would ring, and it was his old boss, yelling into his ear because he didn't meet their targets for the quarter, why didn't he meet those targets?

And just when Jay started to scream and want to get out, asking the empty air for his mystery partner to help him out, the door would burst open, and Carmi Martin as Jeanette Bayag from *Four Sisters and A Wedding* would walk in, saying, "Vanjour! Halu halu halu!"

That always managed to wake him up in a cold sweat.

"The nightmare lives on because you let it," Alex pointed out, shaking her head. "And it felt like bad vibes to put the wedding sort of in your hands."

"I thought you didn't believe in vibes," Jay muttered. He was a little hurt by the concern. "Alex. Just because I don't believe it for me, doesn't mean I don't believe in it for you."

One of the easier lessons he'd learned in his adulthood was to let people be people. That included who they wanted to be with, what they enjoyed and what they chose to do with their lives. Mostly because it had nothing to do with him, and good for them, if that was what they wanted.

And if he was asked to help, then he was going to make use of every skill he had to help them out.

What he learned recently, after his long Tagaytay back and

forth, after seeing Mara's determination for her sister, was that having a wedding was a call for support. Asking people to come to your table and celebrate what they had. So when Alex told him she was getting married, he gave her his full self, his full support. Because his friend deserved nothing less than what made her the most happy.

It was that easy.

"I am here because I am your friend. If you said you wanted an Under the Sea themed wedding I would have asked if you preferred to be the Little Mermaid or Ursula the Sea Witch," he said. Still pouting. He pulled Alex up from where they were sitting, each of them retrieving a bucket of flowers as he led her to his room. "What made you change your mind?"

"Because I wanted you to be here, duh," Alex said, hiding a small smile. "And because you might be leaving."

He didn't deny that. After several emails and negotiations, a couple of video calls, Jay was offered his old job at a higher salary, to start sometime around Q3 if he wanted. His official word back to the bank was, "I'm considering the proposal," and it was enough to maybe buy him some time. Some time for what, he had no idea.

But if his gut feeling told him "not yet," he was going to listen. Maybe it was finding out he would have to pay 25 percent more on his old apartment if he wanted the old place back. Maybe it was something else he really hadn't figured out yet.

"Also I wanted a cute flower girl."

"Luna *is* the cutest. Can't get cuter than my inaanak," Jay said. He knew Alex was going to be fine, and if she wasn't, then he was going to be there either way. "We practiced."

"I know you and Ate Irene freaked at her reaction to me," Alex said, "but I have to admit, I thought it was so funny. And freaking adorable that she wanted to be the prettiest."

"Yeah, I don't think it's going to be as adorable when your guests are all watching." Jay opened the door. Cool air blast from the inside, his eyes adjusting to the darkened room's lighting. "I'll introduce you to the floral designer. She's amazing."

"Before you think it's bad juju," Mara announced, not looking up from her spot on Jay's bed, surrounded by deep red, pale pink and purple flowers, blocks of foam, rolls of pale blue ribbon and tissue paper. She was holding a floral cutter in one hand and a spray bottle of water in the other. Apparently she'd showered and changed when she realized the size of the favor Jay was asking. Her cheeks, a bit of her forehead and her nose were a little red from the sun. "Beyoncé is an excellent musical motivator, and *Lemonade* is an even more excellent album."

Then she looked up, and Jay was struck with the urge to kiss her, to make her smile. Her eyes were wide, and her mouth was formed into a little O of surprise.

"I wasn't going to disagree, but personally I'm more of a *Renaissance* guy myself." Jay grinned as Mara's cheeks flushed red. He stepped to the side so he could properly introduce Mara to the bride. "Alex, this is Mara, she—"

"Huy, Barretto," Alex exclaimed, expertly weaving through the flowers and arrangements scattered around the room to throw her arms around Mara, who smiled and hugged her back. "Seat mate!"

"Seat mate!" Mara looked just as surprised as any of them, scooting over to make room for her friend. Jay watched in equal parts amusement, fascination and a tiny dash of worry at what was unfolding before him, because it didn't mean anything good for him. "Oh my god, I didn't know it was you! You're the bride?"

"One of." Alex grinned, and there was that familiar, "I am *so* in love" smile that Jay had missed seeing on his friend's face. "Wait, did Jay fly you in?"

"Nope."

"Al, I love you, but not that much."

"Jay knew I was staying in the hotel next door, so I was vacation-napped into completing the arrangements. My friend agreed to come in for tomorrow for the setup, and I thought I would get a head start on the arrangements."

"Told you I had it handled." Mara shot him a smile. And if his heart leaped in his chest at her little acknowledgment, he hoped it didn't show. "How do you two know each other?"

"High school. How do *you* two know each other?" Alex's brow rose, but Jay knew she was asking so she could tell him exactly why her friend deserved better, and not because she genuinely wanted to know. Alex was well aware of the existence of his curse. "Did you kiss her? Jay!"

"Alex, I can meet people without kissing them," Jay sassed.

At the same time, Mara began to explain, "Wait, you know about his kiss thing?" Which made Jay groan and wish the flowers currently surrounding them would just bury him now, please and thanks.

"Marrying Tori tomorrow will officially make me number…eight?" Alex said, raising her eyebrows playfully at Jay, who only made a strangled sound that seemed to satisfy her for confirmation. "Have you—"

"Oh, no. I think I'm his first failed vector," Mara said. He didn't miss the flash of regret in her eyes, the little wince Alex made in reaction. "We're friends. Right, Jay?"

"Friends that aren't dating," he agreed.

"Nobody's made you sinok yet, huh?" Alex asked, giving Mara a friendly, knowing smile. Wow, Jay did not remember being *that* close to his high school seat mate. "Aww, beh. I know you've wanted it for a while."

"Oh my god. I can't believe you still remember that."

"Oh my god, what?" Jay asked, suddenly wanting to desperately be part of the conversation. "Sinok?"

"Just Catholic school girl things." Alex laughed as Mara buried her hands behind her face, because she was still giggling and blushing profusely. Jay had never seen her so flushed. "We were made to sign chastity vows when we were in senior year of high school."

"Not that any of us actually took it seriously." Mara snorted. "I mean there weren't exactly a bevy of boys waiting by the school gates, because—"

"Everyone was dating each other," Jay said dreamily. The girls ignored him.

"And the teacher saw Mara's vows and read them out loud to the class as an example of what *not* to do," Alex continued, shaking her head.

"Look, in my defense, her chastity mad libs had a lot of room for interpretation."

"Yeah, but we were supposed to write shit like, 'when we're married,' or 'when we got tired of masturbating'—"

"Ringing the devil's doorbell!" Mara corrected her and giggled.

Jay had the sense that he was seeing Mara totally unguarded. Generous with her smiles and little touches, scooting over so Alex could sit next to her. He wasn't going to lie—he was a little jealous. Alex hadn't mentioned Mara around him before, and the way they hugged made it seem like the seat mates hadn't seen each other in a while. Yet they were so comfortable with each other.

"What were Mara's conditions to break her chastity vow?" Jay asked as Alex slid on to the bed next to her, their shoulders pressed together. Mara started grabbing flowers from her piles and declared that, lalalala, she wasn't listening.

"We needed to list three whens, basically conditions to when breaking the vow was okay," Alex started. "Instead, Miss Lover Girlie here listed three conditions to falling in love."

"Love and sex were intrinsic to me! In *high school*." Mara gave Alex a scathing look, muttering something about not having proper sex education and having to learn it all from fanfic.

"First, kailangan there's a *magical moment*." Alex emphasized the words to sound like she was in a soap opera, or a nineties-era teen movie.

"Oh god." That was Mara, still pretending to ignore them. She bent over, trying to reach for one of the roses, which was just out of her grasp. Jay plucked it from the bed and handed it to her. Neither of them caught Alex observing the interaction and trying to hide a smile.

"What's a magical moment?"

"Oh, you know." Alex waved a hand around. "The world falls away, all is quiet, '214' by Rivermaya is playing."

"Grabe 'to." Mara nudged her. "I'm more an Ebe Dancel girl."

"The second condition. Mara, what was the second condition?"

Mara said something, but she spoke it so softly, and with her head turned away, that Jay had no idea what it could possibly be.

"Right! You said you wanted your heart to skip a beat." Alex nodded.

Then she looked around the room. "Why the hell did we order so many flowers?"

"Because you love love, just like me," Mara teased. Alex didn't argue. Instead she started to wander the room, looking at the arrangements.

"Heart skips a beat. That's easy enough," Jay said. "And the last?"

"The sinok," Alex declared. She then plucked a hot pink gerbera daisy and whirled to face them.

"The what?"

"Hup!" Mara made a little noise, like she'd swallowed air too quickly.

Jay's brain did the connecting for him. Sinok. Hiccup. Mara's eyes widened in surprise, and their eyes met across the bed. A magic moment, a heart skipping a beat and a sinok.

All simple things that happened…well, most days. But as they gazed at each other across his bed, on a completely different island, Jay had a feeling that Mara's high school self had somehow called to him. Dreamed him up somehow.

All she needed to do was ask. Out loud.

"Why are there still loose flowers, though?" Alex's curiosity pulled them both out of the moment. Mara's cheeks were pink as she picked up the bouquet she'd been working on, spinning it in her hands.

"Because we still needed the bridal bouquets," Mara explained. "This is yours."

She grabbed one of the roses, long stemmed, the big red petals clustered close together, and slowly teased open the petals with her fingers, folding it back to look less like a fluttering heart and more like one that was bursting open. It was captivating to watch. She added it to the bouquet, doing it a few more times before she held it up to her friend.

"Wow," Alex gasped, taking the flowers and cradling them in her arms. The baby blue of the ribbon popped against the deeper berry flowers, a collection of gerbera daisies, carnations, roses and eucalyptus, and in Alex's hands, it looked like a heart, bursting out with love. "Roses are my birth flower."

"I remember." Mara nodded, tenderness in her eyes. The look they exchanged spoke volumes that Jay only ever hoped he would know about her. "But I know speaking from your heart was something you didn't find easy back then. Maybe the flowers can speak for you, you know?"

"Yeah." Alex caressed the blooms gently.

Mara was so good at this. Jay longed to squeeze her hand,

tell her how good she was at this, but let the two reunited friends keep their moment instead. "Seat mate. Come to the wedding tomorrow."

"Oh, I wouldn't want to—"

"I want you to," Alex insisted, squeezing Mara's hand. "I want you to meet Tori. And Jay doesn't have a plus-one."

Both Mara and Alex turned to him in varied expressions of, "Oh, I completely forgot you're here," and, "You are *so* welcome," respectively. Jay narrowed his eyes at Alex in response, because he didn't *need* her help. But this was Alex's big day, and since Jay was fully committing to being the supportive friend (and honestly, because he would love to spend more time with Mara), he slipped his hands in his pockets and shrugged.

"I'd love to be your date."

And that, ladies and gentlefolk, was how Jay Montinola ended up at another wedding with Mara Barretto.

They both laughed about it, later that afternoon when Mara needed a break from the flowers, and after they managed to clear a path from the bed to the door. Jay had needed to run out of the room a few more times—once to taste test the food (amazing), one time to assure Luna that she was the prettiest flower girl he had ever seen, and one *more* time to grab Mara's glasses from her hotel room. It was getting dark, and the hotel's moody villa lighting wasn't helping her.

"Let's take a walk," he proposed.

"But—" she protested, pointing to her small pile of arrangements. She just finished speaking to Kal of Tropikal Flower, and he agreed to step in and take over the contract.

What Mara needed to do, and she was currently rushing through, was create the smaller arrangements using the buckets of loose flowers scattered around her.

Aside from Alex's bouquet—which she thankfully took with her—Mara made a bouquet for Tori (with bright red gerberas in the center, a symbol of lasting love), a little basket for Luna full of purple flowers (no red for her, just so she feels a little more special), and boutonnieres for Jay and Ava, at the request of Tori. She still had a lot of flowers left over and was contemplating making Luna a flower crown when he decided she needed a little break.

"Oh wow, the people are *out*," Mara said as she followed Jay to the beach. It was sunset at golden hour, the island's most magical time of day. So magical that it lured Filipinos from their hiding spots from the sun, just to bid it good-night.

The sky was a mix of pale yellow and steely gray, the waters reflecting a dull teal in the fading light. The shore had receded far enough that people still swimming looked like dots on a horizon, paraw boats and their blue sails even farther chasing the last of the sunset. Most of the sand they were walking on was wet and firm, but Mara suddenly grabbed his arm the closer they got to the shore as her feet sunk in fully.

"I can hold your sandals if you want to take them off. Least I could do."

"One of many things you owe me." Mara chuckled, using his arm as an anchor to keep her steady as she took off her sandals and handed them to him. She grinned as her toes sunk fully into the sand. He looped the straps of her sandals in his fingers and held a hand out for her, the two of them making their way toward the water to join the beachgoers' pilgrimage.

"So," Jay started, "Alex."

"Yeah, Alex." Mara's face brightened. "I had no idea she was getting married. Which is what I get for not keeping up with people, I guess."

"People get busy," Jay defended her. Friends came and went all the time.

"That's true. I used to think they just didn't like me enough to stay friends with me. But nowadays, I just kind of accept that it is the way it is. People come into your life and sometimes aren't meant to stay. The wrong thing would be to refuse them when they come back."

"When they show up on your fast craft?" Jay asked hopefully. They knew they needed to talk about it, meeting each other. About the last time they spoke to each other, and what it meant that they were here now, on the beach together.

"Crystal kayak for the couple, sir? Sunset paraw sailing?" one of the locals offered. They shook their heads no politely. Eventually they reached a spot just far enough from the crowds, but still a good enough place to view the sunset. Mara breathed a sigh, and it sounded like deep, sweet relief. Or maybe like walls breaking down. "I was angry with you," she admitted, eyes focused on what was in front of them. But Jay couldn't look away from her cheeks, at the light that bounced off the tops of them, at the press of her lips as she formed her words. "After you kissed me. I thought I was angry that you just proved that I was undesirable, because I am apparently immune to your kiss thing—"

"Mara." How fucking untrue that was. How utterly impossible.

"But," Mara said before sighing so deeply that Jay wished he could smooth the creased lines on her brow with his thumb. He settled for squeezing her hand instead. Reminding her that he was here, that he would listen. "I realize I was more upset that you rejected me." *Oof.* "That you kissed me hoping I would go away, and off to someone else's arms."

A chill went through Jay's body, as guilt sank in his stomach. He'd been so concerned about making her feel reassured, feel good—and even that he'd spectacularly failed —that he ended up making her feel worse. Could he *ever* do anything right by Mara?

"Please don't apologize," Mara said. Like she could tell exactly what he was thinking. "You asked me why I was angry with you, and that's why."

"Are you still?" Jay asked, hope in his voice, small and yet so present.

Someone once told him that hope was not a measurable thing. It was there or it wasn't. And just the presence of that bit of hope—like a bright sun in a darkening sky—was what drew people to the beach, couples to the shoreline, families to sit and play together. A person proposing to their person. And tomorrow, his friends promising each other forever, in a country that wouldn't let them put it on paper.

"No," Mara admitted, and the hope in his chest warmed him all the way to his toes. "I'm not angry. But I am tired. *So* tired of love, and I haven't had anything to do with it yet."

Now it was Jay's turn to frown. How could she even think

that? Mara, whose eyes shone when she watched her sister dance with her new husband. Mara, who made up the conditions for her to fall in love, without having any notion of it. Mara, who jumped into a job because someone needed her. Who deserved so much more love than Jay could give.

"Selena Guerro is my ex," he announced. Mara's unchanged expression told him that she probably already knew that about him.

"Weird flex," she still said. Having the most familiar face on every billboard from Monumento to Pasay was no great feat in their circles. Not when Mon was dating an actress recently nominated for a SAG Award. But Selena's name was everywhere, even for those who didn't want to see it. "What kind of ex was she?"

Jay knew Selena before she became a household name. She was fun, liked to laugh and liked to dance. They were together for five years, when he just started working in Makati.

"The I-thought-I-was-going-to-marry-her kind of ex." He laughed now, but he'd been completely serious about it at the time. That she was the one, that his life would revolve around proving to her that he was worthy of her love. It was only a matter of funds. Of time.

After the breakup, the ring fund quickly became "Jay's Future Inaanak Fund," which wasn't due for maturity until Luna started grade school.

"The start of the pandemic changed things way too quick for everyone," Jay continued. Some more than others, obviously, but this was just part of the story. "And the more protocols were placed, the more important other things became, and one day she called and said she didn't miss me. That she loved someone else."

"Ah, so she made that post." Mara wrinkled her nose. "The hard launch of the boyfriend that went viral."

Jay winced, because he realized the irony of that. Selena hadn't exactly tagged him, but she didn't keep him a secret, either. And in a post that first featured her with her new partner, she said all the things she hadn't told him—that she was sorry, that she loved growing with him, but they had to grow apart now.

"She called your kiss her good luck charm," Mara said.

That was where the whole kiss curse thing started. When Selena declared it to be the truth, that declaration gave Jay and everyone else the power to believe it to be true. It didn't bother him at first. He leaned into it sometimes, just because it was better than making Selena the villain. It was neither of their faults that they hadn't worked out.

"Oh, Jay."

So wasn't it even worse that he'd made a meme out of Mara? He was certainly paying karma through the nose now.

These were old hurts, ones that Jay didn't carry around anymore. There were more important things to care about.

"Oh god, don't feel bad for me," Jay told her, shaking his head. "I wasn't the same guy anymore anyway. Between taking care of Luna and my Ate, suddenly having a household that needed me, I changed. I was happy to change. But I wasn't the guy she loved anymore. I was more scared that I realized that it was totally possible to fall out of love with someone so quietly."

They had touched the top of Willy's Rock now. Keeping a tight, but ephemeral grasp on the day. Jay sighed, willing it to stay just a little longer.

"My point being," he continued, "I kissed you that night because I selfishly wanted to. And if Selena could make me believe that I could kiss someone into true love, then I wanted to kiss you and make you believe that you could, too."

The sun faded away, and the island was plunged into darkness, the low bass of an unidentified song already playing from a restaurant in the distance. Suddenly it was too cold to swim, too dark to enjoy the beach. But neither Jay nor Mara moved from the spot. Jay could have watched years and thousands of suns set like this, their eyes to the wide, vast, endless sea, and Mara contemplating it all at his side.

"I'm not asking you to fall in love with me, Jay," she said, finally.

"But—"

"No buts." Mara's lips formed a smile, but she kept her eyes on the horizon. "All I asked for was a learning experience. Hands-on experience."

Yeah, he was at a loss for words. He kept trying to find them, but they would just kind of close up. Like makahiya leaves when you ran a finger across them, tucking themselves away until they were ready to open again. No, wait. He had a word.

"What?"

"Look." Mara finally turned to him, her arm bumping into his as she hadn't realized how close they were standing together. She didn't move away, though, and touched his arm.

"Thank you, for telling me about Selena. It makes sense, why you believe in this kiss thing."

"Thank you."

"But you not thinking that you're capable of love, or think that you can't decide to choose someone, or that you can change without another person knowing… I personally think that's bullshit." Mara squeezed his arm, as if trying to soften the blow of her words. It helped. "But that's your journey."

"It is?" he asked, his voice sounding too small in his own ears.

"Of course. It's how you feel. To be honest, I don't know how this will make me feel. I always thought I wasn't the kind of person who could separate love and sex, but I could be wrong." The hand that was on his arm moved to his chest, to touch the hem of his sleeveless shirt. "This doesn't need to change us. It can just be about experiencing this. Each other."

"I'll be your first," he warned her. She was still fascinated by his shirt, and his body shivered when her fingertips made contact with his collarbone. She nodded, but she was smiling, as if she knew he was going to say that. "You'll be emotional."

"You'll be crazy for me." She snorted, like just the thought of it was completely ridiculous to her. "But you'll be good for me."

"You'll fall in love with me," he said. Warning her again. Her last chance to tell him to stop, to back off, to walk away from this.

"I think you'll fall first," she told him, looking up to meet his gaze, her eyes sparkling with mischief and desire. Jay's heart stuttered in his chest, very confused, but very, very turned on. He felt a little lost as to where this was going to go.

But Mara was never one to be lost. Her hand splayed over the front of his shirt, and she gently tugged at the material to get him to bend down and kiss her.

The kiss felt like relief. Like a breath taken after holding it for much too long. Jay wrapped his arms around her, keeping the hand gripping her sandals low as his other slung around her neck. He was trying to keep the kiss gentle, like a first kiss you would give a date.

Although. This wasn't their first kiss anymore, was it?

He kissed her harder, deeper, and Mara opened up to him. She gripped him tightly, trying to keep them steady even as she tried different angles, copied the way he slipped his tongue inside her mouth. He wanted her to leave her mark on him, on his skin, with her lips.

Mara pulled away suddenly, quickly, her eyes wide like his very thought had projected into her brain to scandalize her. But just as Jay was about to ask if she was okay…she hiccuped.

Ten

Mara never told anyone this, and never actually entertained these thoughts—except when she was alone in bed, absolutely sure that nobody could intrude on said thoughts—but she had always wondered what it would truly feel like to be this adored. To have someone who wanted to keep you next to them because they couldn't get enough of you, because they found places on your body they wanted to kiss.

Because they wanted to, you know, wanted you to *feel* that in that moment, you were the only object of their desires. And that for the moment, there was nothing in the world more important than making sure you knew it.

And today, Mara learned that not only was this feeling really, really good—it was intoxicating. It made her fully understand phrases like "weak in the knees," or "lost in your eyes." But she also learned that it meant losing a bit of control, allowing another person to adore you as they wanted. As she wanted.

She laughed at the idea as she leaned against the door of her room, hands wound around Jay's neck while he kissed the skin of her cleavage, generous as it was and trying its best to burst out of her top. In the lazy haze of pleasure, a thought occurred to her.

"We don't have condoms."

"You don't always need them," he gasped. Admonishment was on the tip of her tongue when he suddenly looked up, his cheeks pink, his lips a little swollen. He was debauched, and it made Mara's insides feel warm that she'd turned the cool, smooth Jay Montinola into this. "Breathe, Mara. We're not having sex tonight."

Oh. Was she disappointed or relieved? Unclear.

"But there are…other things we can do."

"*Oh.*" Now it was Mara's turn for her cheeks to feel hot, as she pictured the other things in question. "I like the idea of other things."

"Okay, good." He grinned, and Mara tore her gaze away from him to unlock the door to her room. They left their sandy shoes by the door, careful not to track any more of the beach into the room. Jay caught her from behind, his hands on her waist and skimming across the skin of her belly when she turned to face him. Mara tiptoed up to kiss him, kindling the low flame of heat growing inside her. "Just to be clear, you know the basics?"

"Birds, bees, bunnies, trees," Mara recited. She barely held herself together at Jay's incredulous expression. "I haven't had sex with anyone else, but I've tried things. I've experimented with a few toys, lube, that kind of thing. I do it to sleep sometimes. It helps."

"You have to let me know if I'm doing something you don't like," he warned. "Anything remotely uncomfortable, we can stop."

"I'll make sure we will." She nodded. She was the one easing into the experience. Of course she was going to tell him to stop if she needed him to.

"Is there anything you want to know, or want to clear up before we do anything?"

"I just…" Mara frowned, trying to think of the proper words to say. She was aware she was giving away a part of herself with that confession, but it was a necessary part to give away. "I want you to know that I'm doing this because I want to know what sex feels like, and I want to do it with someone nice. Someone kind, if not trustworthy."

"And I fit all three categories?"

"Well, enough," she lied. But she wasn't kidding when she said that Jay was nice. Jay was kind. And if he wasn't? Well, Mara had a new brother-in-law who could track him down so Mara could make sure he regretted it. Safety nets, people.

"Who do you picture when you do?" Jay teased, stroking her cheek with his fingers, a touch that was now becoming familiar, and only made her melt more. "Someone tall, handsome?"

"Mmm, Colin Sheffield." She named a white boy actor, and Jay rolled his eyes.

A jolt of heat ran down her spine when Jay's hand rested

low on her back. She shuddered in delight, causing him to raise an eyebrow curiously.

"Air-con," she lied.

"I can warm you up," he said. But then he winced. "God, that was such a Scott joke."

"Well, now I guess I'm going to think about Scott Sabio tonight. Mmm, shoulders," Mara said. Jay quickly refocused on his task.

When his hand slid under the strap of Mara's dress, her hands suddenly felt ice-cold. She froze as he slowly pulled the strap down, stopping completely when she felt the top of her dress loosen, a strange, unfamiliar tingling sensation on her nipples, her breasts. They were heavy, cumbersome things most of the time. She had no idea that someone else's touch could feel so…intimate. To add to it, she wasn't wearing a bra, but that wasn't what made her stop.

"Wait," she gasped suddenly. Her hands flew up to her chest as Jay's hands shot to his side like he was fully expecting Mara to pull a gun out of her cleavage.

"Mara?" Jay kept his hands up, but his gaze was worried as he tried to read her expression.

She should say something, but the room was suddenly too hot, her heart was beating too fast and her fingers were too cold. Maybe she should say something about the air conditioning, about needing more water, about being hungry.

None of that was the real reason why she'd stopped. Why she needed a second. She was panicking, just a little. The kind of panic she had when a situation felt out of her control.

Why out of her control?

"I—"

It was extremely difficult, having to explain a feeling she'd never encountered before. Usually (always) she had her sisters to help her break it down, parse it into words that she could repeat, words that she believed to be true. They were always a closed door, a dining table or a group chat message away. Ready anytime she needed them. But her sisters weren't here right now, and Mara didn't know why she felt unstable. Thank god they weren't here, but also, *oh god*. They weren't here.

"I'm okay," she said, willing it to be true, as she continued to think about what happened. Jay had undone her top. Touched her in places that nobody had touched before and... oh. Nobody had ever touched her like this. He would be the first person who would ever see her naked, would touch her body with passion, with desire.

She wasn't ashamed. Despite not having any kind of proper, formal sex education, Mara learned. From books and movies that danced around the topic, to friends who explained things nobody else would.

Contrary to what people assumed, Mara did not *hate* her body. She wasn't always in love with her body, but she was grateful she had it. Knew how to use it, knew its limits. But her fear, her panic, came with being literally exposed to someone who would see more of her than she could control. A view of herself that she wasn't ready yet to expose.

"You're breathing really hard." Jay sounded worried, and she wanted to lie again. Tell him she was fine. But it wasn't right. She reached for him instead, and he pulled her in close, placing her hand on his chest. She could tell he slowed his breathing for her benefit. Although if he had told her that, she didn't remember hearing it.

"There you go. Good girl." He pressed his lips to her temple as Mara's fingers steadily warmed. As words came back to her, and the feeling of his chest anchored her to the moment, to explaining how she felt to him. "You okay? Seemed like you went like, far away."

Mara chuckled but said nothing.

"We can stop," he said, his voice suddenly serious, eyes studying her carefully. It made her heart melt, how kind and patient he was. How caring.

"No! I don't want that," Mara assured him. It was with the usual 100 percent surety of everything she undertook in her life. There was no doubt in her mind that she wanted to do this with Jay, but what *this* was had lines and limits that she hadn't learned yet.

"But?"

"But nothing," she insisted.

"Hey," he said, the gentlest of admonition as he lifted her chin with a finger, making her look at him, even as she knew that she could, at any time, turn away. "I need to know what you're thinking, Mara. Communicating with your partner is lesson one."

Ah yes. Communication. The thing she was genetically predisposed to be absolutely terrible at.

"Okay," she said finally, pulling away from him to sit on the bed. Her back rested against the pillows and the headboard, her feet together butterfly style. Her dress wasn't long enough to drape over her legs. When Jay sat beside her, his thumb brushed against her bare thigh, just above the knee. That felt good. It felt *nice*. He looked worried, and Mara wanted to kiss him more, move past this without analyzing it. But he was right. She needed to learn to say things out loud. *Por dios por santo, help po.*

"So." Mara had no idea what to say next. Ah, words! The elusive chanteuse. "Nobody's ever seen me naked. Not in recent history. And when you undid my top, I realized that I wasn't ready for that to change yet."

"Oh." Jay's mouth formed an adorable heart shape when he said that. Mara groaned and leaned against him. He made no arguments, made no list of things to tell her why she was wrong, or why he thought her body was worth showing. Instead he kissed her temple again. And that did more to reassure her than any longer thing he could have said. "For the record, I find you attractive. Very attractive."

"I know." She nodded. "I think so, too. I just need a little more time."

"What would you like to do?"

He was asking *her*? Waiting to hear what she had to say? How weird. Were all men this considerate when it came to sex? This giving? Everything she heard about it seemed to say that she was currently experiencing the exception, not the rule. Which was just the sad state of affairs in this world, and—

"Mara?"

Right, right. Focus. Her desires. Her wants. Because he was treating her like she was special. Like she mattered very much. She could get used to this, definitely.

"I want… I want you to touch me."

"Mmm. Where?" His lips moved to her ear, a whisper that sent a shiver down her spine, reigniting the heat that had started to cool inside her body. "Kasi, I'm touching you now, Mara. Is this the right place?"

The roughened skin of Jay's palms spread over her knee, not enough to contain it but enough to send her heart racing. A warm haze had fallen over the world, and there was no one in it but them.

"No," Mara said, placing her hand over his, guiding it higher. Up her thigh, closer to where she wanted him. No other sound echoed in the room save for the hum of the air conditioner and their attempts to control their breaths.

"Here." Mara leaned in, his hand on the inside of her thigh. Her skirt was tucked below her stomach now, and Jay's palm brushed over the front of her underwear, already damp. He made a satisfied noise.

"Do you like touching yourself here?" he asked. Mara fell back on the bed, spreading her legs for him. His fingertip brushed the inside of the seam of her underwear, and she jolted. "Mara?"

"Y…yes."

"Here?" Jay asked again, tracing two fingers up and down her labia, skimming the warm, wet skin there in gentle strokes. And Mara, who had never been touched by anyone else, who had always been in charge of her own pleasure, was thrilled by the idea of Jay touching her exactly where she wanted, and how. It was almost like controlling a chaos meant to be wild and reckless—at her own pace.

"No." She shook her head, breaths coming in quick as she held back her moans. "I like playing with my clit, Jay."

"Oh, you do?" He seemed delighted, and Mara's faint laugh was more because this felt a little absurd and surreal. He adjusted his position so he was lying next to her, a thigh over one of hers, his free elbow supporting him just above her head. She couldn't see his hand under her skirt, but *god*, she felt it, curling inside her. And the way it sent flashes of heat and tension up, down, around and through her body was delicious. So new, and so familiar.

Mara squeezed her thigh, feeling her body sink deeper in the bed. She worried for a moment that she was too careless. That maybe he was uncomfortable, maybe he didn't like his hand feeling around in the dark. But Jay only chuckled when she asked him about it, shaking his head.

"You're getting distracted," he told her, resuming his ministrations. "I'll let you know if I'm uncomfortable, and you do the same. Communication, okay?"

"Oki foine," Mara mumbled, but the effect was lost by his fingers finding her clit, and her entire body stiffening, fingernails digging into his arm. Jay laughed, moving his fingers low to catch the moisture she'd released, spreading it around her clit as he swirled in slow circles.

She hardly recognized the sounds she was making—gasps and pleasured moans, huffed breaths. A familiar feeling of heat rose up her body, and the delicious sense of something inside her getting tighter and tighter made her twist in bed. The angle was different, the pressure harder, but she knew this feeling. Liked that she didn't have to awkwardly angle her hand because her stomach was in the way.

Everything burst suddenly, the tightness peaking and slowly letting her go. She was panting, Jay's hand pulling back. She lay back in the bed and looked up at him, and he blinked at her. He seemed confused. Why?

"What?" she asked him. "I was done?"

"Were you?" Jay asked.

"Yes...?" she said, uncertainly. His tone was that of genuine surprise and confusion, but it did nothing to make her less confused. "Why?"

"I don't know how to say this without sounding like an ass." Jay's nose wrinkled cutely as he tried to come up with a better turn of phrase. Mara had a feeling he was not going to succeed. "But when I've been with other people, they usually can barely move after. It's like the rush of being caught after falling, or something exploding inside you, in a good way."

Mara frowned. "You're right. You do sound like an ass." If she hadn't been embarrassed before, she was now. And she'd been so confident that she actually knew this part, at least!

"Do you... I mean, could I try something else?" He was being sheepish and polite. What else was there to try? She shrugged. This *was* supposed to be an experience. "Mara. I need you to say it, please."

"Okay, you can try your way," she finally said, sighing like this was a huge imposition for her. But really, *if* there was more to the orgasm than what she had experienced...well. It was an intriguing idea. And Jay was being direct, but kind, and she appreciated that, at least. "Wow me."

"Okay." His face brightened, like a puppy given permission to play. He scooted closer so she would naturally turn on her side and encouraged her to hook her left leg around him. Mara felt something hot and...erect low on her back. God, he was hard. She'd made him hard. And knowing she had the power to make Jay Montinola slightly uncomfortable was a little satisfying. Enough to make her feel a little less embarrassed.

Jay encouraged her to open her legs, the hem of her dress pooling on her waist. She was still wet between her legs, and Jay resumed the same ministrations as before. Except his fingers were going lower, deeper inside her. They started to move in earnest—her body against his hand, and his body against hers. She could feel something wet start behind her.

"Jay, you're...you're really into this," she said between gasps of breath. She slid her hand between her legs and drew feathery light circles on her clit as Jay's fingers made the same motions inside her.

Mara's entire body shook. The heat rose up inside her again, but it didn't feel gentle or familiar this time. It demanded her attention, her feeling, and she made a whimpering sound.

"Don't stop," she breathed.

"You're surprised?" he asked, deliberately pressing deeper into her, a little lower than where he'd been playing with her clit. A place Mara only touched when she really needed her toes to curl, her body to heat up, her heart to race. "You're sexy as hell, Mara. You tell me what you want, and I want to keep making it happen."

"I bet," she said between labored breaths, "you say that to

all the girls." He said nothing in response, but when he stroked her clit in light circles, she gasped sharply and said, "Harder."

He complied. She told him again, gripping the arm that was exploring her harder, rubbing herself against his cock. Because she wanted him to know, wanted him to feel how good this was for her. Did he like this? Was he having fun yet?

"Hngh!" She stopped herself from moaning, clapping a free hand over her mouth. She needed to keep it down. This was too intimate, too private for anyone else to hear. They were definitely rutting against each other now, and Mara liked the bounce, the resistance, the little leaps of her heart. She was getting tired, but it was the good kind, the kind that made your heart race and gasp, and moan. She wanted to surrender to the twisting, building fire inside, but didn't know how. Not yet, not yet.

"A man…likes to hear if he's doing a good job," Jay told her. She liked that he wasn't totally unaffected by all this. "It's just us, baby. Let me hear you."

Then the heat burst, and Mara's mouth opened in a shocked gasp. She didn't recognize the sounds she made—sexy and delighted and tortured at the same time. As if her body was waiting for that release, she came. She came in a way that felt like a burst, a release that she'd been holding back with a tight iron grip. It lasted as long as she needed it to before she came down from her high with little whimpers and laughter because, holy *shit*, that was fucking hot. *She* was fucking hot.

Outside of that room, beyond that island, universes were born and remade in explosions just like this, and Mara could feel that with certainty as her body shuddered and Jay's touch slowed. And Mara knew two things for certain. One, that she made the right choice in Jay Montinola. And two, that this felt right because it was with him.

"Okay," she said, tucking her cheek into the pillow. "*That* was an orgasm."

"Good girl." His voice was husky and slightly pained as he pulled his hand out from between her legs. His fingers were wet with her juices, and the vague, post-orgasmic thought of, *what if I licked that?* ran through her head. "Really good."

"I've always been an excellent student," she said, still catching her breath as she shifted in bed to face him. He still looked wound up, his lips in a tight line, his jaw strained. *He hasn't come yet.* "Valedictorian in grade school, salutatorian in high school. Student council president pa."

"C-college?" he asked as he turned to lie on his back, his erection looking very, very tense.

Mara sat up on the bed, frozen and fascinated by the sight of him—his chest was red like a blossoming sunburn, his muscles strained. There was nothing in the world that seemed to relieve him, until he put the hand that had just been inside her down the front of his pants, and he breathed a sigh.

"I…" Mara was in shock and awe, fascinated at the sounds he was making, at the speed and movement of his hand. "I slacked off. Small fish, big pond. Can I help you?"

"This is good," he assured her, although the voice was strained. His cheeks were flushed red now. Then his eyes opened, dark and wild and hungry with desire. More so when he realized she was watching him.

What could she do? How could she make him feel like

he'd made her? It was almost like a test, one Mara was determined not to fail.

"Now, Jay," she said, making a decision. She reached out
and experimentally flicked her hand over where his choco
chips peeked out from under his sleeveless sando. Jay jerked,
and she smiled. "What happened to communication?"

"Mmph," was his only response. Mara liked that she was
making him squirm again. She held out a hand and waited
for him to nod, send a smoke signal, do *something*. "Please."

She undid the drawstring on his beach shorts. Jay groaned
when she peeled back his shorts, unearthing his hand and his
cock under the layers of cotton and…whatever guys' beach
shorts were made of.

Mara's eyes gasped and took it all in—the movement of his
hand, the grip, the cock itself. It was longer than she expected,
a little thicker. His balls contracted as he fondled them. Poor
baby was doing a lot of the work.

Mara put her hand under his and copied his motions until
he let her take over. They were slightly cool, and strange, but
Jay seemed to like it. The tip of his cock was wet, and with
her free hand, she circled her finger around the tip in the same
way she liked to touch her clit. The sound Jay made would
follow her to her dreams, to the next time she touched herself and pictured this.

Her hand accidentally squeezed his balls at the thought,
and Jay came with a shout. Beads of hot, white liquid shot
out of his cock, over his hand and a little on her. Jay sat up
almost immediately, looking every bit as debauched as she

felt, both looking at each other like it was the first time anyone had ever come.

"Sorry," Jay said in between gasping, heaving breaths, brushing his hand on his shorts before he wiped off the rest of the cum that splashed on her legs. Then he collapsed back on to the bed. "Are you okay? That was—"

"Jay," Mara said, waiting patiently.

"Do you need anything?" he asked. He looked like he really, really wanted to get up but couldn't because he was too tired. "Sorry, I just need to catch my breath. Mara, that was hot. That was really, really hot."

She wasn't going to disagree. But seriously. He wasn't going to...?

"Jay." His eyes were already drooping shut. "Jaysohn!"

"What?" he asked, opening one eye. And maybe he was glaring, but it made Mara laugh. She grabbed a pillow and smacked it lightly on his face.

"Wash your hands," she told him, lying back on the bed and rolling on to her stomach so she could plant a long, lingering kiss on his lips. "You dirty boy."

His mouth hung open, and he looked like he'd been frozen. Mara laughed at his shocked, slightly dazed expression and pushed at his arm to get him to go to the bathroom. Jay closed the door behind him, and Mara sunk her face into her pillow, suppressing her giggles and kicking feet.

If this was lesson one, she had a feeling she was going to come out of this class with a perfect uno.

"How long did you say you were going to be in Boracay?" Jay asked, as he emerged from the bathroom with clean hands.

"I'm here until Monday, so four days," Mara said a little loud, on her back and looking at the ceiling.

She felt…good. Really good, and still wholly herself, which she was grateful for. She knew that masturbating someone else (was that the correct term?) wasn't penetrative sex, but it was intimacy, and it was good to know that she liked it.

Enough to do it again? To do more?

"Then why do you only have two bathing suits?" Jay came out of the bathroom with an incredulous look on his face.

"Judger," Mara teased, sticking her tongue out at him. "How long are you here for?"

"I fly back Sunday afternoon," he said, pouting as he joined her on the bed, their shoulders and thighs touching. He held a hand out to hers and squeezed it. Mara recognized the satisfied smile on his face. It was the same as the one on hers. "And I brought four beach shorts."

"Oh my god." Mara laughed. "I should have known. You're a—"

"Say it. Say it!"

"An over packer," Mara gasped, and they both laughed. The same stupid laughs you release when you and your friends just don't want the night to be over, but you're all too tired to do much of anything else.

But was Jay a friend? Because Mara didn't let her other friends make her come the way he had. She never let them see this part of her, the part that wanted pleasure and liked the idea of sex. Was that what made Jay different?

"I'm glad we rode the same boat to Bora," Jay told her, his gaze fond and sentimental, and Mara had a brief vision of many, many more nights like this. Nights in a home that they made together, where they could go to sleep at night together, and wake up still knowing who the other person was on the other side of the bed, knowing that they loved you just as much as you loved them.

She shook her head to push the image away from her mind. None of that, now.

"Even though you made me work this weekend?" Jay looked genuinely abashed by that. Mara shook her head. "Kidding. I like being useful. I'm happy I get to help Alex."

"And this?" Jay asked, using his pursed lips to point at their clasped hands. "This is okay?"

Mara nodded. She didn't quite have her thoughts together to express how she felt about starting this with him. She was comfortable but still a little nervous. She was relaxed, but there were still some boundaries she wasn't ready for Jay to cross. It was a good place to be. Somewhere new, but still comfortable.

"I should go back to my room," Jay said. "Flower thieves are notorious for acting at night. Also there's a despedida de soltera for the girls at the hotel. Oh god, I just remembered there was a despedida de soltera for the girls at the hotel."

"You mean the entire reason you went to Boracay?" Mara giggled, fully getting up to go to the bathroom herself to clean up. "I admire your dedication as a best man."

"Do you want to come? I'm sure Alex would love to catch up with you."

"Nah. Let them enjoy the evening with their guests. There's a Thai restaurant near D'Mall that my sister recommended that's supposed to be really good," Mara said from the bathroom, running the sink to wash her hands. Then she'd brush her teeth. Pee.

Just hygiene things after you sort of, kind of give someone a half a hand job.

Mara put a clean hand over her mouth to cover up her sudden fit of giggles. God, they did that, didn't they? She couldn't believe it. It felt good. Really good, to have someone else touch you. To have someone warm and kind, and make you feel desirable, and beautiful. Mara could do all those things herself, certainly. But it was different, having Jay there, too. A shared pleasure.

"And I wanted tom yum!" she added.

"Can I come with you?" Jay yelled, presumably from the bed, still. "We can practice your date skills! I can give you a flirting lesson over pad thai."

Right, Mara reminded herself as she finished brushing her teeth. Admittedly it did make her happiness dim just a little, like a lower setting on a lightbulb. But she shook the feeling away, because she was a big girl, and this was all part of the agreement they made with each other. And to be fair to Jay, she was learning quick.

"I think we should take a little school break tonight," Mara said, leaning against the wall to face Jay as he lazily lifted his head from the pillow. "You're here to be a friend to your friends. I'm here to eat Thai food. We can reconvene tomorrow at the wedding?"

It was the smarter thing to do, surely? Yes, of course Mara wanted to spend more time with him, but that was a selfish desire she didn't want to give in to. And if Jay was hurt by the suggestion, she didn't see it in his face.

"Sure," Jay said, leaping off of the bed (wow, energy) to wrap his arms around her, squeezing her tightly while making a small high-pitched noise. Hay. He was caught by gigil. Mara made a little "hmph!" sound and turned around, only for Jay to wrap his arms around her neck, pulling her back against his chest. He rested his temple on the back of her head. "I'll allow you a night off."

"Allow, allow," Mara snorted, rolling her eyes. "Suddenly I regret everything."

His hold loosened on her, like he was afraid she would slip away. "Do you?"

Mara smiled and pulled his hands back down on her shoulders. "Definitely not. We'll see each other tomorrow, okay? I'll be the random wedding guest in the back."

"Not just any wedding guest," Jay murmured. "My favorite kind. My plus-one."

Mara giggled and lifted her gaze. There was a mirror hanging on the back of the door, and she could see herself in it. Her hair was a dry, post-beach, wavy mess, her skin had just started to get dark, and the beginnings of a bit of sunburn were already starting on the tops of her cheeks and the tip of her nose. Her dress was wrinkled, and Jay's arms were long. She could see him smiling as he cuddled her, that happy, satisfied look on his face.

She could get used to being a plus-one.

Eleven

The following morning saw Mara having breakfast at the restaurant on the first floor of her hotel. It was a gorgeous spot with creamy white walls and a tiled floor; the table was cool under the breeze of several ceiling fans working so hard they all looked like they were about to spin out of their axes. The space was made even more chill by rattan furniture and warm wood tables, blue rattan place mats and a bar to the side that had a cheeky mermaid that winked at you from under a nipa hut awning.

Mara sat facing the ocean. And having that same image as the backdrop on her tablet while paying her bills…well, it was a bit sad, but it helped greatly to bask in the real-life version.

Dinner last night was amazing. But admittedly Mara felt a little lonely enjoying authentic tom yum goong by herself. She sent her family photos of her food. Certainly this wasn't her first time eating by herself—it was still there, though, that feeling of something missing. Of wanting someone by her side.

Jay: Good morning, sunshine!
I'll be the handsome one in the best man barong later.
Save me a dance? ☺

Mara: Are you…sliding into my DMs?

He sent back a GIF of a squirrel sledding down a snowy hill. And if Mara had a hard time wiping the ridiculously kilig smile off of her face, well…nobody had to know. And no one was going to know, because no one else was there.

She paused, looking up from her laptop where she was in the middle of paying for Wildflower's utility bills on one tab and partway through reviewing Alex's contract with Tropikal Flower on another. On the table next to her was a planner with a to-do list written beside the words "Boracay break!"

It felt impossible to focus on anything today. Not with the crystal blue waters of the sea right in front of her, not with the sway of the palm trees beckoning her to drop everything and head out for a swim. Not with a plate of grilled ensaymada, parma ham and quezo de bola, a cup of coffee *and* dalandan juice sweating off its coolness. Not when she was still thinking about last night, the sounds she made, the grip of his hands on her body, when she touched him. She was all distraction today, and maybe it was time to accept it.

So she called Marina. Her sister was really good at distracting her even more.

"—so I asked him," Marina said a few stories later, "'Honey, why is there a Gundam in the linen cabinet?'"

"Let me guess," Mara said dryly, closing her tablet a few

minutes later. Of course she wasn't going to immediately tell Marina what was going on. Marina needed to sense that something was up and then wheedle her into telling. "He asked what the linens were doing in the Gundam cabinet."

"Exactly!" Marina laughed, her voice coming crystal clear through the call. "He's so funny."

Mara was suddenly hit by a strong wave of missing her sister. It really wasn't the same, not having Marina around. Even when she spent her weekdays in Makati and weekends in QC, at the very least they had a Sunday meal together.

But now she belonged to—sorry, *with*—David, and even being a call or a message away, Mara still felt the distance greatly. She and David had just declared themselves settled in a new condo in BGC, a gift from David's parents. The place was tiny, and there was very little place to hide, but they were happy. And even better, they had parking.

"Ate," Marina suddenly said, as if apropos to nothing, "just to clarify, no one in our family is hurt, dying or in trouble, right? Did Mom mistake turquoise for tortoise at the glasses store again?"

"No, everyone's fine," Mara assured her sister. The memory of their mother being absolutely perplexed in a sunglasses store always cheered her up. "What a random question."

"Not really random. You *called*."

"You make it sound like we never talk on the phone," Mara grumbled, nibbling at her triangle of queso de bola.

"Ate, Gen Zs never call," Marina said, which made Mara roll her eyes. Mabel and Marina *always* tried to lecture her on the ways of their generation, as if the three of them didn't grow up in the same household with the same Wi-Fi password and VHS tape rewinder. "Everyone is fine. Which means whatever you want to say to me isn't urgent enough to be an emergency, but urgent enough that you needed to call. So what's up? Tell me everything."

Mara leaned back against her seat, squirming so her thighs didn't press up against the legs of the chair. She wasn't sure how to explain herself, or even begin to tell her sister about what happened.

So she said it in point-blank terms instead. That she met Jay in Boracay. That they "did things" last night. Let Marina fill in the blanks whatever way was comfortable for her and react accordingly. Which, on her part, turned out to be a screech that was heard all over Boracay and the rest of the Visayas Islands.

"Anak ng kabayo, Marina," Mara hissed. "Hala sige louder pa bes! I don't think God heard you!"

"ATE, YOU SLUT!" Marina sounded absolutely delighted, cheering. "I am so happy! I freaking knew you and Jay would be good together. I *told* Mabel—"

"Oi, oi, no, we're not together," Mara clarified. "We didn't exactly put a label on it, but it's not serious. We were just…"

"Not seriously carried away by passion. Mmm-mhm, mmm-hmm." Mara decided not to correct her little sister, shaking her head instead while she couldn't see. "Pero Ats, you sure with the casual relationship stuff? I always thought you were a true love kind of girl."

"I mean, it's fine for now." It was what Jay was willing to offer, and at this point, Mara wanted to stop waiting around for things to happen and actually give…whatever this was a try. She didn't regret it so far, which was a good sign. She was being cautiously optimistic. Saying this made Marina snort. Her sister didn't believe her at all.

"Wait," Marina said suddenly, "are you calling me to ask for my blessing or something, because that would be weird."

"Weirder than you marrying my friend?" Mara asked wryly. It was the first time she'd hinted at being uncomfortable about the situation. They were finally at the point where she could joke about it and feel only happiness for them. Which she did. "No, I wasn't asking for permission. I just feel a little overwhelmed."

"Uh-huh." Marina did not sound like she believed her sister one bit.

"Why didn't you guys work out?" Mara asked. Not because she was a glutton for punishment or anything. She was just doing research. Continued research on matters of relationships and why they failed, on what she could do to avoid those pitfalls in the eventual moment that she met someone else. "You and Jay. Was it just because you wanted David more?"

"Well, there was that," Marina mused. This was probably the first time Marina seriously considered her past with Jay. "But I had this feeling that Jay was waiting for me to cut him out. What's the word for that? Like he was weighing and measuring the way I felt about him so he could run before I could."

"Naninimbang," Mara said, the word a sigh on her lips. That sounded about right. She felt it last night, when he was watching her, waiting. And it could be a good thing, in the current situation that they were trying to navigate. But would they always be like that?

She shook her head. It didn't matter. Jay wasn't willing to give her more than introductory lessons on the topic. Regardless of what his issues with relationships were, they weren't in one. Mara wasn't supposed to feel anything more for him than a fond gratitude.

"Yes, tumpak." Marina pulled Mara from her thoughts. "He was holding back. And I didn't get a chance to figure out why, or try to get him to let go."

"Gets." Mara sighed deeply. What her sister described was a mountain of emotional unpacking, and Mara had never been one for sports. Or hiking.

"But you feel good about this, Ate?" Marina's voice was gentle over the phone, soothing in a way that Mara usually tried to sound for her. "I know it can be scary, and you resisted being in a relationship for so long."

"I don't think it was resistance so much as nobody asked," Mara reminded her, trying not to think back to the old crushes she held on to and just…let go. To the guys she liked who never saw her. She didn't regret letting them go. Some of them turned out to be completely different people. But she never *did* anything about it.

"Yeah, but you didn't ask, either." Goddamn it, her sister had a point. "Even 'just sex' needs a certain amount of vulnerability, and you've never liked things that have no absolutes."

All fair. But did that necessarily explain why her kilig also made her just a little bit anxious? Was this what it was going to feel like if she was with anyone else, or was Jay somehow different?

"Is it *always* going to feel like this?" Mara asked her sister. "Just sex."

"Feel like what?" Mara thought she sounded just a little bit condescending, like she was speaking to a child. But it was fine.

"I feel relaxed," she said, speaking the feeling into reality and forming it around her. "Cared for. I feel really good about this, and it's not supposed to be… I mean we agreed that it wasn't going to be serious. But do I feel this way because of him, or because it's always like this?"

"Hmm. I can tell you now, it's not always like that," Marina mused. "Even with someone you really know. Even with someone you've been with several times. Mileage varies, and there are so many factors, you know?"

"No, I don't, actually." Mara laughed. "Are you telling me there's no way to guarantee that what I have right now is replicable with someone else?"

"Well, it helps if you know what you're into," Marina pointed out. "If you trust the other person enough to tell them, then you can work on it. But I guess that's the thing we learned, being our parents' daughters, right? Relationships are always going to be work. I think love is a matter of wanting to put in that work."

Mara sighed, because her sister wasn't wrong. They saw it every day with their parents, the things they did and refused to do with each other.

It was one of the bigger takeaways of her thirties, that

friendships and relationships were not a given. That as much as you could walk away from them when they didn't serve you, you needed to put in the work to make sure. She supposed even what she had with Jay now—something that was supposed to be a casual sex education—meant that there was work to be done. Vulnerabilities to be given away on her part.

She was still thinking about this when Marina declared she needed to go to the bathroom and passed the phone to David, who gave her chismis on Mon Mendoza (he used to have a Mohawk in high school, rebel siya eh), Scott Sabio (once gave a reading of *Othello* that made their English teacher cry) and, of course, Jay.

It was always easy and pleasant to talk to David, he was one of the rare men who was good for gossip. Usually guys would be all, "Oh, I didn't ask," or, "Guys don't talk about that stuff."

"Have you ever seen Jay dance? Like really dance. Choreography and everything," David asked, and Mara had to admit, no, she had not. "He was, like, *the* dance guy when we were in high school. I think he still has a bunch of videos on YouTube. Look up Hopia Street and you should find him."

"That is the dumbest name I've ever heard." Mara laughed, but she did make a mental note to tease Jay about it.

"Well, he was pretty hot shit back then. I think that's why Selena Guerro fell so hard for him."

Mara was aware. She remembered Jay's story about failed expectations, broken plans. Learning the hard way that love wasn't easy. It was pretty difficult to forget.

"Oh, Marina's coming back," David noted. "But I wanted to tell you nga pala, Mar. I'm setting you up with someone."

"Bolero ka." She snorted, because not once in their at least five years of friendship had David ever set her up with anyone, and she never asked for it, either. A rejection was on the tip of her tongue...but Mara had to admit she was curious.

"I'm serious!" David insisted, like he couldn't believe Mara was doubting him. "He's so your type. The kindest guy you'll ever meet, is so tall he kind of ambles in that way you like..."

Mara knew exactly what he meant. It had been a whole discussion she had with Marina, with David watching in fascination as they described the way Adam Driver was so tall that he walked with absolutely no regard to posture. It was a thing.

"And he's extremely cool. Extremely rich. Plays the drums. Has a dog," David continued. "You'll like."

"I," Mara said, the phrase *"already have someone"* on the tip of her tongue, "don't remember you ever mentioning this stellar personality."

"He's been out of the country," David said by way of explanation, as if that actually explained anything. But that was David for you. "He told me he's looking to settle down, put down roots and all."

"He sounds perfect," Mara admitted. He certainly ticked off box after box, in a list that she would have come up with had anyone asked her.

"He's eager to meet you. He's in Boracay right now actually, attending a wedding."

Mara decided to chance it. Why not. "Let me guess. Alex and Tori?"

"Yeah," David said enthusiastically. "Wow, that really must be, like, fate, huh? Maybe you'll meet Perry there!"

Mara snorted. "Is that his fatal flaw, his name?"

"Hey, Perry is a great guy. You've always wanted to fall in love, right? I think finally we found someone worthy." David laughed and passed the phone back to Marina.

Mara talked to her sister a little more, but she had to admit that David's words lingered in her head. *You've always wanted to fall in love, right?*

So then what the hell was she doing with Jay?

Mara sighed and stared at the beach for a little longer. She knew this wasn't complicated at all. That Jay had warned her she would feel things for him that might not be necessarily real. But she needed a bit of time to figure it out, and the wedding was a perfect opportunity.

"Holy fuck." Mara gasped as she approached Shorewinds Hotel from the beach. The setup was incredible. Clearly Kal of Tropikal Flower had decided to throw all of the original floral designer's plans out the window and made his own thing, which was absolutely unheard of. But to his credit, it looked great.

There were circular banigs on the ground, creating a make-shift aisle. It was framed by baby's breath, which were daintily tied together in huge, bush-like bouquets with lacy blue ribbons. The aisle led to a table that faced the beach with palm trees framing the scene.

To the front, he'd arranged the flowers in a half circle at the center, like a floral tiara facing out to the beach. Above them, rattan basket lights were set up in neat rows, with twinkle lights in between. It was gorgeous, and even better that he'd done it on such short notice.

"Kal," Mara said to her friend when she saw him walk back from speaking to his staff. "There was a plan!"

"Oh please. The original plans were mid. I got the couple to see my vision, and I think it worked out naman. Pagoda nga lang." Kal winked at her.

Mara and Kal met at a wedding fair two years ago, when Mara just started Wildflower. She was picking up on an industry that had barely made it through the pandemic, and Kal was one of the few stylists that was eager to share his knowledge and not be a gatekeeper. They were industry friends, the kind who liked to gossip about everyone else and help each other out. Tropikal was still in recovery from the pandemic, but with the boom in weddings, he was recovering fast.

"You learn to move quick on jobs when you need to snap them up," he said.

He'd taught her how important community was when it came to this industry, and Mara never hesitated to mention him whenever a client asked for a recommendation. Clearly this had been a good call.

"And you," he exclaimed, holding a hand out so he could examine Mara from an arm's length away, "just happened to have this dress on you?"

Mara laughed as she looked down at the sapphire blue dress she was wearing. It was made of a soft cotton that blew in the breeze and had a ruffle along the top. She'd brought this dress along to wear to dinner at the Italian restaurant next to her hotel, but she didn't mind putting it to this use. She'd gathered her hair in a sleek bun and put on a pair of gold hoop earrings and all three necklaces she brought.

To be fair, it *did* look good enough.

"You know me. Always prepared."

"Mara." Jay's voice sounded excited as he called her name, making Mara and Kal turn to him.

You would think it was his wedding day, the way he absolutely radiated happiness as he walked to them. He was wearing a linen suit with a jacket in the exact same powder blue as the accent ribbons in the decor. His camera was hanging from a strap on his wrist, and he pointed the lens on her to take a photo. Mara stuck her tongue out and rolled her eyes. He smiled at her through his sunglasses—a different pair than the ones he wore yesterday, along with a shirt with one extra button intentionally left open, showing off the parts of his body that Mara had yet to fully explore.

In short, he looked absolutely delicious. She was so fucked.

"You came," he said brightly as he approached. There was a moment where it was absolutely clear on his face that he didn't know if he was supposed to kiss her on the lips or on the cheek. To be completely honest, Mara didn't know, either.

So he settled instead for taking her hand, lifting it to his lips and kissing the back of it. And honestly she didn't know if that was better or worse, because Kal's eyes widened like he'd just witnessed an important event in world history.

"Of course." Mara's cheeks grew hot as Jay lowered her hand and didn't let go. She felt like she was floating, or like she'd drunk champagne and now the bubbles were popping in her stomach. "I couldn't miss my one and only ex getting married."

"I *knew* it." Jay laughed. "Alex isn't *that* affectionate with me, and I dated her for a month."

"Okay, I'm going to need you to tell me this whole story later," Kal announced, squeezing Mara's arm as he passed her. "I'll see you later."

"See you." Mara smiled at her fellow floral designer, then turned to face her plus-one. "So is that how you met Alex? You dated her?"

"Once upon a time, the algorithm decided we would work out. I guess it was only partially right." Jay sighed dramatically, making Mara laugh. "And now she's marrying Tori, and now the both of them will love me by annoying the shit out of me for the rest of my life."

"Aw, a happy ending all around," Mara teased, poking his side with a finger.

"Long live the lesbians." He nodded in agreement. Then he kissed the top of Mara's head like a greeting, and she caught a whiff of his scent. Mmm. Sandalwood. He took a quick selfie of them, and they continued walking.

She tugged at the collar of his blazer. "Did you get this jacket made specifically for this wedding?"

"Yeah." He shrugged nonchalantly. "Fabric is cheap in Taytay, and my go-to sastre in Kamuning keeps telling me my shoulders are too skinny for ready-to-wear."

Mara shook her head in disbelief. But what she didn't say out loud was that *of course* Jay had blazers and suits custom-made. He seemed the kind of guy who was particular about his look, and she had to admire the dedication. Getting things custom-made wasn't as easy as it used to be, and this was coming from someone who never fit in anything locally made. There always needed to be a special occasion to justify the price, like Marina's wedding.

But she supposed that if you had the fabric, and you had a go-to tailor in the garment district, you really could do wonders. Why *not* have a linen suit made especially for you, right? It certainly produced the, uh, desired effect.

Especially if someone was taking it off.

Um.

"Are you blushing because it's hot?" Jay asked, more out of concern than because he could tell Mara was trying to keep her attraction to him at bay. She assured him she was fine with a wave of her hand. It was actually a perfectly cool and breezy afternoon at the beach. The sun was warm but not oppressive, enough that you didn't mind so much that you weren't neck-deep in the ocean at that very moment.

Jay led her to the seats for the guests, particularly the one next to Irene, who was bouncing Luna on her lap and playing Sawsaw sa Suka with her. Luna's little giggles were infectious, and she looked extra adorable in braids with baby blue ribbons and a little crown of baby's breath. Mara saw Jay hold up the camera to take the photo. He showed her the image immediately after, and it really looked like a stolen, happy moment. The colors were gorgeous, thanks to the sun.

"Nong!" Luna burst into giggles as Jay immediately subjected her to a tickle attack while Irene held on to keep Luna from tumbling off of her lap. "My dress!"

"Is very pretty," Jay assured her, smoothing out the creases in the blue linen, the fabric matching his suit. "Are you ready to walk the aisle with me?"

"Yes." She threw her arms up in the air, and Mara had the sudden urge to tuck the girl into her pocket. She was like this with all of her friends' kids, especially when she saw them on social media. Usually because they were all fucking adorable, *and* she didn't have to be the one to deal with them when they had a meltdown. "I'll be the best flower girl ever, right, Tita Mara?"

"Tita Mara?" Irene echoed in amusement, giving Jay a knowing smile as she and Luna waved at Mara. "Are you keeping me company while these two leave me?"

"Someone has to take a video while you take a photo." Mara smiled, moving the empty chairs around to give her the room to sit next to Ate Irene without jostling her or Luna. Jay didn't comment and put the chairs back, shifting so he was standing behind her, casually leaning while his hand was on the back of her seat.

"And someone has to tell her all the tea about everyone else," Jay teased.

"What makes you think I know?" Ate Irene asked innocently.

"Ate, don't at me. You know. I know you know."

"I do know." Irene sighed dramatically, leaning back against her seat. She looked absolutely chic in a pale blue halter dress that had a large bow in the back. Her shoulder-length hair was styled so that it flipped up at the ends, and with her drop pearl earrings, a diamond ring on her left hand and a pair of black sunglasses, it was obvious that style was a game that the Montinola family could only slay. "In return, I won't pepper Tita Mara over here with invasive questions about why I had to tell your inaanak that no, Ninong was not sucking Tita's face at the beach, he was just being friendly."

Mara's jaw dropped, and Irene looked entirely too pleased with herself while Luna snickered at their expressions. Jay opened his mouth to retort, but someone up front was signaling him to come forward. So he glared at his Ate instead.

"Okay, I'll make sure to walk on this side of the aisle so you can't see Luna when we walk later." Jay had an evil glint in his eyes. Well, she imagined he did behind those sunglasses.

That made Irene gasp. "You wouldn't."

"Would I?"

"You would not," Mara said, chuckling as she poked Jay's stomach. "Now go and be the best man ever."

Jay grinned and leaned forward so he was face-to-face with Mara. "What if…I would rather stay here with you?"

Mara's valiant attempt to glare at him failed so miserably she had to look away, and his grin got even bigger. She rolled her eyes and grabbed the sunglasses off of his face, which was probably worse because now she was looking right into his dark brown eyes. They shimmered with amusement and mirth, but there was a low heat there, too. One that tempted Mara to make it burn hotter.

"Ui," he joked. "Kinilig. You should get used to this, Mara. Practice."

That deserved a playful threat. "Sige ka. I won't take any photos of you."

"Ooh!" Irene sounded intrigued by the prospect, steepling her fingers together like a Disney villain. "Truly evil."

"Hey," Jay protested, standing back to his full height and pouting. "I promised I would populate the hashtag! AlexLovesToriBabyJustSayYes!"

Mara laughed, because one had to give flowers to the longest hashtag of all time. "I don't think they meant for you to populate the hashtag with your face."

"Between me and Scott, someone has to."

"The wedding coordinator just tapped her watch," Irene said, yanking the hem of his blazer and flapping it like a loose sheet. "I think that's the universal sign for come the fuck on, Bridget."

Jay, Mara and Luna gasped. Even Irene looked surprised at herself, blinking up comically at them.

"Mama said a bad word!"

"Exactly, and that's why we're going to go na." Jay picked up his inaanak and pretended to shield her ears as Luna laughed hysterically. Irene gave her brother an exasperated look, but she still took the camera from him.

There was a brief moment where Mara thought the look the Montinola siblings exchanged was wistful. Like they were missing each other while they were both on the same beach. But it was gone before she could find a way to ask about it.

"We'll be right back." Jay turned to Mara, swinging himself and Luna toward her. "I'm going to need to approve any story you're going to post. For the integrity of the hashtag."

"Just go." She was going to say more, but Jay beat her to anything else by swooping down, fully supporting Luna with his hand on her back as he gave Mara a quick kiss on the lips. So quick that his lips were slightly stained with her color, Make A Mauve. Well. Impressionist Cosmetics did advertise it as a lipstick for kissing.

Mara was still in slight shock as Jay and Luna headed toward where the rest of the wedding party was assembling. It felt like her lips were tingling, her toes curling in her sandals. She couldn't seem to remember where she was, forgot what day of the week it was, what time. None of that seemed important at the moment, not even whatever it was that Irene just asked her.

"—like him, Mara?"

"Ha?" Mara asked, confused.

"Nothing!" Irene laughed, her chic bob shaking as she shook her head. "Jay just seems really happy."

"Of course he's happy, we—" *gave each other hand jobs last night* "—we're in literal paradise, and nobody has to work." Mara chuckled. "The conditions are ideal. Never mind that we didn't speak for three months before that, and *that* was the first time we actually got along, ever."

"Really? He was so mopey for those three months, though. Always sighing and talking about Girls' Generation." Irene shrugged. "Also, any kind of happy day is a good day. God knows he could use some of those."

It occurred to Mara that regardless of if she wanted to hear it or not, Irene was about to tell her something very private and intimate about the man she was definitely not dating. She didn't want to be rude, so she settled instead for saying a very vague, "Hmm?" to get Irene to continue.

"We both hate it, but it wasn't easy that the eldest-born son was the youngest child," Irene began, both of them barely noticing that everyone was starting to take their seats. "It was a thing. People expected things of him that I was already doing, or I was held back from certain things because he had to do it first."

"Like what?" Mara was genuinely curious. As Jay explained it, he and Ate Irene were a few years apart. Certainly there were some things Ate Irene had to do first.

"I didn't get a driver's license until I was, what, twenty-five? Because my parents insisted it wasn't safe for a single woman to drive around the city by herself. So Jay had to drive me around for most of college, until I put my foot down and got a license for myself."

Mara winced. She could understand the feeling. One where you didn't want to be the burden on any of your siblings, because it was your job to do things first. As well as the reality that, knowing as much as your parents loved you, they could also be absolutely irrational and ridiculous. That sometimes, you needed to ignore their shit to get what you needed.

"Well, I don't totally regret it, because we got pretty close because we kept getting trapped in traffic." Irene chuckled. "But you get what I mean? He feels a big amount of responsibility that I personally think is undue. When our parents separated, he was the one who spoke to the banks and the lawyers, because I had to be the one to manage them emotionally. When I got pregnant and the pandemic hit, he stayed with me. We had swabs up our nose every week, went to the doctors, and he was in his PPE for the whole time I was in the hospital."

"It must have been scary for both of you," Mara sympathized. The Barrettos were lucky none of them needed serious medical attention at the time—more than lucky, really. But she remembered the string of weddings, wakes and other family events all over Zoom too well. Even then she couldn't imagine the risk of having a baby in a hospital at the time.

"He made me feel less scared. Jay's a scaredy-cat most times, but give him something to focus on and he'll power through with flying colors."

That felt oddly reassuring.

"Our parents needed money so they could move as far away from each other as possible, so when they sold the house, he was the one who bought a place in Pasig for us all to live in." That made Mara's mouth widen in surprise. It was no easy feat to outright purchase a condo, especially if it was a recent purchase. "When Luna started day care and needed someone to pick her up, he renegotiated his job with his Hong Kong firm to scale back his hours, because my job declared a return to office."

"That sounds…" Mara tried to think of how to respond. It all sounded like good things. Great things. Things that would have been major hurdles for other families, the kind that would require bigger sacrifices or adjustments. Quite frankly, it was incredible that Jay had done all of that for his family, and definitely made her respect him more. But the way Irene said them made them sound like they weren't great things at all.

"He's never complained, and if he ever felt pressured, he has never, ever shown me," she continued.

Suddenly she knew why Ate Irene wasn't happy about it. Because *she* was the older sister. The panganay in Mara knew that it wasn't a good feeling, needing to rely on your sibling so much. That feeling of thinking, *This should be me!* and feeling guilty knowing your sibling was having a hard time, while also feeling guilty about needing them more than they needed you. "And he keeps finding more to do, when I never asked him to!"

And it was no one's fault, really. Certainly no one's character flaw, loving their family. But it did add a lot of pressure to an already complicated situation, she could only imagine.

"It's like he's trying to meet someone's inflated expectations. All while fully convincing himself that he can never meet them."

What did it take to convince a guy so good at making people love him that he was terrible at love? She hadn't fully believed that it was just the Selena Guerro thing. But add to that separated parents, a jilted older sister and a family that needed him more? She understood. It felt like she was standing outside a tower of Jay's boundaries. She was in his territory but not quite fully inside his court.

The music started to play from a string quartet, all of whom were wearing rainbow scarves in various ways. That was cute, and clearly a signal that the ceremony was about to begin. But Irene was too deep into her story to stop.

"I'm getting married in two months," Ate Irene said, turning to face the altar, her arms crossed and her shoulders slightly defeated. "It took a while for my fiancé and I to figure out that we really loved each other, what it meant that I already had a kid with someone else. So all of a sudden Jay has a three-bedroom condo to himself when he never really wanted one, he has all this free time, and I..." Her voice caught, and Mara remembered the wistful look that the siblings had exchanged earlier. "I just want him to be happy. I want him to live his own life. Luna and I will still be in it, but..."

"It's not going to be the same," Mara said. It was funny how much she understood Irene, despite this being the first real conversation they'd had. Maybe it was a Montinola thing, having such deep conversations so early on? "My sister got married three months ago, and it's not the same. But I know that as hard as it is for me, it's harder for her. It's not life if it doesn't have change in it, I think. I'm still learning that lesson myself."

"It's a hard one," Irene admitted with a small smile. "He loves fiercely, my little brother. He's just really good at convincing himself that he's bad at it."

In that moment, she was filled with the sibling urge to hug Irene. Mostly because it felt like someone was echoing a lot of her own emotions back to her, and Mara of all people could understand that burning need to make sure your sibling was happy. But also because what Irene had shared about Jay was incredibly personal, the kind of story you didn't tell just anyone. Mara appreciated it.

"I think you'll be good at falling in love with him," Ate Irene said happily, as the violins started to play for Alex's entrance.

But in the back of Mara's mind, she recognized that every-thing she knew about Jay so far, she had heard from someone else. How much had she told him about her fears, her inse-curities and her worries, in comparison? It wasn't a competi-tion, but surely, surely it had to be a little...even, at least? Jay didn't tell her any of this himself for a reason. Irene was tell-ing her all of this because she assumed that Jay had decided to fully open his heart to Mara.

And if she sprung a couple of tears when Alex walked the aisle, it was easier to believe it was fully because her old friend looked absolutely gorgeous, and so incandescently happy. It was always a good moment, seeing two people vow to be to-gether. And while the yearning in Mara's heart wasn't new, it seemed to hurt just a little bit more today.

Twelve

There was not a single dry eye on the beach when Tori Bonifacio swore to love and cherish Alex Suarez for the rest of their lives. It was a marriage of two powerfully independent women, who just wanted to be together. Who wanted to celebrate that they were together, and have all of their family and friends witness it. Tori's "my heart knew yours the moment we met," was matched by Alex's "you're my dream girl," and the rest of the ceremony was a blur of more happy tears and laughter.

Jay had to admit that even he shed a little tear (okay fine, he fully wept, but it wasn't just him!). Talking about destiny and the magic of love was usually overrated. But hearing about magic and destiny from a queer couple made him feel extra fuzzy and warm, mostly because to a lot of people, they weren't allowed to have magic and destiny.

To be honest, Jay loved a wedding, almost as much as Mara, maybe. But something in the back of his mind always made it feel bittersweet, like knowing that the bride would be moving away from the family she was close to. Like knowing that as happy as Tori and Alex were, their best option to get any kind of legal recognition was to move to Quezon City (where neither of them worked) and get a legal document that basically allowed them to make medical decisions for each other, in Quezon City.

Weddings were commitments to the sweet and the bitter, he supposed. But it was easy to forget the bitter when there were flowers, when there was a beach, when there were people cheering you on.

"Stop frowning," Scott said beside him, as the wedding party gathered by the beach for pictures. It was golden hour once again. How the hell did time move so fast on the island? "You're distracting the camera with your face."

"Oh, what is that I'm hearing? Do I hear the sounds of Scott Sabio admitting someone is more handsome than him?" Tori asked from the front of the posed group, the sparkling sun making her seem like she was glowing. Or maybe it was just what happiness looked like on her.

"Only when he's brooding," Scott clarified. "Look at him!"

And so Jay was granted the honor of the entire Bonifacio-Suarez wedding party turning to study his face. Which immediately made him flash his most charming smile and give them a little wave. Jay was not a brooder. Not at all.

"I don't know," Ava mused as she leaned her head back against Scott's chest. "I think if anyone looks good while brooding—"

"Aw, thank you for the vote of confidence, babe," Scott

cooed, kissing the top of her head—only to make a face because what he tasted was all hair spray.

"Well, actually I was going to say it was Mon." Ava indicated their much taller, larger friend whose naturally neutral face gave way to the possibility that he was the more handsome brooder. But because he was in a good mood, Mon instead made a stellar display of his adorable dimples, while his girlfriend Olivia Angeles told him to smile and keep looking cute.

But Ava's declaration had its immediate effect, and it sent the rest of the wedding party into a flurry of circular arguments, ungkatan ng past and lightly sprinkled insults that Jay had learned was common in big groups like this.

Oddly enough, after the photographer yelled, "Okay, candid!" all of them looked absolutely fake as they opened their mouths pretending to laugh. It was fun, though, he had to admit, and it got him totally distracted.

"Hey, did your job ever get back to you about relocating?" Scott said suddenly. "I have a couple of friends who could help you find a place, something closer to Wan Chai."

"I'm negotiating the relocation package," Jay explained, recalling the video call he had just before they left for the airport. "They weren't too excited when I asked for a higher raise to move to a more expensive country, since I'm essentially doing the same job."

Scott winced. "That's going to be rough. But whatever you decide, let us know, ha?"

"Scott, I already told you, an annual pass to Disneyland is nontransferable, and I haven't renewed mine since I moved back here."

"I know that!" Scott frowned at him, and it was hard not to see the belligerent high school kid that Jay had known. "But what about your emotional feelings journey with Mara?"

"Who put you up to asking me about Mara?" Now it was Jay's turn to pout.

"Mo—me," Scott said, after throwing a sideways glance at Mon, which revealed that the man was doing a terrible job at pretending he wasn't eavesdropping. "It was all me. We just think you guys are cute together. We saw you hanging out at the wedding."

"I thought you both thought she was scary," Jay argued.

"*You* thought she was scary," Scott reminded him, shaking his head. "But that's a standard part of the trope." At Jay's confusion, Scott shrugged. "Like I said, 'here na me, you not yet.' I get it."

"I don't know." Jay's shoulders sagged. "I still don't feel like I can give her what she wants."

"You think any of us do?" Scott chuckled, shaking his head as Jay watched his friends wrapped up in their significant others. "Feeling you can or can't do something is different from knowing you can. Or realizing that making someone else happy is never going to be easy. But you let yourself try anyway."

"I did try, remember," he said, kicking the sand a little and pouting. "I tried and I was left being celebrity chika for being a good luck charm."

"And look how many people you've made happy since then," Scott reminded him, nudging his head to where Alex and Tori were whispering and giggling at each other. Tori was shaking her head as Alex kissed her new wife's knuckles. "You could be so good at loving Mara if you let yourself. But to love is to be brave, Jay. And I know you're such a cutie-pie that you get scared of ocean seaweed—"

"I thought it was a *snake*, okay!"

"But you're no coward," Scott said, giving him a friendly pat on the shoulder.

After the photos, they all headed back to the reception area to grab a few drinks before dinner.

It was too late for merienda, but too early for dinner, which Jay had recalled was a major dilemma when planning the wedding. The solution had come in the form of mini Jamaican patties from a stall in D'Mall, and pairing that with the resort's afternoon iced teas and their famous mojito slush. Given the atmosphere, Jay quickly realized it was as good a solution as any.

He was about to make his way to the Jamaican patties— he'd heard good things about the cheesy beef flavor—when he spotted Mara talking to someone. Someone tall, with hair that flopped in a Korean-drama-hot-guy way, wearing a beige linen suit, a silver bracelet and fancy but laid-back leather loafers. They were both laughing at something, in that way people did when they were being polite but enjoying themselves. Jay could tell—whoever tall guy was, he was checking Mara out, keeping his eyes on her whenever she turned away from him.

Meanwhile Mara's cheeks were flushed, like she was either hot from the blazing sun or…blushing. She laughed heartily, but she always laughed in conversation. The guy's hand was resting on the table, near where she was leaning her elbow.

Maybe they were touching?

"Jay," Mara said brightly, her cheeks pink from the heat as she smiled at him. It made Jay's heart do a little flip, but he ignored that. "Here he is, the best man himself. Are you off duty?"

"Not quite yet, but I think we'll make it through." He chuckled, putting on his charm armor. He plucked out the orchid from his boutonniere and held it up to Mara for a second before reaching to tuck it behind her ear. If his fingers tingled, if his heart skipped a beat in his chest, nobody else had to know. But the surprise on her face was clear.

Jay put his sunglasses back on and smiled to the new person. He was very tall. Much taller than Jay, and more broad in the chest. But his smile was polite and easy, the kind of guy who knew how to meet people.

"This is Perry," Mara said, introducing them. "He and David know each other, and apparently he's Tori's new boss at Fox Gallery."

"Unlucky for her," Perry (Perry? Seriously?) said sheepishly. "I love Tori's vision, though. We were just talking about what we could do that was a little more interactive, but still a kind of piece people didn't need a whole context for to appreciate."

"I've always thought modern art was confusing. I'm an easy guy. I like when something is big and shiny. It makes my heart race in a weird way."

"Just like a Girls' Generation song." Beside him, Mara

chortled. Perry was excellent at hiding his confusion, but Jay laughed along.

"Modern art is what you make of it. Doesn't have to be that deep." Perry shrugged. "Honestly, my favorite piece is this portrait I had commissioned of my dog, Rita." He was sheepish as he held up his phone screen, showing a frankly excellent painting of a happy looking golden retriever. "But I was just actually asking Mara if I could commission her for a floral piece for the next exhibition."

The red hue on Mara's cheeks deepened, and Jay didn't have to be a part of the flower industry to know that she was being offered something big. Tori had told him about her work at Fox Gallery in Salcedo—how it was a job she held on to by her fingernails because rare was the gallery that could tread the line between the rich people's favorite while also feeling welcome to all. Apparently Perry's family really saw Philippine art as their pet cause, and it showed in their current success.

"That sounds amazing," Jay enthused, turning to Mara. He had no idea what Wildflower needed or did as a business, but given her work that he'd seen so far, the way she made Alex's eyes widen at the thought behind her bouquet, and the thought she gave behind her sister's flowers… Mara knew more about the meaning to flowers than any book. "Did you say yes?"

"I'm still trying to work my magic on her." Perry smiled. It was a slow, gentle smile, and Jay understood why his eyes were only for Mara. "But that neck piece you made for Alex is exquisite."

The three of them turned to look at Alex, who was talk-

ing with a group of people while Tori had a hand resting on
the small of her back, skin-to-skin contact thanks to a very
convenient backless top. Mara had made Alex a little necklace at the last minute, a few carnations and a rose on a long,
pale blue leather cord. It softened Alex's usual stern expression, like the flowers were deep feelings for Tori that she
couldn't keep hidden.

"I'm still thinking about it," Mara admitted. She was gorgeous in the golden sun, and he wondered vaguely how many
more times he would get to see Mara like that. He'd hoped
there were more. "I've got—" she glanced at Jay "—a few
things on my plate I'm still trying to handle."

Jay wanted to tell her to just go for it, that their arrangement surely had nothing to do with her work.

"Something we should probably discuss over dinner sometime?" Perry asked. "I would love to discuss a future together
with you, among other things. I think you would love 06/13.
Best tasting menu in Manila."

And then, it happened.

She *hiccuped*. Once. Twice.

It seemed to catch her by surprise, and clearly the guy
thought it was fucking adorable, and—Jay's stomach twisted.
He knew that feeling. He had it whenever he was anxious
or when he ordered mala noodles one level of spice higher
than his usual.

From the look of utter shock on her face, Mara didn't miss
Perry's very thinly veiled question. He was asking her out on
a date to the restaurant with the most chic tasting menu available in Manila. With that single sentence, he promised a nice

evening where they would discuss flowers and art. Then he would tell her all the ways she was wonderful, make her feel beautiful and desired, and that would lead to more dates, more getting to know each other, to falling in love, and—well.

This was what he'd kissed her for, yes? This was what Jay wanted for her.

As he remained a bystander in what was likely the first time someone asked Mara out to a date, a darker, quieter thought emerged. *She can't fall in love with him. I was falling for her first.*

Jay refused to entertain the thought now. He didn't want to let it fester and grow, or turn into something bitter and ugly. But he also knew that he didn't want to hear her answer. Not even a little bit.

"I…think my sister needs me," he lied, taking Mara's empty glass and handing her his untouched drink. Then he took off before either Mara or Perry could say anything because he was, what, friends? Jealous? A coward? All of the above? Correct.

"I see you guys have met Perry," Alex said, coming up to them with a sweating glass of iced tea in one hand and a Jamaican patty in the other. What a vibe. "You know Tori fell for him so hard she almost married him, but I asked her first."

"What?"

"That was a joke, Jay. My wife's a lesbian. Are you okay?" Alex actually looked concerned. "I thought you said yesterday that you and Mara weren't dating."

"We're not," he said, but then his stomach did that other weird thing it did whenever he lied. The one where it was like someone thrust a hand into it and squeezed. No wonder he'd never been known for being a good liar. "We're not dating, we're…" *Learning how to fuck each other?* "Not dating."

"O-kay," Alex said doubtfully. "So you don't mind if Tori and I set them up? We were just talking about it last night, that they would actually be good together. I mean, they look cute diba, with the height difference and all."

Jay made a funny sound from his throat, like a teeny, tiny frog had leaped out of it suddenly. This Perry guy was so tall he had to lean in to Mara to listen to her talk, but he didn't seem to mind, and Jay wanted to stop them.

But he reminded himself that this was what Mara wanted, wasn't it? To find someone, learn how to flirt, be better at asking for what she wanted. Which, he supposed, could lead to something like this, which was a good thing, right? One did not simply become a grade school valedictorian without being able to pick up on a lesson quick.

"He's exactly the kind of guy she should get after a kiss from me," Jay said, his gaze unfocused.

"You don't mind?"

"Why would I mind?" he asked the currently spinning universe in general.

"Yeah. Why nga," Alex repeated, and Jay knew his friend was trying to bait him. But his pride and…prejudice? No. Whatever, his inner self was only just a little bit Perry—goddamn it—*petty*, and refused to own up to what he was currently feeling.

He did, however, hear the hosts for the reception call the wedding party to the stage. It distracted him, but not enough that he missed Perry leaning in to kiss Mara—only for the display to be blocked from his sight because a group of, like, five people clustered together in front of them to take a selfie with the back camera of the phone! Youths!

"Huh," Alex mused beside him. "I wonder where he kissed her. Sa lips? Sa cheek? Or sa neck?"

"Set them up! It's fine," he said to Alex, kissing her on the cheek, ignoring the way she was totally taken aback as he jogged up to where the wedding party was gathering.

"Jay!" Alex exclaimed, following after him again. "Jaysohn Montinola, do *not* make me run in this dress!"

Jay stopped, hands in fists on his sides as he turned slowly to face Alex, who crossed her arms over her chest and glared at him. She wasn't wearing a dress at all, but instead had chosen a comfortable-looking halter neck top in white and soft, flowy pants. The flowers on her neck really were lovely.

"You're wearing pants," he said, coming out of his daze, and he kind of felt like he could see straight again. Ironic.

"Yeah, I am," Alex said, looping an arm around his. "I just wanted to catch up to you and tell you that you're being an idiot."

"Well, by all accounts, I'm never *not* an idiot, so you're going to have to be more specific."

"Why are you threatened by Perry?" Alex asked, hands on her hips.

"I'm not threatened by him." Jay shook his head. "He sees exactly what I see when I look at Mara. Someone creative and funny, someone who you want to be in your corner because she will make you feel like the best person in the world. Someone beautiful and gorgeous and shy, but wants to love you as much as you want to love them." The words tumbled out of him. He'd been holding on to them for the longest time, and it felt like he was pulling out an extra limb for Alex's examination.

"That's...that's beautiful." Alex blinked at him in surprise. "But you make it sound like a bad thing."

"I just..." Jay was pacing in front of his friend now, on her wedding day, making her focus on his problems. He hated it. He hated himself for making Alex confront him because he was being petty and jealous. "I kissed Mara the first day I met her. Because she wanted true love, and I told her I couldn't give it to her."

"Why not?" Alex asked, confused. "You're the most loveable person I've ever met. You shine on everything you touch."

"I... That's the sweetest thing anyone's ever said to me," Jay told her, his shoulders slumped, and Alex rolled her eyes.

"Please, Jay, I'm a married woman." She scoffed, but it was clear that she found saying that out loud really nice, and Jay was happy for her, so much so that he started to ask her more about how it felt to be committed to Tori. But before he could, Alex already hit his arm with the back of her hand. "Focus. So you think Perry is Mara's true love?"

"I mean, he could be," Jay exclaimed, looking back at the two of them. Yeah, they were on their second drinks, still laughing at whatever the heck a guy with an art gallery and a floral designer had in common. "You're right, they do look good together."

That was the part that was stressing him out.

"So make a choice." Alex said it so firmly, like the solution was obvious. "Either step aside or fight back. Have some backbone, Montinola."

As it happened, there was little time to go up to Mara and show he had a backbone, because there was one last thing requested of him as a best man. One thing that he agreed to because Alex told him he didn't need to make a speech...if he did this.

Jay had always been better at talking with his body than his mouth anyway.

"Dude." Mon winced, shaking his head.

"What?" Jay asked, having no idea why Mon was laughing.

"You seem..." Scott started, but seemed to wisely choose not to say anything as he, Mon, Jay and a couple of other members of the wedding party—including Tori's twenty-year-old brother Jake, who had the cutest little baby eyes but could outdance them all—took their positions at the back of the venue.

"Excited?" Because like the queens on *Drag Race*, a fire had been lit under his ass, and he was determined to show off what a fine ass it was.

"Not the word I would use," Mon said, wiping his brow. The man in question had performed on stages bigger than this, had literally been to red carpets viewed by way more people. He'd just married the couple less than an hour ago with an introduction that started the collective waterworks on the beach. Surely *he* wasn't nervous. "I'm sweating through my shirt."

"I was just supposed to be a wedding guest," Teddy Mertola piped up from behind Mon, absolutely pouting. He wasn't thrilled, but the guy had attended every practice session, asked

Jay about the choreography after each session and picked it up
much faster than Mon and Scott.

"At least we got our flights free." Van, an artist known
more famously for his work than his dance moves, slung an
arm around his boyfriend, Min. He knew Tori from the gallery, and Jay was willing to bet that a flight to Boracay wasn't
a big blow to his bank account. "And it's a one night only
thing."

The idea to form a one night, one performance only boyband had been Tori's, a wish fulfillment thing she had in
her head. She also knew that the only time she had enough
power to exert such an ask on these hapless guys was on her
wedding day, and had been very vocal about making her one
day unforgettable.

One day. Today.

What had started as the seven of them grumbling about
what they were willing to do to secure Tori Bonifacio's love
resulted in everyone committing and doing a pretty decent
job, at least by Jay's standards.

Mara would not know what hit her.

The crowd's enthusiastic cheers got them moving into position. Tori and Alex were sitting at the center, with Ate Irene
holding up her phone camera behind them and Mara sitting
with Luna close by. Jay grinned and made eye contact in a
way to make Mara absolutely sure he was doing it for her,
and the music began.

They chose a pop song that took inspiration from Michael
Jackson, with the kind of sexy choreography that was still appropriate to the crowd. It was pretty cheesy, and a far cry from

what he used to do when he was younger, but Jay still loved to dance. He could feel it in his body, the way it strained and stretched, that this was right. This was good.

But more importantly, he wanted Mara to know that he was dancing with only her in the audience—at least in his head. When Tori's brother was lip-syncing (quite excellently—where the hell did this kid come from?) his solo, and Jay stood to the side, he turned around and made sure to give Mara a little wink, and a "hey."

The way her jaw dropped open was going to count as one of the biggest wins he'd ever achieved. Much to his credit, her jaw was absolutely on the ground by the time they made it to the dance break, and he was absolutely feeling himself at that point. The movement was freeing, and it really did do an ego good, to know that someone had their eyes on you when you knew the moves. God, he really did miss dancing.

When the song ended and the seven of them hit their last pose with heavy breathing, the entire crowd had gone crazy, especially Tori, who stood up and hopped over to them declaring this was the best wedding she'd ever attended. Jay joined the guys in giving her a slightly sweaty group hug made up of delirious laughter and a promise never to do this again (their greatness had to be contained, Scott said). They dispersed from the stage, and Jay walked toward his family to applause, with Luna imitating his moves and begging Nong to teach her. Mara handed him his camera.

"I think we should let Nong catch his breath first," Ate Irene said, reaching out for her daughter. "Come on, kiddo. Let's get some Cocomo."

Jay waved them off. But as soon as he did, he turned to Mara and crossed one leg over the other. He leaned against her and took a selfie of them. Mara crossed her eyes and stuck her tongue out at the camera.

"Keep doing that and your eyes will stay like that," he joked, but Mara pretended to ignore him. He decided on a different approach.

"What did you think?" He casually put his arm on the back of her chair, leaning in a little. Thank god he had extra clothes on hand. He took a deep sip of his water while Mara was just staring at him, her eyes dark. He saw her throat work as if she'd swallowed a lump in it. She was absolutely staring at his panting mouth, his collarbone. Jay felt himself shiver from the want in her gaze. "Yeah?"

"Yeah," she agreed, and Jay felt that her hand on his thigh was reward enough, mostly because Mara was that bold with how he made her feel. "That was sexy. Like…really sexy. You're very bendy."

"That's something." Jay laughed, feeling his heart patter at Mara's slight squirming. Her cheeks were flushed, and he could tell there was a question she wanted to ask him. Every part of Jay's soul told him that whatever it was, he was going to say yes.

"Jay," she said carefully. "Can we advance my education tonight?"

"Your education? In what subject?"

"Mechanical physics? Aerodynamics?" At his confusion, she sighed and finally said, "Blowing."

OH. Neurons and pathways in Jay's brain lit up like Las

Vegas lights, flashing and spinning. If this was what it was like to fight for what you wanted, he definitely didn't mind rushing the battlefield. He grinned. Mission achieved.

"Whatever you want," he said, leaning in just close enough that the tip of his nose grazed hers, that his hot breath was on her skin. "Whatever you're ready for."

She squeezed his thigh, and Jay had to regulate his breathing even more just to make sure he didn't pop a boner in the middle of a wedding reception. Which probably wouldn't be the first time, but linen pants, dude.

Because the universe hated him, and because they truly wanted to live up to their name of being the banes of his existence, Alex and Tori turned in their seats to face them, knowing looks on their faces.

"What is all this whispering?" Tori teased, which made Mara snort. "Are we witnessing a miracle?"

"More than the miracle of two people finding each other in marriage and love?" Mara asked, which only made Tori giggle and whisper something in Alex's ear.

"They're not dating, they said," Alex said playfully. "Not dating, my pancake ass."

She took her wife's hand and led her to the dance floor, missing Mara calling, "Alex, I've always thought your ass was lovely!" behind her.

Mara had only seen moments like this happening to other people. She'd always thought it was so romantic when a couple snuck out of a party because they were so wrapped up in each other.

Well, she found out this evening. The rush of sneaking out, leaving behind the revelry and happiness of people to have more of her own. Whispering things like, "You're so beautiful," "Are you going to make me come tonight?" "Can you feel how much I want you?" into ears. Giggling because they were so lost in each other. Feeling drunk without taking a sip of alcohol. Being unable to keep her hands off of Jay's hips, because something inside her woke up at the press of his erection against your thighs.

The couples who did this in movies, books, TV, always looked so happy and carefree. Like there was nothing in the world more important than this. Slipping away to kiss someone you found irresistible.

"Mauve is really your color." Mara wiped the transferred lipstick off of the corner of his mouth with her thumb. Jay grinned and gently took her wrist to move her fingers over his lips. With a hum, he kissed the pad of her middle finger before he slid the finger between his lips, sucking gently.

"My sister always did say I was a winter deep." He grinned as if he hadn't almost made Mara come in her panties there and then.

They made it to the glass doors that led to his villa, finally tucked away from everyone else. Their shoes remained just outside the door as Jay unlocked it. He placed his phone, keys and camera on the side table.

Mara stepped out of the hot, humid summer night to the cool stillness of the bedroom. The cold blast of air did nothing to cool her skin, especially not when Jay stood behind her and crept his hand over her stomach and up her breasts.

Mara gasped at his touch, her body arching into the hands that barely contained her. Jay's hips pressed against her back, and her lower body clenched, aching for more.

"What did you want to do again?" he asked, flicking his fingers at the crest of her breasts until Mara realized what he was looking for. She gently guided his fingers to where her nipples were peaking under her dress, under the scrap of cloth she was using as a bra tonight. "Tell me."

"You know you're spoiling me for anyone else," Mara pointed out, experimenting with grinding against Jay's front. The sound that resulted made her think that her instinct had been correct. "I've been told it's not like this for everyone. With everyone."

"Dapat lang." She thought she heard him say more, but it was kind of hard to focus when all she wanted was to put her hands down her underwear and touch herself until she came.

"I think it's about learning what will make the other person feel spoiled," Jay said as Mara sat on the edge of the king-size bed, her feet hanging off of the side.

He turned to close the glass doors, then the curtains over it. Mara watched as he turned on the tall lamp in the corner, filling the room with the kind of soft, romantic lighting that made her think of declarations of love, of swearing to be with someone. This was a place where she could scream in all the pleasure in the world without caring who would hear. A place where she could allow herself to just…be herself. "And anyone who finds you as sexy as I do will want to make that effort."

"So it's about effort," she noted with a determined nod.

He took off his blazer and left it folded over the arm of the lounge chair. Jay chuckled as he undid the cuffs of his sleeves. Two more buttons of his shirt.

"Desire and effort." Jay took off his belt with quick movements. Mara felt a lump in her throat and swallowed thickly as she observed him. There was no mistaking what the bulge in his pants was. And she supposed that was a literal manifestation of effort. "It's caring about another person's pleasure. And I guarantee I'm not the only one who will want you, Mara."

But you're the only one I want, she almost said out loud, but kept it to herself, settling herself on the top of the bed, her skirt somewhere around her waist as he sauntered to her. The desire in his eyes was unmistakable. This was a man determined to find out what made her feel good.

She supposed it was vulnerable, too, exposing himself to her like this. To have the evidence of his desire so present, and nothing he could do could hide it. And she knew how to repay it.

"Ditto," she said. Trying to go for casual. But maybe she sounded a little nervous as she sat up, took her dress up and over her head, tossing the swath of blue fabric to the side, leaving her in a tube bra that wasn't doing much by way of support or coverage and a pair of panties.

From where she was sitting, she could see the curve of her stomach; he probably couldn't tell her the color of her panties. These were things she was taught to resent about herself, to hide away and cover up. But she wanted Jay to have this, to know this part of her as much as she did.

"Mara." If the hunger in his voice wasn't enough to send a thrill down her spine, the way he gazed at her was. Like she was a woman worth his worship. "What the hell does a Pokémon have to do with any of this."

That sent her into a fit of giggles so hard she needed to lie back on the pillows and turn away from him. What a way to relieve the tension.

"Hey!" Jay pretended to sound wounded as he hopped on the bed, making her body bounce. And very suddenly she was caged in his arms, his legs, his straining cock. "I thought we were doing... What did you say?"

"Mechanical physics?" Mara asked, her laughter dying down a bit. "With a bit of tongue technology?"

"We can absolutely do that." Jay nodded, his fingers already skimming the band of her underwear.

She opened her legs for him, inviting him to touch her there. His hand was warm, the fingers rough and now familiar to her. Mara gasped and arched into the sensation, feeling his cock stir somewhere along her leg. Jay's mouth pressed hot kisses on the exposed parts of her cleavage, moving down to her stomach. He looped a finger under the side of her panty. "May I?"

Mara could only nod, her body shivering as he slowly slid her underwear off, and she shuddered. Jay placed a hand on her arm, making her look up at him with hooded eyes.

"You okay?" he asked. Mara nodded and sat up to kiss him, reassuring him that she was fine, that she wanted this. Her, the girl who always followed the rules, who never had a hair wrong, who did what she was told. It made her feel beautiful and desired; it made her want him even more.

"My vagina is cold." She snickered, because it was the only

way she could describe the sensation of feeling this exposed. Jay chuckled and undid the button of his pants, keeping his briefs on.

"Lie back down," he said before he pressed his hands down on the tops of her thighs and licked a strip up her labia, her hair tickling his nose.

"Oh!" Mara shouted, her hips arching up. "Oh my *god*."

"Oh my god, yes, or—"

"Oh my god, keep going." She squirmed, twisting so she could see him at least. She could barely see anything but the top of his head between her legs, and god that was a sight she wasn't going to forget anytime soon. "Please."

He hummed a response, and spread her labia with his fingers before he flicked his tongue at her clit.

God, she thought she was sure that there were no further surprises to get with Jay without him entering her, and yet, here he was proving her wrong with a little flick of his tongue. She heard herself moan and gasp, her cheeks getting hotter and hotter as Jay pressed his tongue against her clit, as his other fingers curled against the spot where she was wettest.

"Fuck!" Mara groaned, her thighs tensing as the pleasure made her tighten and thrash. She realized she'd never done it like this—her arms weren't long enough, and any other equipment she had didn't feel *this* good. But it pressed a button she didn't even realize she wanted pressed so repeatedly and thoroughly. "Jay. Oh god, Jay."

She raised her legs, planting her feet on the bed. Dimly aware that she was thrusting fully at him, as her fingertips brushed over the top of his head. She could feel him moving against the bed, too, matching the rhythm of his one, two, three fingers inside her.

Jay sucked her clit.

Mara was an absolute goner, coming in a shout, in a burst of white like a fuse had exploded in her head. And with one final curl of his fingers came the last of her breath.

She collapsed into the bed, hand idly reaching for Jay. He was panting as he caged her in his arms. She kissed him lazily, letting him thrust his covered-up cock between her legs. His hand was still wet with her juices as he stuck it down his briefs.

Mara experimentally dug her fingernails into his reddened chest, flicking his nipples with her other hand, and he was coming, too, soaking the front of his briefs, a couple of drops on the bed. Jay collapsed next to her and dropped the laziest of kisses on her shoulder, his pants open, his shirt still on.

Mara had never felt so debauched in her life, and god help her, she liked it.

"You're a terrible teacher." She chuckled once her breath came back, letting him curl up against her, his arm around her stomach. "I don't think I learned anything from that aside from, 'Wow, I really liked that.'"

"That's the point," was all Jay said, his voice sounding sleepy and tired. "So you know you like it." And the unsaid words hovered in the air around them. *So you know you like it and tell someone else.*

Mara closed her eyes so she could ignore them, but the night felt too full of silence, and she wanted to push it all away.

"Marina told me I've never been in a relationship because I was reverse manifesting it," she told him, letting her words fill the room instead of the ones they refused to say out loud, casting them out. "But I think I just wasn't brave enough to ask. When I was younger it was because I thought I wasn't pretty enough or thin enough. Now I just... I don't want to get hurt. I already have to live through so much without that risk."

"Ah. Like shitty governments. Wars just outside our door," Jay said. Just open up any feed and find ten things to ruin your day. Live in this country and experience how bad it could be. Live elsewhere and it was just as bad, but in different ways.

"Yeah." Suddenly it didn't sound so stupid. It was a hard world to live in. And she didn't think she had the emotional capacity to stake her heart in more pain. "I already feel overwhelmed by life without someone else in the picture. Maybe I'm just weak."

"You're protecting your heart," Jay reminded her. "You're still letting people in. That's a good sign."

"Maybe I'm protecting it a bit too much," Mara admitted. "It feels like such a privilege, being able to do that. To have a choice, even, of having anyone at all."

"It is. They say admitting to a privilege is the first step in using it for better things."

She sighed and let his words wash over her, feeling the weight of her confessions lift from her body and stay in the air.

"I don't know what I'll do with myself once Ate gets married," Jay said, adding his thoughts to the mess of hers. "I don't regret anything. I'm happy for them, but..."

"But they don't need you as much anymore, and that sucks."

She knew that feeling implicitly. "I wish I could tell you what to do about that, Jay."

"I don't think there's anything to do about it, Supergirl," he joked, lifting his head so he was looking up at her face instead. "It just is what it is. I was thinking of taking my old job in Hong Kong."

"Hong Kong?" This was the first she'd heard of it. Or maybe David had mentioned it when he introduced Jay to Marina, but she couldn't remember now. "You're moving?"

"Technically, I moved, came back and might be moving again. I haven't decided," he admitted.

Mara sat up in bed, suddenly not so tired or sleepy anymore. Was this why he didn't want to commit to…well, anything? How could you just not know something as big as moving to Hong Kong? It would have kept her up until she made a decision. How could he lie in bed like that and not know? How could he start…this with her with Hong Kong hanging over his head?

"I want a chance to find something more to live for."

"And you're going to find that in Hong Kong," she said. Not quite able to picture it.

She understood the appeal, of course. Living somewhere else where you didn't have to be beholden to anyone. But you didn't exactly have anyone, either. It was hard to picture that for Jay, who cared so much that he woke up the whole island to make sure this wedding happened. Who gave up what appealed to him out there to be with his sister.

"Well, I don't *really* need to move back. I can make the same amount here, and at least here I can actually afford it."

So why are you thinking of leaving?

"I could also become a supervillain and use my kissing powers for evil." He lightly laughed, his eyes fluttering closed. He must be way more tired than she thought, if he was falling asleep that quickly. But also, god. Hong Kong. There were farther places for him to go, sure. But that was still pretty far, as far as she was concerned. She crossed her legs on the bed, trying not to look at him, trying to keep him from seeing her. Because Mara was trying to come up with all the selfish reasons for him to stay. Not that she had any right to it. But it was a good exercise.

"You know, I've come up with a theory about our failed vector," she said, turning to face him.

He said nothing in response to that, but mostly it was because he was already asleep. Mara sighed, shaking her head fondly. His breathing was even, with the occasional snuffle or a muttered word. He'd probably woken up at some ungodly time in the morning, and between this and the wedding? It was understandable that even someone so full of energy could run out of steam.

"I guess I'll tell you later." Mara brushed a few strands of his hair away from his face, and she knew that she was absolutely fucked.

For all her bravery and all her insistence that she wasn't going to let her feelings run with her, here she was, eating her words. Mara decided that evening that it was much too late for her to want to take any of it back. She was going to see this through and figure out how to mend her heart after. She was too far gone for him, and she didn't much feel like looking back.

Thirteen

The worst thing about leaving paradise was how gray everything seemed after. The airport, for example, was quite literally gray. Smog from traffic was gray, as were all the concrete roads that led back home. Something about all of that just highlighted the "back to reality" feeling. Or more accurately sometimes, "Welcome back to the hellmouth."

It was strange to think that just hours before that, Mara was standing in perfect white sand, watching crystal blue waters, perfectly sunny blue skies and eating Cocomo from a half-cut coconut fruit. Hayy, she missed it already. Life just wasn't always fair that way. No matter how happy she had been in Boracay, there was always a day she had to come back.

She'd snuck back to her room on the day of the wedding at an ungodly hour of the morning. So ungodly she thought witches were cackling as she reentered her room. But even as Mara lay in bed, she couldn't fall asleep, her mind whirling about what she'd done, about Jay moving away, about what she felt. Whatever it was she felt, because she still wasn't sure. She sent a message to her group chat with her sisters, calling an SOS.

Need to talk about life. Calling an emergency council when I get back.

And because Mabel was only twenty-five, she was still up at said ungodly hour and texted back. **Roger, boss. Wouldn't want to do it half-hazardly.** ☺

The next morning, Mara woke up with no idea what time it was. When she checked her messages, they included a DM from Ate Irene saying they should meet up in Manila when they were both free, and a message from Jay.

You left. ☹ Sent several hours ago. Probably when he woke up to find her gone. A couple of hours later, he messaged again. **Can't stop thinking about last night. I need to see you again.**

The gasp Mara made caught in her throat, and it became a hiccup. But she couldn't quite find the right words to send back to him, so she decided not to respond and get on with her last day on the beach.

By that afternoon she was sitting in the lobby of her hotel, looking out at the sea while nursing a bowl of the Cocomo Coco Loco with Mango. The dessert was coconut ice cream made with coconut milk, served with toasted pinipig, ripe mango cubes and coconut meat. It was served in a half-cut fresh coconut, which meant you could carve out the meat with a spoon after you ate all the ice cream.

Days at the beach moved like gently melting butter—slow and decadent. Mara's thoughts felt that way, too. Whenever she tried to sum up what had transpired, parse how she felt, or understand why she was already missing something that wasn't hers, her mind would wander somewhere else. She didn't know if it was because she was overwhelmed, over-thinking, or just utterly distracted by the beach. The waves were calming, and knowing its rhythms was a thought that occupied her and made her feel a sense of calm.

That was when Perry showed up. It was always a feat for a guy to look like he smelled good in a country where the sun was your relentless friend. But Perry managed the even more difficult feat of looking like he smelled good while at the beach.

He wasn't sweating at all, the heat leaving nothing but a light, healthy sheen on his skin, and a bit of redness on the tops of his cheeks to make him more approachable. He seemed delighted to see her, and Mara had to admit it made her already melting brain melt a little more. It was always nice when someone was happy to see you.

"Mara!" he said, coming up to her. "I thought you left with the rest of the wedding party."

"And leave the beach too soon?" she asked, shaking her head. "No way."

"I wouldn't want to leave the beach too soon, either." He grinned and took off his sunglasses. And somewhere in this world, a chorus of children sang out a glorious, "Hallelujah." Perry really was the whole package, and a very impressive one, too. "May I?" He indicated the rest of the bench beside Mara.

"Sure." She scooted to the side to give him room, and there was just enough for him to sit with one leg over the other. But she could still feel the warmth of his thigh pressing against hers. Or maybe it was his hand. "I was supposed to be here to not think."

"How is that going for you?" he asked, his fingers firmly clasped around his knee.

"Very badly," she admitted, scooping up the last of her ice cream while digging in to the fresh coconut for more meat. "Too many questions, and I can't focus long enough to answer."

"Maybe you just need a friend?" Perry asked, and Mara had the distinct impression that by friend, he hadn't meant friend, at all. Maybe someone who cared a little differently than a friend would. "I'm a really good listener. My preschool teacher wrote that in my report card and everything."

"A written first account." Mara laughed. "My preschool teacher called me an achiever, which is maybe a kind way to say that I was bossy and domineering."

"Some people like to be bossed around and domineered." Perry seemed to speak from a wealth of experience, and he just had that aura that told you that he knew exactly what he was talking about. It radiated from him, like a heavenly vibe of responsibility and good boy behavior. Huh. David was right. He was exactly the kind of guy she wanted for herself. The kind of guy she hoped would one day look at her and think, *wow*.

"Maybe," Mara echoed, looking at Perry like he'd just announced that he would like to be able to scale up the side of a building one day. It was strange how open he was about his intentions, and Mara didn't mind so much that he was. "Or maybe I'm just old."

"I like to call that protecting your peace."

"Are you in marketing?" Mara asked, tucking one leg under the other so she could lean back against the wall and finish her mango. "You are really good at spinning things."

"That sounds bad." Perry pouted. Cute.

"No, I mean you're good at making things sound better," Mara corrected herself. "You're straightforward and real, but not rude. Sometimes I forget that you can do one without being the other." She sighed and put her now empty coconut between them. "Although you have to be careful. A girl could fall for you without you meaning it."

"Sometimes falling for someone is just falling for someone." Perry shrugged. "Doesn't have to have anything to do with the person you're falling for. It is not your mission to tell them your feelings."

"So what's the mission? If it's not telling them?"

"It's feeling the way you feel, and deciding if you're going to do something about it. Are you going to stand by what you feel? Are you going to ask them if you have permission to do something about it?" He wasn't looking at her when he was speaking, and Mara wasn't really, either. She was more focused on what he was saying, on the way he made it sound so easy.

"I like to think that multiple things can be true at the same time," he continued, without missing a beat. "For example. While it's true that I approached you for art reasons, it's also true that I've wanted to ask you out to dinner since I recognized you at that reception."

Mara's heart caught in her chest. At that particular moment it was hard to decide if her surprise was kilig related, or just the recognition that this was the first time anyone had asked her out on a date. Both things could be true, but they couldn't be more different, too.

"Me?" she asked, which was ridiculous and pabebe. Of course, her. But *why* her?

"Yeah." Perry chuckled like he was challenging her incredulousness. "I've heard from both David and Alex all the reasons why they think we would be a good match, and I happened to agree. I think you're funny and smart, and it matters to me that you and I have a basic agreement on politics."

"Oh, totally." Because that was half the battle, most days.

"I also think you're gorgeous. So I think asking you out to dinner is the least I can do to get to know you better, and it's a good way as any to start a love story."

Oh, he was sweet. Very sweet, and Mara appreciated that he wasn't shy about telling her what he wanted out of her. It was really that easy, she supposed, to put your heart out there for another person to take.

"That's me doing something about how I feel, by the way," Perry pointed out. "Dinner is usually a good way to start."

"It really is," Mara agreed.

"That's it?" Marina asked, as Mabel's jaw dropped in disbelief at the end of Mara's story. "Dinner is a good start? Did you say yes? How did you feel about it? Do you like him? What about the deal with the gallery?"

"What about Jay!" Mabel made it sound like that was the more urgent matter. "Mom already keeps calling him son-in-law whenever we bring it up!"

Mara did not even know that it was a thing that was brought up so often. She had no doubt her parents had some notion of what had transpired with her and Jay in Boracay—their family was too small for any kind of secret to be kept—but her parents were usually all about the broad strokes. Malayo naman sa bituka, their dad always said. But for her mom to have such an affectionate pet name was new.

"Mom already has a son-in-law," Mara pointed out, pursing her lips in the actual son-in-law's direction. "That guy."

"Yes, I'm guy," David agreed, stirring noodles into his sauce like he was making his own version of a dry pot. Marina looked slightly horrified at what her husband was doing. "Also just for the record, I'm here in my capacity as a 10 percent owner of Wildflower. I have no biases in who you should go out on a date with, Mara. Even if Perry literally asked you. And offered to get you to try out floral art, which is something you've always wanted to do."

"Very unbiased, hon." Marina laughed, shaking her head.

"Well, I vote for Jay," Mabel huffed. She crossed her arms in exasperation. "I think Ate is only considering Perry because he's there. Jay makes her all blushy and happy."

"You haven't even seen me with Perry!"

"Also Jay is literally moving to Hong Kong, Mabel," Marina added, stirring vegetables into the spicy soup. "Honestly, the man is amazing at getting in his own way. Just like you, Ate."

Mara sighed and wiped off the steam from her glasses for the third time that evening. The emergency conference with her mother and sisters happened as soon as she arrived at the house. Her father had greeted her at the door, welcomed her home and listened to Mara's complaints about being hungry and wanting dinner. About a minute later, Marina barged into the house, saw Mara watching reels on the couch and said, "Get in, loser. We're going to therapy."

Which was how Mara ended up at a hot pot restaurant, the kind where you couldn't name the restaurant if you tried and simply knew it as "that place, you know the one." Everything was unlimited, you mixed your own sauce and didn't feel like a complete meal without a can of Wo Long Kat. It was comforting and reliable, a literal hot soup to balm her jagged feelings. But it was also perfect, because you needed to eat slow, which gave her time to think about what she wanted to say.

"So?" Mabel was incensed. "He's still here. He can change his plans, if Ate asked him to!"

"She's not going to ask him to." Marina shook her head. "That would kind of be unfair."

"It would." Mara sighed, dipping her meat in her sauce. She liked her shabu shabu sauce with a lot of garlic, soy sauce and satay. By the end of her meal she would dump all her sauce in a bowl of noodles and broth, and it would be glorious. "Even if I did want to change our situation in any way—" she didn't miss the way her sisters glanced at each other, a reaction to a secret conversation they probably had in the car on the way to pick her up "—he's decided to leave already."

"Decisions can be changed," Mabel argued, shrugging like she was talking about the weather. "He's still here. The parameters can change all the time."

But the thing was, Mara had never liked it when the parameters changed. Things needed to make sense, which was why she'd thrived in school. What they never tell you about life after was that the world was as senselessly changeable as life itself. She didn't like the idea of changing Jay's, just because, what, she felt something for him?

"He told me upfront when we met that he wasn't interested in a relationship," Mara pointed out to convince her sisters it was pointless...but really it was more to remind herself that Jay had been explicitly clear with her since the beginning. Just as much as Perry was clear that he wanted to give whatever it was that could be between them a shot. "In fact our entire not-dating arrangement hinged around *not* being in a relationship."

"So what were you doing the whole time you were in Boracay?" Marina asked. "Hanging out with each other, being each other's plus-ones, spending time together?"

"Sounds like a relationship to me," Mabel singsonged, popping a whole cheese ball into her mouth.

"You could always..." Marina began.

"Tell him how I feel?" Mara asked, and her voice squeaked at the notion. She didn't even know how to *begin* to tell him. She didn't have Perry's smoothness or his willingness to put himself out there. Telling Jay how she felt—not that she knew what she felt yet, exactly, because she wasn't in love, probably—seemed like such an imposition on him. It didn't seem fair to him, for her to use the way she felt as a way to make him stay.

And what if he stayed because of her feelings, and she turned out to be wrong? Or if he stayed because of how she felt and realized he didn't feel the same? What if they got married because he'd already made the sacrifice of staying anyway, bahala na, and they never talked about this?

She could picture it suddenly. Both of them sixty years old and waking up in bed next to someone they no longer recognized. Could picture them fighting, their anger and all the words they don't say out loud filling rooms. Could picture herself ranting to her kids, so much that her eldest would literally run away to Boracay just so she didn't have to play marriage counselor. Anxiety filled Mara like all the noodles and veg and balls in their hot pot, bubbling over.

The wooden chopstick in her hand snapped. Her three dinner companions jumped at the sound and gaped at her.

"Anyway," Mara said finally, releasing the anxiety in a long, long exhale. She took a deep, fortifying sip of her Wo Long Kat. "I need to talk to Jay. This can't go on."

As much as she didn't want to be ruled by things that weren't real, she had to admit that there was a reason she was picturing these fantasy scenarios. Much bravery was required, and she didn't think she'd built enough of those stores yet. Love was a leap, love was being brave, love was taking a chance. But Mara had never been one to do any of those things. Not without some indication that she had some chance of success.

Mara could not read the look that was exchanged between her younger sisters. She didn't really know if she wanted to.

Fourteen

It was a hot summer in Manila. That was usually a statement met with sarcasm, like, weh hindi nga, no fucking shit, it's hot. But summer in Manila was the kind of hot that stuck to your skin, the kind where the air was still and humid, like wading through a steamy sauna without the steam.

Thankfully, Jay's building had an air-conditioned lobby. For Mara's sake, and the staff that worked there, it was a really good thing.

Jay's condominium unit was nice. It was the tall, new kind of place that had all the stores you needed at the first floor, plus a bank, a pharmacy *and* a laundry shop (PasigLabandera!), the kind where a short walk could get you to a cute little café that made you feel like you were part of a "community." It was in a part of Pasig that was only just starting to get crowded because they build condos where public infrastructure was built for small suburbs. A good spot, not too far from good schools, big malls and commercial spaces.

Crowded, but not too crowded that walking around on foot was an impossible task.

It was a well-considered place. Jay had chosen well.

Anyway, the important part of the story was that when Jay opened the door to his unit, he was wet and wearing only a towel hanging on for dear life around his waist. Despite the fact that Mara had seen the lobby receptionist call up to the unit and had in fact swiped the elevator key for her.

"What th—*Ate!*" Jay whined in much the same way a bunso child would as Ate Irene emerged from the back with a box full of happy houseplants and an innocent smile. "You didn't tell me Mara was coming up!"

"I didn't?" she asked innocently. Mara couldn't see the expression on Ate Irene's face because a drop of water had pooled at the tip of Jay's hair, then splashed on his collarbone, then started to slide down the middle of his chest, and—oops. Into the happy trail it disappears. Oh wow. Newton had been on to something with those laws of gravity. "Gosh, I must be getting old."

"I would offer to help, but you're trying to escape from me, and I'm naked," Jay announced, glaring at his sister. Mara also realized that this was the first time she was seeing all of Jay's body in the daylight, and wow. It was fascinating to watch his muscles move and tense as he twisted away from her. He was more wiry and skinny than she pictured (than she'd actually held, and touched), but she knew that was the frame of a man who could part her thighs and hold them open while—

"Right, Mara?"

"Hmm?" she said innocently.

"Oh well, I have to go get these babies settled in our unit." Ate Irene shrugged, moving past them. "Our apartment isn't going to make itself cozy."

Mara remembered that Irene and Luna were moving. She'd heard someone mention that Irene's wedding was coming up soon, but she didn't know any of the details and didn't want to press the matter.

"Do you need help, Ate?" Mara was distracted, not rude.

"No, no!" Irene shook her head, butting the box against the wall so she could open the front door, wedge her foot through the gap and move it wide enough so she could pass. Mara held the door open for her so she could change into a different pair of slippers. "The two of you stay. It's literally across the way."

"Your car?"

"Her condo," Jay explained, hand still on the knot in the towel. And no, Mara was *not* going to think about what he was trying to keep out of her view. Nothing she hadn't seen before, and touched, too. "She and Luna are moving to Kuya Nige's place in St. Tropez Court."

Mara had seen it when the Grab car had dropped her off here. It wasn't far at all, but she supposed if you were comparing it to someone being ten steps away, if you compared it to moving all the way to Hong Kong, it was a huge distance either way.

She helped Ate Irene to the elevator anyway, leaving the door lodged open. She came back to the unit to find Jay still standing where she left him, a little less wet, but seemingly a little lost. So she closed the door behind her, and he showed no signs of acknowledging her. Instead he was looking around the apartment, like he was trying to find something that was missing.

"You okay?" Mara asked as she took off her shoes. Jay blinked at her. She assumed that he'd forgotten she was there, deep in thought as he seemed.

"Yeah, I—I just realized that was the last of their stuff." He frowned as he glanced around the apartment one more time. It didn't look empty exactly—most of the major furniture items were still there. Maybe a little big. Spacious, which he probably wasn't used to yet. "My family moved out of the apartment."

"Oh, Jay." It broke her heart to see him so defeated. She took his hand, the one that wasn't keeping the towel tied to his waist, making him turn to face her. Then she pressed a hand to his cheek. Jay sighed and closed his eyes and leaned into her touch. "You want to talk about it?"

"Not—" he started, but Mara was already halfway to saying something else.

"We could order tacos. There's a Takaw Tacos near you, right?"

Maybe he was craving birria tacos. Maybe he'd wanted to have it for weeks. Maybe it was something else entirely, but the way his face changed from a broody seriousness to a soft happiness to a full sunshine smile made Mara's heart flip three different times, three different ways. She liked how easy it was to make him smile. She wondered if it was always going to be this easy with someone else.

"Yes, please," he said, pulling on Mara's hand so he could

plant a long kiss on her temple. He squeezed her hand. "I'll go get dressed?"

What an odd question. Of course he should get dressed. They were going to have tacos. But the way he looked at her, Mara kind of had an idea.

"Oh god!" she exclaimed, shaking her head. "No, no. Jay, you don't have to—I mean unless you want—"

"Do *you* want?"

"I think I want us to talk first." She laughed, shaking her head because she'd been so worried and nervous the entire car ride here, rehearsing things she wanted to say and how she was going to tell him that she was done, he was right, she couldn't do this.

All that seemed to fly out the window now.

But, no. They were adults who could have a friendly, but serious, conversation over birria and horchata. Okay, maybe not horchata. Takaw Tacos's house-made horchata was usually sold out by the time Mara got to them. "Go na."

So there they were, sitting on the floor of his living room, eating tacos and drinking Coke Zeros. One of them was dripping birria consommé on the bare floor, and the other one was Mara because she'd put her tacos in a bowl, dripped consommé over them and ate it all like a rice bowl.

"I don't know what's more unhinged." Jay laughed, wiping the dripping sauce off his lip and licking the tip of his finger. "Your way of eating tacos or me not having a rug."

"I don't think you're using the word *unhinged* right." Mara added more of the tomato thing. It probably wasn't proper salsa. "Why a rug?"

"A rug adds a vibe," Jay argued, whipping out his phone to pull up a Pinterest board. Mara tried and failed to be subtle about peeking at his boards—"Photos," "Interiors," "Outfits." Simple. Jay pulled up the "Interiors" board and showed her what he'd pinned. All the spaces showed sunny, comfortable rooms with soft furnishings, but had very modern touches. The rugs were all checkered and slightly shaggy. The coffee tables were sometimes colored acrylic. Mara was surprised. None of that was currently in the half-empty living room. "See?"

"Mmm-hmm." She nodded, scrolling the board a little more. It was a little too trendy for her tastes (god, some of these rooms had a disco ball), but she could easily picture some of her own furniture pieces fitting in these rooms, too. Her bookshelf. The vanity she'd thrifted that was likely a desk. Vases full of flowers.

She could picture the two of them in that space, eating food on the floor in front of the couch, constantly worrying about staining the white squares of the carpet. Could almost hear her music playing in the background—Maggie Rogers, maybe, while his disco ball slowly spun and made patterns all around the room.

It wouldn't be such a bad life.

"Why didn't you have a rug before?" Mara wondered out loud. Just wanting to stop picturing the life she could have. It wasn't what he wanted. "If it is such a vibe."

"Children are sticky creatures, Mara." Jay tsked like she should have known. "I think every pillow of this couch has been flipped over twice from all the spillage."

"Luna?"

"Some of it was Luna." Jay laughed. "My sister kind of gets distracted a lot, so spillage was inevitable." The smile on his face turned a little wistful, and he looked around the room again. "But the place really is big, huh?"

"I didn't think new buildings had cuts like this anymore."

"I got lucky with the preselling." Mara somehow had the impression that Jay's mind was suddenly far, far away, his eyes focused on some middle distance that wasn't really there. "Maybe I can rent this place out and move somewhere smaller? Or somewhere closer to Ate?"

She gave him a look. Jay sighed. "You're right, I should give them their space. Clearly I have more than enough to go around, though."

"Do you not like the guy she's marrying?" Mara asked, wondering if it was okay to poke at the issue a little more. It seemed like he needed it. "You don't seem very happy about it."

"No, I do! Nige is awesome," Jay insisted, and Mara believed him, because Jay was a terrible liar. "He loves my sister, and he'll be an amazing dad to Luna. I just... I'll miss them, that's all."

He gave her a placating smile, one that was all lips, all cheeks as if to assure her, *"I'm fine, I'm fine."* But perhaps she could push him. Just a little more. Get to the heart of what he wasn't saying, because maybe it could help him?

"Or maybe you'll miss the life you thought you were going to have with them," Mara said, lowering her taco bowl. "It seemed like you were so ready for it."

There was silence.

A beat.

A long beat that could also sound like a line being crossed. Had she pushed him too far? Why was she suddenly so worried about pushing him away, when that was exactly what she came here to do?

She'd come here because she'd resolved to talk to Jay. Not to display her feelings out for him to dissect or examine, but to have an honest discussion of how they were going to move forward with this. Because Mara concluded that while she absolutely enjoyed what she and Jay were doing together, there was no way she was going to be able to actually have sex with someone who wasn't going to stick around. She didn't want to share this with someone who for all intents was just going to add it to a list.

Did Mara know this about herself before she started fooling around with Jay? Maybe. But it wasn't a hard line until she had to cross it, and it was good to know. So this arrangement was about to end. And he was over there wearing a Good Morning towel wrapped around his head.

Because she cared for him, obviously. Because she still selfishly hoped that maybe just sticking around, staying would be enough to convince him to stick around. There was a great guy out there in Makati who wanted to take her out to dinner at a fancy tasting menu place, who wanted her to showcase her art to the upper echelons of Manila's art world. Someone who wanted her and thought she was beautiful.

But then, there was Jay. Jay, who only wanted the best for her, who was considerate and sweet. Who thought she was brilliant and smart. He wanted her to be happy, and he thought she was beautiful, too. And Mara's heart wanted someone it had come to know well, someone whom she knew would treat her with kindness.

"I was," he admitted with a downcast look. "Maybe I'm mourning that a little, right? I was ready for this life where I raised a kid and sustained a family. It was all happening too fast that there was no time to doubt myself or convince myself that I couldn't do it. And I'm not angry, nor do I blame Ate or anything, but yeah. Suddenly my life is different, and I have all this…room."

He sighed, and Mara wanted to give him a hug.

"I think that's why I considered Hong Kong. Where else would I have the least possible amount of space to myself?"

"It's Manila." Mara chuckled. "Get on the MRT at rush hour and find out what least possible amount of space feels like."

He laughed, dropping his head back against the couch.

That was when Mara noticed that the sun was setting behind his head, filling the room with warm, orangey light. Was golden hour the thing she was going to remember most about…whatever this was, between them? She could almost hear a sad, maudlin song playing in the background. Maybe "Nakapagtataka," which was all nostalgia and standing under the rain. How many times could she get away with playing that song out loud before Mabel banged on her door and begged her to stop?

"Exactly," Jay said, wiping his hands with tissue paper,

holding out his palms when Mara held up her handy-dandy alcohol spray for him.

This was it. Now or never. Well, now or later. But if there was anything she learned from her time with Jay (was she already being nostalgic?), it was that you had to say what you wanted out loud. You couldn't expect the other person to guess, it wasn't fair to them, and even worse, not fair to you. Mara didn't know what would happen next, but she was standing by her feelings. There were worse things. Harder things.

"Don't move," she finally said. Jay stopped moving. Actually froze like a witch had trapped him in time, complete with the stunned expression on his face.

She couldn't help it. Her heart melted, and she giggled, pressing her forehead against the crook of his neck as she laughed weakly against his shoulder. Jay's hand immediately went to her back, rubbing soothing circles on it without him knowing what was running through her head.

"I meant don't move to Hong Kong. Because I can't."

"I don't think I asked you." There was a hint of amusement to his voice, like he thought she was being funny. Mara lifted her head to glare at him, and Jay's face moved from amusement to concern. "Wait. Are you asking me to stay?"

"Not to pressure you, I promise." Although it was too late, wasn't it? "I just thought, if you were looking for something to live for. It could be this. You and me."

"Mara…" She didn't know what to make of the way he said her name. But she refused to let him get a word in right now, not when he'd opened a floodgate inside her, and she needed to let it out.

"You're worried about disappointing me, or not loving me the way I need." She placed her now empty bowl on the table in front of her. "But you're not giving yourself the chance, either. Or giving me the chance to find out for myself if we would be a good fit together. Because I'd like to know."

She didn't want to look up and attempt to guess what he was thinking. But she just really, really wished he would hold her a little tighter, make her feel smaller so the things she said didn't have to feel so big.

"They wouldn't call it falling if it didn't require you to be brave," Mara pointed out. "Or if you didn't lose control a little."

"You want me that much?" Jay asked, his hand sliding back down. "It's been three nights, Mara."

"It's been three months for me," she admitted, looking up this time to face him and the truth of the way she felt. "Three months where I sat in that flower shop, waiting for the one that you promised me to walk through the door and fall in love with me. And I was going to be okay with being your failed vector. But the moment I decided to stop waiting, you showed up."

He tried to speak, but all he managed was to open his mouth and make a small noise. He seemed surprised that she was saying this all out loud. She'd planned to go the completely opposite direction with this, but instead all she wanted was to exhaust every option, every word she had in her arsenal to come to a conclusion about all of this.

"So here's the thing, Jaysohn. I'm not looking for forever. But I think I could find forever in you."

His mouth hung slightly open as they looked at each other.

It was such a mundane thing, to speak truths to someone who had taken it all, who had listened to it all and gently volleyed back their own. But Mara felt like her world shifted in that moment. Like this was a moment in time that was to be marked, mostly because she'd given power to her feelings by sharing them. Bravery must always be acknowledged, even if it was just for her.

He smiled. Mara could spend pages and pages of a journal chronicling Jay's different smiles—the ones he gave when he was being polite, when he was trying to hold in a laugh, when his happiness was a small, warm feeling and when he was so happy his face rivaled the sun in its brightness. But the truly incandescent Jay smile, the one that melted away Mara's fears and made her think this was going to be okay? It was probably her favorite. It was the one he gave her when he first kissed her, the one he gave her now that she'd showed him her heart.

He touched her cheek and, still smiling, kissed her. He tasted like birria, but then again, so did she. "I'm staying."

Mara's jaw hung slightly open, too dazed from the kiss and everything to process what he said. "What?"

"You think I could rent out this place for forty-five thousand?" Jay mused, doing a piss-poor job of pretending that he didn't notice Mara's confusion. "Or is that too low? I mean, it has furniture, so that should count for something. I probably need to find a broker, which means I have to butter up Mary June Ang from the admin office, and I am so bad at buttering her up. She's into those fourth-gen K-pop kids. I just *can't*."

"Jay," Mara exclaimed, resisting the urge to poke his side.

"Can you believe my bosses wouldn't give me a relocation package to move to Hong Kong? Basically the offer was to work in Hong Kong for the same salary, which, why would I when the money stretches farther here? And it's not like they actually need me to report to work. I have several colleagues who stayed in Europe and Australia and they were never asked to RTO."

"Are you really not moving?"

"I have no idea what you're talking about," he said, deliberately being evasive as he started to pop his shoulders, his neck, like he was dancing. "I'm a movement machine."

There was no talking to him then. And she had run out of words to say, reasons to make and arguments to give. What was it that Shakespeare said? "Shut up, and let me kiss you"? Probably.

"Jay," she said, putting her hands on his cheeks. If she was pressing just a little more to get him to stop talking, she wasn't going to deny it. But it did force him to look at her and blink innocently. "Shut up."

And he did. Not only did he shut up, he kissed her back. Deeply and fully wrapping her up in his arms. It felt like he was trying to pour his entire soul into his kiss, trying to bring her close and never let her go. They continued kissing, moving closer until Jay knelt over Mara, the coffee table pushed back a little so he had room to put his knees between her thighs. So she could look up at him with dazed eyes and swollen lips. The sunlight was on his face still, and the moment would stay in her mind forever, the day Jay said he wanted to stay.

"What did you call yourself? A failed vector?" he asked,

chuckling as he handed her back her glasses after cleaning them off with his shirt. "I haven't stopped thinking about you since I kissed you that first night. I was so sure I did it wrong."

"I don't think there's a *right* way to use a magic power that could just be coincidence," Mara teased, wrinkling her nose to push her glasses just a little higher. "But Jay. You didn't fail. In the corniest way, your kiss magic is still a thing. It just worked on both of us."

He kissed her again, and Mara could feel that he was torn between continuing to kiss her and smiling, which she remedied by making out with him even harder.

"I know we need to talk more." He brushed a thumb over her cheek. "But I want to give this a try. I want to give this all I can, as much as I can."

"Good." Mara nodded. "Because I want that, too."

And suddenly, Mara knew Jay wasn't going to let her leave his condo right away. He swung himself off of her and stood up, holding out a hand for her. Mara let him help her stand, and he ended up stumbling slightly backward when he popped up, and she pulled him back to steady him.

"Can I show you something?" Was Mara just imagining that embarrassed blush on his cheeks, or…?

"Is it your pet cat?" she joked, and he pulled her toward him with their still connected hands, raising them above their heads until Mara's body was flush with his, before he lowered his head and kissed her. She needed to tiptoe a little bit just so he didn't crane his neck so much.

"Just to clarify," he said. "I was asking if you were ready to have sex with me."

"I figured." Mara smiled. "And yes. Let's do it. I have condoms in my bag."

"What a coincidence," Jay said, moving toward the short hallway to the bedrooms, Mara following behind him, their hands still entwined. "Me, too."

She laughed and wrapped her arms around his chest, hugging him from behind. It may have been the middle of summer, but giving Jay a back hug gave her a comforting kind of warmth. Mara didn't want to admit it, but she'd craved this, holding him in her arms and knowing that it meant something that she could do it.

"Is it in your little squirrel pack?" she joked.

"Hey, the pack contains the essentials! I told you this."

He slowly twisted the knob and opened the door. Mara had to admit that she never really had any thoughts on what Jay's room could possibly look like. Carpeted floors, maybe. Strips of LED lights tucked behind mirrors or a TV. But what his room actually was, she quickly realized, was comfortable. And very, very him.

The first thing she noted was the bright orange donut-shaped lamp hanging on the wall, one she knew was always out of stock at IKEA. Then there was the bed, a large one that had been placed on a platform, with a duvet cover and pillows that had a lived-in texture she was sure it had come with when he bought it. There was nothing on the side tables that was easily reachable to a child, but he did have a Snoopy doll on his bed. Mara spotted a closet, but there was also a clothing rack left out, full to the brim with all kinds of pieces that she was sure he'd carefully chosen.

Her toes settled into the checkered rug, again something he likely selected. His curtains were the kind that were soft and let just enough of the light through, making the room a study of light and shadow at that time of the day. He turned on a stand fan that was in the corner (of course he'd gotten one of those fancy ones made of white metal and fake wood), and the room seemed to breathe a bit better. He also had one of those very trendy floor chairs that she always thought looked like the back of a centipede, but his was dark green so you didn't *really* notice. There were framed photos of family and friends, most of which she knew he'd taken.

"I love your handiwork," Mara said, indicating the large painting placed slightly off-center from the bed, a canvas that had seemingly random squiggles and handprints on it. In the bottom right corner, Mara noted someone had written, "Luna, 3." Or, "Luna's"?

"It was more of a group project." Jay chuckled, his hands tucked into the belt loops of his pants as he looked fondly at the image. He walked to one of the side tables and tossed three things on the bed. A pack of condoms, lube and a sheet of paper that Mara picked up to read and saw were his medical results for HIV and STD screenings. She looked at him, smiling.

"You prepared." She understood his embarrassed blushing now, because she was doing it, too.

"I wanted this experience to be good for you." He explained it like it was a simple thing, to make her feel like he cared about her. But god, based on everything Mara had heard from everyone else, the bar was so low that all she felt was damned lucky that they wanted each other this much. What a miracle to find someone who cared about you, as much as you cared about them.

"And what about you?" Mara asked, putting the medical results to the side as she turned to face him on his bed.

"Well, I am a man. So it's really easy for me to enjoy myself." He bent down to kiss her again, running his hands up and down her arms and making Mara shiver. He undid the claw clip that held her hair back and ran his fingers through her hair before it fell over her face. "But I also have the most annoying sense of pride, so I have this burning need to make you come."

"Burning, wow." Mara giggled between kisses, between shivers of her skin as his nails lightly raked the shell of her ears, her neck. Her top was a crocheted thing that was held together by a front tie, and Jay held the end of the string with his fingers and waited for Mara's permission before he tugged. The front of the shirt was undone, and Mara felt her breaths quicken.

"Did you make this?" he asked, pulling gently at both ties to fully expose the top of her cleavage, her chest rising and falling even more obviously now.

"Yeah." Mara nodded as Jay kneeled on the floor in front of her, gently pushing her knees wide so he could slip in between her legs to lavish kisses on her exposed skin. "It's…it's just granny squares."

"You like granny squares?" He didn't even look up, so focused he was on sucking the skin just where Mara's bra began to cover her up. She heard herself gasp and felt herself shudder, but all her mind could focus on was the head of his breath, the wetness of his lips, the gentle touch of his hand. He undid the second tie, and the third, and Mara was almost panting, aching for him to touch her more.

"They are surprisingly easy to work with," she said, blindly taking his hand, his wrist, and putting it over her breast. He could barely cover it as he squeezed, and Mara gasped. "Jay."

"Hmm?" he said, licking the dip of her cleavage.

"Don't say granny squares when we're about to have sex."

The sound he made was the cross between a splutter and a raspberry, because his mouth had still been pressed against her skin. The unexpectedly funny sound had her bursting with laughter. Jay's shoulders were shaking, and they spent the next few minutes holding on to each other and cackling. And when it faded, Mara knew with certainty that this was not going to be the experience she'd expected, hoped, feared or worried about.

This was going to be so much better.

"Just so you know," Jay said, holding a hand up to Mara's eyes and waiting for her little nod before she slipped her glasses off her face and placed them on one of the side tables. "If anything is uncomfortable, you can tell me to stop."

"I know," she said, nodding.

"I can stop. I can," he insisted.

"Please don't. At least until I say so."

And they really didn't. By the time Mara was on her back in nothing but her slip dress, hips raised slightly by pillows and breathing through Jay watching her with hungry eyes, she didn't want this to stop at all. She pulled down the front of her dress and undid the clasp of her bra in front. It really was easier. Jay helped her loop her arms under the straps, giving him the space to pull the bra away. She shivered when Jay pulled it away, her skin tingling where his fingertips touched her bare breast.

"Oh Mara," he gasped, reverent and gentle as his cool fingertip lightly flicked at her slowly hardening nipples. "You are so beautiful."

"Yes I am." She had no plans of taking off the rest of the slip tonight, but it was comforting to know that she was in no hurry to do it. Because while this would be the first time, she was determined to not let it be the last. "Can I put the condom on you?"

And when Jay entered her, his cock warm and hard, slipping into spaces of her body that not even she was sure she'd ever touched, Mara knew this was definitely not going to be the last time they did it. It was such a new, but welcome feeling. But she loved the weight of his body against her, the way it fought against her but filled her so well. She loved the sounds their bodies made in their joining, her tension melting away as Jay canted his hips against hers, as her body shook and clenched to make him fill her deeper, deeper.

"God, Mara, you're so tight," Jay babbled as they slammed into each other, the bed making a creaking sound underneath them. "I knew it would feel good inside you, I knew it."

She couldn't say anything in response, luxuriating in the feeling that something inside of her was going to explode. Mara wanted to hold it in, to stop it, or contain the feeling. But it was impossible, so impossible.

"Are you going to come, love? Don't hold back, let me hear you. God, I want to hear you."

She had imagined what this would feel like. Oh, she knew it would be wonderful, but she had underestimated how deeply intimate it was, so be this close to a person. To have them know what you sounded like in your most vulnerable moments. In times like this it was impossible to hold on to control, and that freedom was what Mara had not expected to feel at all.

She came with a shout, her hand over her head as it grabbed Jay's headboard for support, her leg wrapped around Jay's hip. He followed her shortly after, slowly sliding out of her to properly dispose of the condom.

Mara blinked up at Jay as he walked back to her, a satisfied, smug grin on his face. The room had darkened, and several floors below, traffic built into gridlocks. People moved to and fro in their own places. All of them blissfully unaware that this magical thing would be inevitable—that Mara Jane Barretto was going to fall in love with Jay Montinola, and she was happy to keep falling for as long as she could.

Sex *was* cool. But knowing you got to do it again with someone you liked? Well, that was even better.

"You okay?" Jay asked, moving to the bed to lie beside Mara, helping her toss aside the extra pillows to his nearby floor chair ("It's the chair I throw everything on. Best five thousand I've ever spent."). He stretched his arms over his head, his toes forward and still naked. Then he bundled Mara into his arms, pulling the rest of her slip over her legs, her knees. "Let me grab your glasses."

He reached over her and grabbed them, and her vision was restored. The world was a lot less blurry, but thank god it was mostly all very much the same. She did feel a little overwhelmed, curling into Jay's chest and letting him smooth his hand up and down her back.

"Next time," she said, looking up. Jay looked a little worried. Nervous. "We eat *after* sex."

His face broke out into a happy, satisfied smile. He chuckled and pressed a kiss to her temple. "Next time," he echoed.

And Mara's heart settled into a peace she had never before understood. But there was peace in feeling so wanted, and so loved.

The room was quiet, but neither of them felt like getting up at the moment. It was in that quiet moment that Jay suddenly asked. "Can I order flowers from you?"

"To give back to me? Just give me money."

"Wow." Jay laughed. "It's actually for this thing happening on Friday. Do you want to come?"

"Wait," Mara said, frowning up at him. "What's happening on Friday?"

Nige and Irene are finally getting married!

*Civil ceremony to be held
at Leo's Deli at the Kontra*

San Juan City

Fifteen

Nothing about Ate Irene's love story had been conventional.

She had a one-night stand, got pregnant during the pandemic, reconnected with her best friend when things opened back up and decided to marry him after three years. They had opted for a civil ceremony—a church wedding could wait until Luna was in first grade and the Catholic school (if they chose it) made them do it.

Ate Irene had always been a fan of architecture, which was why she chose to get married at the Kontra. The building was housed in a corner lot that used to have an ancestral home turned restaurant, but now had become an incredibly chic, modern hub of cafés, restaurants and shops. The space was built with thin columns of steel painted white, which looked industrial but still tropical.

The bride and groom were married in the middle of all, on top of a set of steps, surrounded by fiddle leaf plants and underneath a gigantic ceiling fan.

"The bride wore a dress by no one." Jay's mother sighed beside him as they stood as her witness for the blessed event. Nige had an aunt who was a city judge, and she believed that a civil wedding ceremony was a quick wedding ceremony. "But then again, nothing about our family has been conventional."

"No. But it's better this way, I think," Jay said, shaking his head and trying not to get distracted from Ate Irene looking into Nige's eyes. "Have you talked to Dad?"

They were both blatant about staring at the man seated a row behind them, his eyes fixed up front. Jay looked a lot like his father, but he hoped he would have a little more fortitude than the man who cheated on his wife and decided it wasn't worth fixing.

"Forty years, and I still have nothing to say to him." His mom shrugged. "I would much rather be talking to your plus-one."

"She's amazing, isn't she?" Jay said fondly, letting his mother be the obvious one this time, as she smiled and waved at Mara, who insisted on sitting in the back row. Jay turned just in time to catch Mara awkwardly waving back. He stifled a laugh, and she was close enough that he could still see her blush.

"The moment she showed up with those flowers, I knew," his mother declared. Jay was willing to give her that. Ate Irene had wanted no fuss, not even a bouquet. And so when Jay came to pick up Mara that afternoon at Wildflower, she'd showed up with a hand fan that she'd attached a few orchid flowers to, white blooms with bright magenta centers to match the building. "It gets pretty hot at Kontra. If she wanted, she could have a fan to stay cool."

And so Ate Irene got married in a dress by no one, and without a bouquet.

Jay thought that his Ate never looked more beautiful than she did the day she married the love of her life, wearing a soft pink dress with delicate straps, a lace front and a drop waist. The stylist had tied and retied the ribbon in Irene's hair until it was Mara who had stepped in and made the bow perfect.

And of course Luna was beside herself with excitement, and the girl was practically out of rose petals when she and her ninong stood at the end of the makeshift aisle. Mara secretly pulled a rose from Luna's flower crown and pulled out the petals to place in the basket, the awe in the little girl's eyes nothing short of miraculous.

Jay was enjoying how Mara was slowly fitting into his family's life. How he was fitting into hers, as well.

"I'm just glad the two of you aren't so fucked up about love that you swore off of it." His mom sighed beside him. "I thought your dad and I doomed you when we broke up, when I moved away."

It wasn't exactly true. It had taken Ate Irene a *long* time to decide Nigel was the one for her, and even Jay still had days where he didn't think he deserved all the happiness Mara gave him. But Jay was old enough to know that there was no point in contradicting his mother's headcanon, especially when he knew better.

"Well," Mara said after the short ceremony, when the witnesses finished signing the marriage certificate, when Nigel signed an application to legally adopt Luna. Jay stood apart from all that, and he thought he would feel lonelier today, but any loneliness he had was completely eclipsed by how happy he was for all of them. "What did the judge say?"

She was wearing a sleeveless wrap dress that had a tie on the front right side of her body, like a modern take on a hanbok. She let her short dark hair down, pulled back only by a little clip. She had an orchid tied to her wrist, "just to be a little more weddingy!" Jay wrapped a hand around her waist and pulled her close, breathing in the lovely gardenia perfume she'd put on today.

He realized that before today he'd felt guilty about noticing these little things about her, because he didn't think he had any right to it. But now that he could enjoy them more fully, he started to notice even more things about Mara he loved—that she had a signature everyday scent, but wore other perfumes when she thought the occasion was "special." That she considered pants as "work wear" and would have preferred to wear dresses daily.

"Unfortunately, despite being an official witness, I am *not* their ninong sa kasal." Jay sighed dramatically, pretending to be devastated by this turn of events. "Scott will be so disappointed."

"Scott lang ba talaga?" Mara teased, and Jay playfully poked her side to make her laugh. They made their way to the reception place, the Italian restaurant in the basement run by a Sicilian chef that usually said no to private parties, but one does not underestimate the power of Scott Sabio and his charm. And Jay's power to convince Scott to do things.

The dinner was divine, of course. It just didn't get better than a five.

But as cool as Ate Irene and Nige were, as elder millennials they still had a bit of cheese and tradition in them, because they chose "Got to Believe in Magic" as their wedding song, and neither of them objected when the even older people in the room came up to the couple and started safety pinning thousand-peso bills into the bride's dress. A very old, but still very much appreciated, tradition. All of the wedding guests knew the song, clearly, and there was a moment where everyone was singing along to the song as Nige and Ate Irene held on to each other.

Jay found himself on the dance floor shortly after, swaying with Luna in his arms, the little girl making a valiant effort to pretend like she knew the lyrics. He spun them around and ended up facing the spot where Mara was sitting, smiling at them with a fondness in her face that Jay had only recognized because he looked at her like that all the time.

"Are you taking photos?" Mara playfully rolled her eyes

but pulled out her phone anyway and snapped pictures of him dancing with Luna. He reached out a hand for her and pulled her into their little dance circle, Luna lazily keeping a hand on Mara's shoulder as they danced to the song. Jay treated them to some of his singing, because why not.

"...in a world that's full of stranglers..."

"Strangers," Mara corrected him.

"Something stronger than the dudes above..."

"Moon!" She laughed, just in time for Nigel and the de-moneyed, de-pinned Ate Irene to pick up Luna so they could dance as their own family. Irene quickly threw her arms around the both of them, said, "I told you so!" and went to go dance with her husband and daughter.

"You think you still have magic powers?" Mara asked him suddenly, as the two of them continued to sway against the music. There was barely any dancing, but Jay didn't mind.

"Oh, suddenly it's magic powers when it works on you?" he teased. "You know we've only been together a week. You could still be wrong. The love of your life could still walk into your life."

Mara scoffed, completely dismissing the idea. Jay could only wish he had her absolute confidence. Was that an older sister thing? "Maybe. But at the moment, I don't think I could be pulled away from you."

He smiled and enveloped her in his arms, tilting her back a little so she would look up at him. Jay never thought he would end up in this moment with this incredible woman. And he was willing to spend his lifetime being worthy of the task.

He was never going to kiss anyone else again.

★ ★ ★ ★ ★

Author's Note

If you haven't seen "Got 2 Believe," please go watch it now (it's available online!). It's one of two top-tier Filipino romcoms for me, the second being "Isa Pa With Feelings" (watch that one too!). The movie is definitely a time capsule of the early 2000s, aka my formative teenage years. Just like Toni, I wanted to be the independent business owner, with friends, with a shop and a happy relationship with her family! Yes she was a bit of a princess, illusyonada, masungit, maldita for sure. But so was I. I wanted what she had, shiny eyeshadow, too light concealer, and all!

And god, it really didn't get more charming than Rico Yan in those days.

It's a little more difficult to picture a Pinoy romcom life in my thirties, but the feeling of wanting to be my own person, and yet still be so connected to everyone and everything is something I think my generation can relate to. We were told to want things, and expect things (sometimes via family myths and legends!) but the journeys are all our own. As much as I wanted to celebrate a cornerstone of our cinema culture, I wanted to explore what that story would mean if the characters were older, if they had different choices.

The more I write these books the more the question of what "Filipino happy endings" are supposed to look like pops up into conversation. And to that I say, what do happy endings look like in general, because I think we all want the same things! A nice person we adore, who also adores us. Sometimes that's more than enough. Sometimes, that's revolutionary enough!

Anyway. I hope you enjoyed this, as much as I enjoyed writing it! Time to rewatch the movie.

Thank you to KB, Danice and Layla, who cheer me through the books always, and for this in particular.